CW00520506

BROTHERS LOST AND FOUND

Charles Satchwell

Best wishes John
Charles Satchwell

IBSN: 978-1973412595

Dedication:

I'd like to thank John Costello, Ann Evans, Bryce Parker and Sue Wilson for their help with this book.

Inspired by the songs of Steve Earle

Cover design by Oliviaprodesign

Chapter 1

Chet Carter was driving his Dodge pickup cautiously, unlike last night when he was tearing down the highway without a care in the world. Yesterday the truck was empty, and Chet was full of whisky. Today it was the other way around. The radio was blasting out a song and he sang along, '*we gotta get out of this place.*' His brother Aaron had escaped this godforsaken town when he joined the army. Chet felt as though he was stuck in a rut.

Chet turned off the highway onto a dirt road. The bottles in the back of the truck chinked together every time he went over a bump. Soon he pulled into the driveway of his uncle's house, parking the pick up next to the barn. Uncle Bart was shuffling around the yard feeding chickens with Duke, his faithful old hound, at his heel. The dog was devoted to the old man. Chet climbed out of the Dodge and Duke ran to greet him, tail wagging enthusiastically. Chet made his usual fuss of the mutt, stroking him and rubbing his belly the way he liked.

'Delivery go well?'

Bart spat out some tobacco juice, the yellow liquid disappearing in an envelope of dust.

'Yep.' Chet replied.

'Everyone paid up?'

'All except old man Williamson. He's been sick as a dog all week. Betty said they'd pay double next time.'

'You ain't gotta worry about old Tom. His son Jamie earns good money. Even if Tom's not earning Jamie will cover him. Don't suppose Tom wanted any this time?'

'That's what I was thinking but Betty said her old man was still sipping his usual quota. Said he calls it his curing medicine.'

'Moonshine's been curing old Tom ever since I've known him.'

Bart picked up a piece of copper pipe he'd just sawn and filed the edge. He took it over to a barrel to check that it fitted into the hole that he'd drilled.

'Is old Tom your longest serving customer, uncle?'

'Reckon he could be.'

Chet lifted one of the empty crates off the Dodge.

'How long you been making moonshine?'

'Since I was about eighteen. Was younger'n you when I bought the still from Jake Schneider. Jake inherited the setup from his pappy. There's been moonshine in Jackson County since prohibition.'

'Why'd he sell up?'

Bart took off his cap and scratched his head.

'Problem was, Jake's eldest boy upped and married some girl out of state. His other two kids lived nearby, but they didn't seem to give a shit about the pappy that brought them up. I do believe Jake's ex-wife soured the mash. When Jake's health went downhill his eldest boy persuaded him to leave the town he'd lived in all his life. The old man had no one to take over the family business, so I took over. Seems like blood is thicker than liquor.'

Bart laughed at his own joke until his chewing tobacco got stuck in his throat. He coughed and spat out the wad. Then he took a swig of moonshine from a nearby jar. Chet shook his head and smiled affectionately at his uncle.

'Guess that's why I'm working for my uncle, because the pay ain't nothing to write home about.'

'You ungrateful son of a bitch. Took you in like a stray raccoon when Jethroe disowned you.'

'Just kidding Uncle Bart, appreciate living with you and being second in command of this prestigious organization.'

'And here was me thinking you were just the delivery boy.'

Bart laughed like a drunken teenager. He may well have been supping all afternoon. The old man's cackling made Chet smile. He gave his uncle the takings and unloaded the empty mason jars into the barn. He wondered how his uncle could have afforded to buy the still at such a young age but thought it best not to ask as Bart would more than likely cuff him around the head again.

Chet's favorite room in his uncle's house was the den in the basement. Bart had set up a small bar down there, stocked mainly with the company's homemade liquor, which Bart jokingly liked to describe to rare guests as the house wine. The rest of the den was furnished with a large screen television, a sofa and three arm chairs. In the corners were big floor standing speakers. Chet picked up his guitar and played a Buddy Holly song. He'd been practicing it for weeks in order to add it to his repertoire of songs for the Sunday session at Guthrie's.

Daydreaming, Chet saw himself playing at big auditoriums, or football stadiums. Thousands of wide eyed girls staring up at him, screaming his name. Coming back down to earth, the reality of his life slapped him in the face. His chances of making the big time were slim living in this backwater town in the Smokey Mountains. If the truth be known, he was going no place except to one of two bars in this one-horse town. Chet spent most weekends downing beer in Guthrie's. On Sunday, he drank less to remain sober for the free and easy session where he usually played a few songs. This was the highlight of his week. He didn't get paid for it, but the regulars applauded wildly which gave Chet a buzz. On other nights, he played pool with his friends. A big plus about Guthrie's was that his father, Jethroe, never went there. On the odd occasion Jethroe did go out he went to 'The Rustler' to catch up on gossip, but he never drank alcohol.

Chapter 2

The bar had an open front with tables on the street, but the soldiers were sitting inside. An overhead fan provided a cooling respite from the oppressive heat. It was early evening and the bar was not yet crowded. The soldiers liked it because the beer was cheap, and the girls were cute. Petite, skinny Thai girls in skimpy dresses working the tables, serving customers and flirting at the same time. Sergeant Hammond was buying the beer for Aaron, Brent and Tyler. They'd become a close knit little group since they met at basic training. The soldiers were extremely fit looking guys. Hammond's neck was as thick as a big man's thigh. Brent and Tyler's muscular arms and legs were reminiscent of men who lifted weights. Aaron Carter was taller and slimmer than the others. His muscles were well defined but not as big. If the others were heavyweight, he was light heavyweight in boxing terms.

At a nearby table sat a group of men with British accents. The contrast between them and the soldiers was evident. Two of them were considerably older, all of them had pot bellies and they didn't look as though they were in shape. The only lifting they did was the beers they were swigging. A waitress was talking to the soldiers when one of the Brits tried to butt in.

'Come over here, darling. It's about time you spent some time with us. We're your regular customers. These GI's are here today gone tomorrow. Sit yourself down on my lap.'

Hammond gave the man a stare that would make a sober man think twice before answering back. 'This girl's waiting on us, fella. Try someone else. Better still go find another bar.'

The Englishman got out of his seat. He scowled and pointed aggressively at the Sergeant. 'Who do you think you are coming in here and throwing your weight around?'

'We're US army enjoying some rest and relaxation. You'd be wise to do the same,' Hammond replied.

The Brit walked over to the table and looked Hammond in the eye. 'You're not welcome in this bar, Yank. Why don't you go back to your own country?'

Hammond sat more upright in his chair. 'You're pushing your luck, limey. The US army don't take orders from the likes of you.'

'I ain't scared of you, soldier boy.'

Hammond realized from the glazed look in the Brit's eyes that he'd had too much to drink to be thinking right but he gave him another warning anyhow. 'If you've got a lick of sense you'll go back to your table.'

The limey grabbed the waitress by the arm and attempted to pull her to his table. Aaron immediately leapt to his feet, and turned him by his shoulder. The limey let go of the girl and aimed a punch at Aaron, who dodged it and hit him hard with a left jab. The scraping of chairs on the tiled floor signified to any other customers that the fight was about to intensify. Aaron continued hitting the mouthy limey with a combination of punches to the head. The man staggered and fell, as if his legs could no longer support his weight. Four more Englishmen stood ready to join the fray. The Sergeant and the two other soldiers stepped in to intercept them. One of the Englishmen threw himself on Aaron. Another hit Hammond. He didn't even flinch. He put the man in a headlock and pummeled his head with his other hand. Aaron shrugged the man off him and pushed him away to give him room to throw some punches. The limey held his arms in front of his face to protect himself, so Aaron punched him in the stomach and the ribs until he dropped his guard. Then he hit him in the face with hard, accurate punches that made the limey's head rock backwards. Brent and Tyler stood with fists bunched facing the remaining Brits. The eldest Brit kicked Brent in the shin then waded in, arms flailing. Brent exchanged a few blows then used his bulk to wrestle the man to the ground, pinning him down with one hand and punching him with the other. The remaining

Englishman had seen enough. He backed away, hands in the air, clearly wanting no part of the onslaught. Hammond hauled the, still head locked, limey outside. His face was badly messed up. Taking a lead from his Sergeant Aaron pushed the man he was fighting into the street as well. When Hammond came back into the bar he approached the man with his hands still raised and pointed at the man who'd started the fight, spread eagled on the floor.

'Get your buddy out of here.'

The limey bent down and shook his friend to try and rouse him. He was out cold. Aaron helped drag him through the door and deposited him on the ground next to his buddies. Brent picked up the man that he had been fighting by his collar, as if he was a rag doll, and dumped him outside too. Tyler hadn't needed to do anything. The fight was over quickly with a minimum of disruption. The bar owner came out and threw a glass of water over the drunk trying to revive him. The man came to, spluttered and lifted his head. Hammond stood over him.

'Time, you boys found somewhere else to drink.'

The bar owner nodded in agreement. The Brits faces were cut and swollen. All except for the sensible one who hadn't joined in. They eased themselves up and two of them lifted the man who had initiated the fight to his feet. He was still unsteady, so they carried him between their shoulders, like a shirt on a coat hanger. The bar owner, a native Thai, walked up to Sergeant Hammond.

'I no approve of fighting. Lucky for me no damage.'

'Those guys had it coming,' Hammond replied.

'I no blame you. Soldiers still welcome in bar. My girls no like those men. Sometimes they very rough. They too much trouble.'

The soldiers nodded in agreement. They went back to their table and sat joking with each other, as though nothing had happened. After the bar owner returned to the bar, Sergeant Hammond looked Aaron square in the eyes.

'Where'd you learn to punch like that, Carter?'

Aaron shrugged his shoulders. 'Guess I just know how to handle myself. Been known to bust a few heads back home.'

'You get into many fights?'

'Only when I gotta get my little brother out of a fix. He's got a temper and he ain't the sort to back down. Where I'm from we tend to hit first and ask questions later.'

'Think you might be interested in boxing for the Battalion?'

Aaron took a swig of his beer.

'Maybe.'

'When we get back to base I'll make a few calls,' said Hammond.

Aaron still had his eye on the girl who was the object of the dispute, gliding silently around the bar almost ghost like. Her name was Choi. She had short black hair and delicate features. He'd spoken to her many times enjoying listening to her broken English which was just good enough to hold a conversation. She smiled sweetly at him and he beckoned her over.

Aaron said, 'Sorry about that. Some folks ain't got no manners.'

Choi spoke to the whole group although she kept her focus on Aaron. 'You guys need drink?'

'We're okay for now but we'll need some more beers soon,' said Hammond who was accustomed to speaking on behalf of his men.

'Okay, be back in short while.'

Aaron touched her arm.

'Wait, I got some questions.'

The other soldiers smiled at each other and Aaron blushed as he became aware that his buddies were watching him. He pointed to a nearby table. 'Gonna sit over there a while, guys. Need a little privacy.'

He took Choi's arm gently and guided her to a table for two in the corner of the room. Choi was reluctant to sit down. Aaron knew that she was only allowed to fraternize with a customer if he was buying her a cocktail. He said, 'You want a drink?'

'Okay,' she replied and turned to go.

Aaron touched her arm. 'When you get back I'd like to get to know you a little better.'

She returned with her drink and placed the bill on the table. Aaron looked at the total and put more than enough money on the table to cover it. They sat facing each other, intimate and cozy, far enough away from the others that they wouldn't be overheard.

'Got a three-day pass coming up. I sure would like the pleasure of your company? Must be some interesting parts of Bangkok I ain't aware of?'

'You want me take night off work?'

'Yeah.'

'You pay bar fine?'

'No problem.'

Aaron was rubbing his right knuckles with the palm of his left hand as he talked.

'Is hand okay?'

'Guess it's bruised some from hitting those jerks. No worries. It'll be fine. Pick you up here on Friday at eight?'

'Okay. You must pay bar fine before I allowed to go with you.'

Aaron nodded. They finished their drinks and Choi went off to serve some other customers. Aaron went back to his friends. Tyler noticed him rubbing his hand.

'Injured your fist, Carter? Hope she's worth it.'

'We weren't fighting over the girl. The reputation of the US army was at stake.'

'Take your word for it, Aaron,' Tyler replied.

'Some folks need to be taught a lesson, Tyler.'

Hammond butted in, 'From now on let someone else do the teaching. You need to look after those hands if you're gonna box for the army. Besides the girl will appreciate you having soft hands.'

The guys laughed at the Sergeant's comments. Aaron was smiling too.

'Next time we go drinking I'll put on boxing gloves and drink out of a straw.'

'No need. Just let me sort out the trouble makers. I'll let you know if I need any help.'

'Sure thing, Sarge.'

Chapter 3

Guthrie's was one big room. The middle of the room was filled with tables and chairs spread out in a random fashion. On the right was a recess that was used for a stage. On the other side was the pool table. There was only one bar, up against it were a row of bar stools. Hanging from the ceiling and attached to the walls were all sorts of artefacts. A copper kettle, old farm implements, rusty tools, advertising posters, dolls and other old toys, even an old tin bath tub. It was as if someone had died leaving all their possessions in the house and garage to be cleared out. Obligingly, the owner of Guthrie's probably loaded up his wagon and brought all the useless items to his bar where he nailed them to any empty space on the walls, or ceiling. He called it décor. The locals called it junk, but they couldn't care less as long as he served them cool beer.

Chet and Bobby were playing pool and their girlfriends, Rita and Grace, sat nearby watching. Bobby rarely beat Chet, but this game looked like being his as he stepped up to put down the black. It was a straight shot, but he was hitting it almost the length of the table. Bobby concentrated hard, taking his time, his chin almost touching the cue. He hit the ball well, but it rattled in the jaws of the pocket failing to drop in. Chet stepped up to pot the black and win the game. He slapped Bobby affectionately on the back.

'Should've finished me off when you had the chance there, Bobby.'

'That black should've dropped.'

'You hit it too hard. Believe that means you gotta buy me a beer, Bobby boy.'

'What's new?'

Bobby went to the bar. He'd been friends with Chet since school days. Rita has been Chet's girl for a while, but when he started seeing Grace Chet fixed her up with Bobby. Chet held his beer in one hand, his other arm was around Grace. She looked at his smart jeans, white shirt and thin neck tie. His hair was slicked back like Elvis Presley. As usual on Saturday night he still had some money left. Sometimes they would go to a drive-in movie in the next town. On the way home, they invariably made out in the back of the station wagon. Grace was in her last year of high school. Chet didn't graduate as he dropped out in his last year. Skipping school gave him more time to do the moonshine runs.

Johnny set up the balls as he was playing the winner. Chet was likely to get beat this time as Johnny was the best player in the bar. Chet wasn't a bad loser, nor was he one of those players that lorded it over you when he won. While he chalked his cue, he noticed a loud-mouthed stranger at the bar. He looked at him even harder as he came over.

'How about you boys being hospitable and let a newcomer play?'

Chet looked the man right in the eyes but continued chalking the cue. 'We play winner stays on here. Put two quarters on the table and you get to play next.'

'Guess you ain't hearing too good. I figure on playing this game,' the stranger replied.

He was well over six-foot-tall with a large sun-tanned face and a big square chin, arms the size of tree trunks, heavily tattooed with foreign writing. His hair was buzz cut, army style. What stood out most were his penetrating blue eyes which were surrounded by wrinkles, as if he had spent his whole life squinting into the sun. He stared back hard at Chet with a fixed grin on his face. Johnny intervened to avert the stand-off.

'I'll partner the new guy, Chet, and we'll play against you and Bobby.'

Chet shrugged and blew excess chalk from the tip of his cue. The stranger nodded in agreement and picked up a cue. When Johnny put the triangle away he looked over at Chet.

'Break them up, Johnny, said Chet.'

'That all right with you, big guy?' Johnny asked the stranger.

'Sure.'

Johnny smashed the white into the pack. Chet watched the balls flying around the table as Bobby returned from the bar carrying the drinks with Rita close behind.

Chet said, 'Looks like we're playing doubles, Bobby.'

'Sounds good to me, Chet.'

As Bobby put the drinks on a nearby table the stranger spoke.

'Name's Joe Sullivan. How about introducing me to the little lady?'

Bobby had a worried look on his face. He glanced over at Chet who had his chin on the cue lining up his shot. Then he replied in a faltering voice. 'This is my girlfriend, Rita.'

'Pleased to make your acquaintance, Rita.'

Sullivan lifted Rita's hand and kissed it, but kept hold of it. Rita was clearly embarrassed, but no one said anything as Chet took his shot and sank a ball. He potted another ball before missing a more difficult shot. 'Your shot, Sullivan.'

Sullivan let go of Rita. As he got down to hit the ball it was plain to see that his bridge hand was unsteady. The smell of whisky on his breath encircled the table. It was a relatively easy shot, but he missed. Bobby took his turn, but he failed to sink anything either, leaving a difficult shot for Johnny, who, predictably, put the ball down with ease and proceeded to sink four more balls. As he hadn't left himself an easy pot, he played safe. Chet had no obvious shot, but he went for a difficult cut anyhow. He missed leaving a ball close to the pocket for Sullivan, but he missed gain. He slammed his fist on the table and said, 'That ball should have dropped. This pool table's a piece of crap.'

Bobby also missed again. Johnny smiled as he surveyed the table. The balls were spread nicely, and he preceded to clean up. As he put the black down Sullivan slapped his leg and gave a raucous laugh. He walked up to Chet with his hand outstretched. Chet took the offered hand. The man had a grip like a vice.

Sullivan said, 'Looks like we gave you a whupping, son. Let's go again, double or quits?'

'We're done, the table belongs to you and Johnny,'said Chet as he picked up his beer and walked away from Sullivan.

'Where you going, boy?'

Chet stopped dead in his tracks and turned.

Sullivan said, 'You lost the game so you gotta pay up.'

'It was just a friendly game, Sullivan. No one said anything about playing for money.'

Sullivan walked over to Rita and grabbed her by the wrist. 'If you ain't gonna pay I claim this little beauty as my prize.'

Rita's contorted face showed that the big ape was hurting her. Bobby rushed over.

'Hey man, get your hands off my girl.'

'Butt out kid. This girl's coming home with me tonight.'

Rita tried pulling her hand out of Sullivan's grip. 'Get him off of me, Bobby.'

Bobby pushed Sullivan, but he didn't budge. It was like pushing against the side of a house. He glared at Bobby who screwed up his face as the fumes of Sullivan's whisky breath invaded his nostrils. Suddenly, Sullivan let go of Rita and grabbed Bobby by the throat with his large left hand. Bobby looked frightened to death at the prospect of what was coming next. Rita gasped as the brute threw a right hand towards Bobby's face. At the same time, the thick end of a pool cue smashed against Sullivan's head, so hard that it snapped. Sullivan dropped to the floor as if he'd been shot by a Colt.45. Chet stood over him with the broken thin end of the cue still in his hand, wielding it as if he'd just hit a home run. Sullivan was out for the count. Bobby held Rita in his arms, while the onlookers crowded in to get a closer look at the big ape lying on the deck. No one said a word until the barman, Maurice, came over. 'This guy's been drinking heavily. It was only a matter of time before he caused trouble. Even so you better hit the road, Chet.'

'If you knew he was drunk why didn't you throw him out, Maurice?'

Maurice didn't answer. Chet knew he had done him a favor, but he also knew that Maurice wasn't about to admit it. He was obviously worried about how Sullivan would have reacted if he'd asked him to leave.

Maurice said, 'Need to call 911. This guy needs treatment. The cops are gonna be here soon, so you and your friends best get out of here, Chet.'

Chet knew Maurice was right. Rita and Grace were using fake ID. Only Chet and Bobby were twenty-one. He took Grace's hand and escorted her to his station wagon. Rita climbed into Bobby's Chevy. Soon they were all sitting in the den at Uncle Bart's house sipping moonshine. There was a knock on the door and uncle Bart walked in.

'Bar run dry tonight?' said Bart.

'Had some trouble with an out of towner, uncle. Big ape tried to molest, Rita,' replied Chet.

'What did you do?'

'Hit him with a pool cue. Seemed the best way to stop him.'

'Guess you gotta do what you gotta do. You're like your daddy. Jethroe was always getting into fights when he was younger.'

'Jethroe got into bar fights?'

'Me and your Uncle Luke came to his rescue many a time.'

'Always thought you and Luke were the fighters in the family?'

'Only fought when we had to.'

Chet wanted to know more about his uncle's misdemeanors. But he decided not to press him in the presence of the others. The similarity between the two generations of brothers was striking. Bart used to look out for Jethroe, just like Aaron protected Chet. The difference was that Aaron and Chet were still close, while Bart and Jethroe were no longer on speaking terms.

Unlike Chet, Aaron had done well at school. He'd been the high school star quarterback and a football scholarship took him to college where he majored in law. It was a surprise to everyone when he enlisted in the army. Chet was looking forward to the next time Aaron came home on leave, as army homecomings are a big deal in this small town. Chet didn't know why he was still hanging around.

Bart left the youngsters on their own and went upstairs. Although they were downing beers in the den as usual, the banter and fooling around was missing. Grace fiddled with her hair and Rita was twitching nervously. Chet resorted to what he always did when he was feeling down and played the blues. His guitar twanged out the chords like it was crying, which did nothing to lighten the mood. Bobby had been sitting quietly listening to the music, but when Chet put down the guitar and drank some more beer he spoke up.

'You sure hit that bastard hard, Chet.'

'Needed a mighty blow to stop that brute, Bobby.'

Rita looked at Chet with admiration in her eyes.

'I'm pleased Chet knocked him out. He was hurting me, and god knows what he'd have done to Bobby.'

The frown on Grace's face told a different story. She kept her head down, absorbed in the act of peeling the label off her bottle. Bobby put his arm around his girl.

'Nearly crapped my pants, Rita. Last time I saw anything that big was a grizzly bear in National Geographic.'

Chet grinned at Bobby's joke. 'When'd you start reading National Geographic?'

'Whenever I visit the orthodontist.'

Bobby opened his mouth wide to show Rita his straight white teeth, then continued. 'Fact of the matter is, Chet saved me from a beating.'

'We look after our own, Bobby,' Chet replied.

'We sure do, Chet.'

Grace fetched herself another Bud from the cooler and took a swig. From the look on her face you'd have thought she'd just swallowed a bug. She joined the conversation.

'I ain't denying Chet's got balls, but when you get in a difficult situation it ain't always right to lash out.'

Bobby let go of Rita, sat forward, and stared hard at Grace.

'How would you have handled it, Grace?'

'Not hit him with a pool cue, Bobby, that's for sure.'

Rita said, 'How else was he gonna stop Sullivan?'

'I'm tired of seeing Chet in trouble,' said Grace.

'Chet didn't start the fight, Grace. That brute grabbed hold of Rita for no good reason,' said Bobby.

Grace didn't reply. Bobby and Rita were both looking at her as if she was stupid. After a while she asked Chet to take her home.

Half way to Grace's house Chet pulled the station wagon into a side road. It was one of their usual haunts, a quiet place Chet often parked when he felt horny. He turned off the engine and leaned over to kiss her. She responded at first but then pulled away.

'I'm not in the mood tonight, Chet.'

'What's wrong?'

'I just don't feel sexy. Guess I'm unsettled by the trouble in the bar. I wanna go home and think things over.'

Chet was looking forward to sex with Grace to relieve the tension, but he wasn't in the right frame of mind to argue. One fight was enough for tonight. 'Okay.'

Grace turned towards him and stared him in the eye. 'Maybe you oughta take a good look at yourself.'

'What are you getting at, Grace?'

'The fight at Guthrie's for starters.'

'Sullivan had to be stopped. End of story.'

'Is it that simple to you?'

'Pretty much.'

'Do you ever think about the bigger picture?'

Chet tensed up and sat forward, raising his voice. 'What bigger picture?'

'All we ever do is go to Guthrie's.'

'What else is there to do around here?'

Grace sat up straight as rigid as a statue. 'If this is all we got then we're going nowhere fast?'

'You got some sort of problem, Grace?'

'I'm tired. Let's just sleep on it.'

She turned away from him. Chet felt frustrated, but he didn't want to lose his temper. Grace had been getting more and more moody, lately. He dropped her off at her house and went home. As he lay in his bed he thought about what Grace had said about them going nowhere fast. Whenever he reminisced he always came to the conclusion that Jethroe was the source of his problems. He'd never been his daddy's favorite child. He seemed to remember that his mother doted on him some, although she died when he was only nine years old. It was after his mom died, during high school, that his troubles began. Before his mom died Chet remembered feeling good about himself. He was the star batter in his little league baseball team. Popular at grade school, with a big brother admired by everyone. Aaron was the apple of his daddy's eye, whereas Chet was his worst nightmare. Chet was always getting chastised by Jethroe for not completing his homework, back chatting and fighting. Every little misdemeanor meant he was in for a whupping. That is until Chet had become too big.

He remembered well the day that the beatings came to an end. As his daddy was taking off his belt Chet had picked up a bicycle chain that his brother had left on the ground, after cleaning, and swung it around menacingly. Jethroe had looked deep into Chet's eyes trying to figure out whether Chet was bluffing or not. He was not prepared to find out and simply put his belt back on and walked away. Retaliation had been building inside Chet for a long time, but he didn't know for sure what would've happened if Jethroe had tried to belt him. If his father had moved one step closer, he may well have wrapped that chain across the old man's face and the whupped boy might have been doing the whupping for once. Chet hadn't set foot in his daddy's house since that day.

Chapter 4

Guthrie's parking lot was deserted. Chet had finished his hooch run early so he wandered in to get some information from Maurice. Looking around he saw old Don sitting on a bar stool, his pot belly stuck out so far it prevented him from resting his elbows on the bar. He was having his daily alcoholic appetizer before, or instead, of supper. Jack Daniels had become his soul mate since his wife left him a few years back. Or maybe him and Jack were tight before she went. There were a couple of old boys playing pool, otherwise the place was empty. Chet nodded a howdy to Don, who reciprocated. Maurice breezed over surprised to see Chet in the bar at this time of day. Worry lines etched across Chet's forehead, like grooves in a record.

'Look like you just won the lottery and lost your ticket,' said Maurice.

'Having a whole lot of luck lately Maurice, and it's all bad.'

'Guess you wanna know what happened after you fled the scene?'

'Yeah, I'm anxious to find out about that Sullivan guy.'

Maurice continued wiping glasses as he talked.

'The big guy regained consciousness but he wasn't with the program. Paramedics came and carried him out on a stretcher.'

'Was he hurt bad?'

'Who knows?'

'Suppose the cops showed up?'

'Yeah, they grilled me some.'

Chet sat forward on his seat. 'What did you tell them?'

'Told them the fight started when Sullivan grabbed hold of a girl,' said Maurice.

'What else?'

'They wanted to know who hit him.'

'You tell them?'

Maurice put down the clean glass and picked up another. 'Told them I didn't know the folks involved.'

'Did they believe ya?'

'Probably not.'

'They talk to anyone else?'

'Interviewed some of the regulars. Wouldn't surprise me if someone let on it was you swinging that cue. If you wanna find out about Sullivan why don't you go visit him in the hospital?' Maurice sniggered at his own joke. 'You buying a drink, or just come her to chat?'

Chet's face still wore a frown and he didn't comment. He didn't appreciate Maurice's flippancy. He took out his bill fold but thought better of it and put it back in his pocket. 'Think I'll hit the road, Maurice.'

'Probably best you stay away from here for a while.'

Chet raised his eyebrows. 'You barring me, Maurice?'

Maurice kept wiping the glass. Checking it over and over for smears in an over exaggerated way, rather than looking Chet in the eyes. 'Just think it's wise you keep a low profile until this whole thing blows over.'

Chet leaned forward his voice becoming more threatening in tone. 'You should have thrown out the drunken bum before he got a chance to manhandle Rita.'

'Had my eye him but you jumped in before I could do anything.'

'More like you were shitting yourself hoping he'd fall down drunk before he caused any trouble.'

'Either way, you assaulted the guy and the cops are sniffing around, so you'd best go to ground, Chet.'

Chet nodded in agreement and Maurice moved away to refill Don's glass. Chet felt a hand on his shoulder and turned around. 'Hey Rita, what you doing here?'

'Finished work early. Been in the Rustler with a couple of girls celebrating a 21st birthday. When we came out I saw your Dodge in Guthrie's parking lot, so I thought I'd join you. You gonna get me a drink?' Rita replied.

'Was going home but maybe a beer wouldn't hurt.'

Maurice had just put Don's Jack Daniels on the bar when he saw Chet raise his hand and flick his fingers together. When Maurice came over Chet looked at him hard in a challenging manner. 'Get me a couple of Buds, Maurice.'

Maurice lifted two bottles from the shelf. Chet looked at Rita's face to see if she was happy with what he'd ordered. Bobby and Rita usually drank Budweiser. Her smirk and the fact that she wasn't complaining told him she was fine with Bud. Maurice flipped the tops off the bottles and grudgingly placed the beers on the bar. Rita picked up a bottle and took a slug. 'Ain't like you to be here this time of day?' she said.

'Checking on what happened to Sullivan after we left,' Chet answered.

'Find out anything?'

'Maurice reckons Sullivan's in hospital and the cops are looking for me.'

Rita moved closer to Chet, so close their bodies were touching. She placed her hand gently on his thigh and slid it up and down his jeans. Her mouth parted slightly, and she smiled. She moved her tongue across her upper lip. He could smell the liquor on her breath.

'Sullivan got what was coming to him far as I'm concerned. Really appreciate you protecting me and Bobby last night, she said.'

'Cops may not see it that way, Rita.'

'They oughta. If they ask me, I'll tell them you were defending me from that big ape. We both know Bobby ain't capable of protecting me. Needed a real man to do what you did.'

'Wish Grace thought the same.'

'She don't deserve you. You need someone who'll stand by your side, like me.'

Rita's hand moved higher up his leg. Chet felt himself going hard.

'Don't think you should be doing that, Rita.'

'Don't you like it?'

Rita was smiling, showing her shiny white teeth, as if she already knew the answer was in the affirmative. Chet was thinking about when Rita was his girlfriend. Grace and Rita were best friends always hanging out together when Chet first met them in Guthrie's. Rita was the first to show an interest, so Chet started dating her. Later he began flirting with Grace and he made the switch. Then Rita started seeing Bobby and everyone remained friends, but there was sometimes tension between the girls. Rita pouted her lips and rubbed the mound that had formed under Chet's jeans.

'Christ, Rita, not in here.'

Chet looked around anxiously. No one else had entered the bar and the few people in the place were not paying any attention. Rita was a sassy little thing and Chet was aroused. She pressed her soft body up against him. It felt good. Her hand was still caressing him, and he gently lifted it off his jeans. She looked up, puzzled, with her eyebrows raised. He still had hold of her hand and he adjusted his pants with his other. Grinning, he let go of her hand and it went right back onto his jeans squeezing his penis through the denim. She moved her lips towards him and they kissed. Then Chet thought better of it and pulled away. 'Hell Rita, someone might see.'

'Who cares.'

She ignored his protest and moved her lips closer and they kissed again. Chet glanced furtively behind and realized that no one was watching, and he put his hands on her soft round butt and pulled her in tighter. She slid out her hand, so she could feel his hard member pressing against her. Chet remembered how she looked naked. He could visualize her curvaceous body moving underneath him.

'Take me, Chet.'

'Where?'

Chet wanted to take her over the pool table there and then.

'Anyplace, back seat of the Dodge. I don't care, she said.'

'What about Bobby and Grace?'

'Bobby's a great guy, but you and me should be together. Grace ain't right for you.'

The thought of Grace and Bobby finding out about any indiscretion suddenly hit Chet like a sledgehammer and his desire started to ebb. 'Can't do this, Rita,'

'I know you want me, Chet.'

'Ain't denying that, Rita, but you're seeing Bobby and I'm with Grace.'

The smile disappeared from Rita's face. 'Grace don't care for you like I do. Fate's put us here together. Let's make it happen.'

Chet knew that Grace's attitude towards him had changed for the worst lately and he wondered if she had said anything to Rita.

'Come on, Chet. You know you wanna screw me.'

'Can't do it, Rita. You're Bobby's girl and I ain't about to cheat on Grace.'

Rita looked Chet in the eyes then lowered her head. She seemed sad rather than angry. Chet didn't like having to disappoint her. Suddenly, he felt the need to get away. 'Time, I was gone, Rita. Gotta visit Uncle Bart in case the cops show up at his place. Best not to mention this to Bobby, either.'

'I ain't about to run off at the mouth.'

'You're a great girl, Rita.'

He finished off his beer, readjusted his pants again, as he was still semi hard, and he walked to the door. As the door swung open Rita hollered at him. 'You'll regret turning me down, Chet.'

He turned and raised his hand. 'Maybe, so long, Rita.'

Chet went quickly out the door and into the parking lot. He drove his Dodge down Main Street, about to head for home, when he saw a road sign for the county hospital. Following the sign post, he turned onto the highway. When he arrived at the hospital he sat for a while in the parking lot, unsure whether, or not, to go in. Eventually he climbed out of the Dodge and walked through the big double doors into the hospital. Waiting in line at the reception he listened to the people in front and realized that, as he wasn't a relative, he was unlikely to get any information about Sullivan. He decided he was wasting his time and walked towards the exit. Glancing down the corridor he saw the restroom symbol and made a detour, as he needed a pee. Further down the corridor he saw a cop sitting outside one of the wards. Chet figured that he might be guarding Sullivan, so he took a chance and went up to him. 'Come to check on the man who got hurt in Guthrie's bar last night.'

'What about him?' said the officer.

'I was there when the big guy went down. Wondered how he's doing, is all?'

The officer sat forward in his chair. 'Are you family?'

'No, just concerned about the stranger.'

'You offering yourself as a witness?'

Chet shuffled his feet. 'Didn't see the actual fight, just saw the guy flat out. Wanna know if he's okay, is all?'

'He'll survive,'

The officer's eyes were burning into Chet. 'We're still looking for the man that hit him. You know who he is?'

'No, sir. All happened so quickly. The guy that did it run off before I arrived on the scene.'

The cop nodded his head.

'Guess I found out what I needed to know, if you reckon he's gonna be okay I'm out of here.'

Chet walked away, but he didn't drive straight home. Instead he took a detour to Grace's house, eager to share the news with her, hoping she would be more amenable than last night. Grace's mother opened the door. She looked as though she'd just smelt a fart. 'Oh, it's you. I'll go get Grace.'

Grace came to the door and stepped out onto the porch. She didn't look pleased to see him, either. 'What's going on, Chet?'

'Just been to the hospital, seems like Sullivan's gonna be okay.'

'Does that mean the cops are gonna back off?'

'Don't rightly know. Think they're still looking for me.'

'They might put you away, Chet. You been in trouble with the law before.'

'Why you gotta be so downbeat, Grace? Was I supposed to let that bastard beat the crap out of Bobby?'

Grace put her hand over Chet's mouth. 'Lower your voice. My parents don't approve of cussing.'

'I'm a little wound up, Maurice just warned me to stay away from Guthrie's. If we can't go there where we gonna go to have fun around here?'

Grace looked down at her feet. 'I've been thinking we oughta take a break from each other.'

'You wanna split up because of last night?'

'Not just last night. Guess I want someone with better prospects.'

'You sound like your mom, Grace.'

Grace looked up. Her eyes were blazing, and she leant forward thrusting out her chin. 'What's that supposed to mean?'

'Let's face it she's never liked me.'

'This ain't nothing to do with her. It's about you and me. We're wasting our lives

'We have fun, don't we?'

'I want more, Chet. What do you really want to do with your life?'

'Play guitar and make it in the music business.'

'Who you trying to kid?'

Chet moved closer and put his face real close to Grace. 'You think I'll be running moonshine the rest of my life?'

'If the revenue man don't shut you down you probably will.'

'Working for Uncle Bart's a temporary situation.'

Grace softened her voice. 'Look Chet, you play a mean guitar but so do a thousand other guys. You need to wise up.'

'I've got a vision and one of these days I'm gonna live my dream.'

'You sound like Martin Luther King. You're going nowhere fast, Chet. You ain't even capable of being faithful to me.'

The scene with Rita flashed through Chet's mind. He looked at Grace with raised eyebrows. 'What you getting at?'

'I know you see other girls every now and then.'

'Is that what this is all about?'

'We just ain't right for each other, Chet.'

Chet clenched his right fist tight in anger. He was grinding his teeth. He was seething but tried not to show Grace. 'Please yourself, Grace. There's plenty more fish in the sea.'

'Mind you don't fall in trying to catch one, Chet.'

Chet needed to get the hell out of there. If he hung around he might only make things worse. He strode towards the Dodge with a face like an angry pit bull. Grace went inside and slammed the door shut. Tires screeched on the asphalt as he sped away. After a while he pulled in at a local truck stop and slumped over the steering wheel. He enjoyed having Grace as his girl. She looked good hanging on his arm. Moreover, she was as wild as a polecat in the sack. He'd just turned down sex with Rita because of her. Now the bitch had dumped him. He walked to the pay phone and dialed Rita's number. Riding Rita would be the best therapy he could get. He was getting aroused thinking about her soft, warm body underneath him. Her mouth open, breathing heavily. Her eyes sparkling. Urging him to fuck her harder. Grunting, screaming as she climaxed.

'Hello.'

Rita's dad answered the call. Chet wasn't expecting that and placed the phone back in its slot. He closed his eyes and shook his head, trying to clear his mind. He felt his world was coming apart. At least he could take comfort in the loyalty he'd shown to his best friend, Bobby. He drove home and went straight to his room where he immediately noticed a letter on the bed. He knew by the postage and the airmail sticker on the envelope that it was from Aaron. He looked at the photograph on his bedside table of Aaron holding the high school football trophy aloft after they had just won the state cup. His hair was windswept, and he had a massive smile on his sweaty face. He ripped open the letter admiring Aaron's neat hand writing. The paper was the thin airmail variety. Aaron had probably purchased it at the same time as he bought the light weight envelope. He got comfortable lying on the bed before reading it.

'Ain't heard from you for a while, Chet. You still supplying refreshments to half the county. How's your guitar playing going? Expect you're still entertaining the good people at Guthrie's? The bars in Thailand may be lacking entertainment but the girls are real cute, especially one, name of Choi. That's my good news. The bad news is one of the battalion got killed yesterday. Boy called Ryan Taylor, I knew him well. His plane was shot down. Only 20, it sure makes you think. Makes you realise how precious life is, and how important it is to live every minute. Don't waste your time doing stuff that's meaningless. Do something with your life. You have a gift, little brother. Keep practicing that guitar. Keep writing songs. One day you might be a famous recording artist with Sun Records in Memphis. It don't just happen though, you got to make it happen. Maybe you ought to spread your wings. There's more to life than the Smokey Mountains, however pretty they are. Looking forward to seeing everyone when I'm home on leave. Give my regards to Uncle Bart and anyone else you see. Ain't heard from the old man for a while. That ain't like him. I'm wondering if he got it. I know you and Jethroe ain't on speaking terms, but I'd appreciate it if you could check up on him. Make sure he knows I'm planning on coming home on leave at the end of the month. Your big brother, Aaron.

Chet smiled with pride as he read the compliments that his big brother had paid him. It was Aaron who first lent Chet his guitar and taught him to play. Later when they both had guitars the two brothers would strum along together, but Chet surpassed Aaron in his guitar playing and started to compose his own songs. Chet compared Aaron's exciting life to his miserable existence. Aaron got away from home when he went to college. Now he was experiencing other countries in the army. Chet rarely went across the state line. Grace was right he was going nowhere, except maybe to prison. He wanted to comply with his brother's request, but he didn't relish visiting

Jethroe. There was a knock on the door. Bart walked in and stood looking down at Chet. ‘You okay, Chet?’

‘Feeling a little down, is all.’

‘Is the letter from Aaron?’

‘Yeah, he gives his regards. He’s coming home on leave at the end of the month.’

‘That’s good. We need to talk.’

‘Okay.’

Chet sat up on the bed and Bart pulled up a seat as if he was visiting someone in hospital.

‘Cops been looking for you,’ said Bart.

‘That figures.’

‘They want you to go the station house to help with their inquiries. They suspect it was you that hit that trucker.’

Chet sat upright. ‘You tell them?’

‘Hell no. Someone from the bar talked, I guess.’

‘They gonna charge me with assault?’

‘They didn’t say.’

‘I was defending Bobby. That brute was gonna to beat the crap out of him and he threw the first punch.’

‘Was Bobby hurt?’

‘Moved his head just in time, the punch only grazed him.’

Bart rubbed his eye with his hand. ‘Maybe you can claim self-defense, but I ain’t no lawyer, Chet.’

‘There’s a cop sitting outside the guy’s room at the hospital. That ain’t usual.’

‘Maybe they are waiting for him to give his account of the incident as soon as he’s able. What you gonna do?’

‘Reckon I’ll sleep on it, uncle.’

Chapter 5

Next morning Chet loaded up his station wagon with a couple of bags of clothes, his precious guitar and his life savings which didn't amount to much more than a couple of hundred dollars. He left the keys for the Dodge in his bedroom with a note for uncle Bart. Soon he would be on the interstate heading to Memphis. In his dreams he'd envisaged this moment many times before. Chet felt obliged to visit Jethroe before he left, to pass on the message from Aaron. It would be the first time he'd been to Jethroe's house since he picked up that cycle chain. He didn't feel good about calling on Jethroe, but from now on he wasn't going to run away from his problems, even though it appeared that was exactly what he was doing.

Thelma opened the door and her eyes nearly popped out. A huge smile appeared on her face as she threw her arms around Chet. His body was rigid, but he put his arms around her to reciprocate. He knew Thelma, but they had never been that familiar, so her intimacy had taken him by surprise. Ever since his mom had died she'd been helping Jethroe, who paid her to clean the house from top to bottom. She was thankful for the money as her husband had ran off with another woman, leaving her to bring up three children on her own. At first Jethroe hardly ever saw her as he was usually outside working on the farm, but Chet remembered the day that Jethroe showed some real compassion towards Thelma. It stuck in his mind because it seemed out of character. She had arrived late and had rushed into the barn where Jethroe, Aaron and Chet were busy with pitch forks moving hay. Chet remembered the conversation.

'I got a favor to ask, Mr. Carter. My youngest boy's ill.' Thelma had said.

'You go right on home and tend to him, Thelma,' Jethroe had replied.'

'Ain't gotta leave right now but I gotta get some medicine from the pharmacist on the way home. Used all my money paying the doctor's fee, so I was wondering if I could I get an advance on my wages?'

'How much you need?'

'I'm not sure but ten dollars would probably cover it.'

'Here, have twenty and let me know if you need more.'

'That's real kind of you, Mr. Carter. Take it out of my pay at the end of the week,' Thelma had said.

'Let's call it a bonus. You've been doing such a fine job I've been meaning to give you a raise anyway,' Jethroe had replied.

At the end of the month Thelma tried to give Jethroe the money back but he had refused to take it. Thelma invited him to come over for supper to thank him.

Looking back, Chet now realized that was probably the start of the relationship, although they kept things low key. Every now and then Jethroe would sleep over at her house, or vice versa, but they rarely went out together. To the best of Chet's knowledge, they never went away for the weekend, or on holiday. Jethroe was kind and generous to Thelma and she was giving towards him, but her priority was her children to whom she devoted most of her time. It was common knowledge something was going on between them. Chet didn't have a problem with that. Everyone was entitled to a few home comforts. He brought his thoughts back to the present as Thelma spoke. 'This is a pleasant surprise, Chet.' Thelma seemed genuinely pleased to see him and Chet was happy she was there as Jethroe was usually in a better mood when she was around.

'Good to see you, Thelma. Is my daddy home?'

'Sure, come in. I'll go get him.'

When Jethroe walked into the room and saw Chet sitting in the lounge he raised his eyebrows, then he screwed his face and narrowed his eyes. Thelma's smile turned to a frown as she saw the look of contempt on Jethroe's face. Chet knew that Thelma hated arguments.

Jethroe said, 'What you doing here?'

'Just got a letter from Aaron. He wants you to write him as he's planning a trip home.'

'Jethroe rubbed his brow. 'Been meaning to send a letter.'

'Reckon you need to write him to confirm the date.'

Jethroe cocked his head to one side. Chet had seen that look of many times before, and figured Jethroe was expecting him to ask for money. 'That all you want?' Jethroe asked.

'I'm leaving town.'

'What for?'

'Wanna make something of myself. Ain't nothing for me here.'

'Heard you broke a pool cue over a trucker's head and the cops are after you. It's my guess you're running scared.'

'It was self-defense, and I ain't scared of the cops, anyhow.'

'Ain't talking about the cops, you oughta be worried about Sullivan.' Jethroe said pointing at Chet,' You picked on the wrong guy this time, the word is he ain't the sort to let things lie, so you can expect a shit load of pain when he gets his hands on you.'

'I ain't gonna be around when he comes looking.'

'Hoodlums like Sullivan don't give up that easily. He'll run you down like a hound dog chasing a raccoon.'

'Ain't telling no-one where I'm going, so you ain't gotta fret about Sullivan.'

'Guys like Sullivan ain't particular about who they pick on. This could bring a whole world of hurt on anyone gets in his way.'

'Who you been talking to, anyhow? You ain't been in Guthrie's for years.'

Jethroe sat down. 'News travels fast.'

Chet held his head high. 'Well, let it be known on the grapevine that I'm out of here. When I'm a famous musician I'll be back to visit.'

Jethroe sniffed. You're living in a dream world, you ain't ever gonna make anything of yourself. You're a lazy good for nothing…….'

Thelma interjected, 'Jethroe, quit being so mean to the boy.'

Jethroe raised his eyebrows in surprise. 'This ain't none of your business, Thelma.'

'She's right. All you ever done is put me down. You're a bitter, old man.'

Almost before Chet had finished the sentence Jethroe stood up and grabbed hold of him by the throat, pushing him backwards until his head slammed against the wall.

Thelma shrieked, 'Jethroe, stop.'

He let go and Chet came swinging at him, but the old man struck the first telling blow, a straight jab to Chet's nose knocking his head back. Thelma quickly put herself between father and son, pushing Jethroe away. Chet ran the back of his hand across the underside of his nose. It came away smeared with blood and he looked Jethroe in the eye.

'All you've ever done is hurt me. Best thing I ever done was moving in with Uncle Bart. Don't know why I even came here, you and me ain't never gonna see eye to eye.'

Chet turned and walked out the door, but paused before he closed the door to listen to Thelma, reprimanding Jethroe.

'How can you treat your own flesh and blood that way? What's the boy ever done to cause you to be so hateful?'

Jethroe didn't answer and when Thelma let go of him he just walked out of the room with his head lowered. Chet wasn't frightened of his old man, tough as he was, but he was grateful for Thelma's timely intervention. For once in his life Chet felt as though he was in the right and Jethroe was wrong. Jethroe had a way of blaming him for everything which made Chet feel guilty even when it wasn't his fault. At the moment, he felt like the world had it in for him. He was no longer allowed in Guthrie's, the one place he could let his hair down, meet his friends, play guitar, and escape the boredom of this one-horse town. Grace had dumped him, and he knew he was nothing more than a moonshine delivery boy. Aaron's letter advised him not to waste his talent. Chet sped out the drive and pulled onto the highway.

Chapter 6

The plan was to drive west on the interstate following the signs for Memphis, once there he needed to find somewhere to sleep for the night. Then he would look for a job and visit the recording studios. Surely life in the big city would be better than living in a hick town in nowhereville. When he hit the outskirts of the city he looked for a motel, nothing fancy but good enough for someone on a limited budget. He settled on a Motel 6 just off the interstate. After checking in he picked up a local paper from a rack in the lobby and scoured the want ads. There were pages of minimum wage jobs that he didn't want and heaps of jobs for which he wasn't qualified, or had no experience.

He thought back to when he had worked in the hardware store. That had been his weekend job while he was still at high school, but he had found it boring. To break up the monotony he used to take his guitar to work and practiced in his lunch break. Sometimes he'd think of a tune and he couldn't wait to pick up his guitar and reproduce the sound that was going around in his head. One day when the store was empty a tune had come to him, so he went into the storeroom where he'd left his guitar and started strumming. The store owner, Brad Thompson, found Chet playing guitar when he should have been upfront waiting on customers.

'You lazy son of a bitch. I pay you for serving customers not sitting around playing guitar.' Mr. Thompson had said.

'Ain't no one in the store to serve, Mr. Thompson.' Chet had replied.

'How the hell would you know way back in here making a racket like a stray tom cat.'

Chet uttered his usual retort when he thought he was being unjustly treated. 'Fuck you.' Diplomacy wasn't on his resume.

Chet had got the job at the hardware store after Aaron had left to work on his daddy's farm. Unlike Chet, Aaron was well thought of by Brad Thompson. He had certainly never been accused of slacking. Chet didn't fret when Mr. Thompson had fired him, as he had never been enthusiastic about working in the store. Getting fired had not only lost Chet a source of income, it earned him another beating from Jethroe. That was before the show down that had resulted in Chet moving in with his Uncle Bart.

Getting back to his current predicament he now began to question the wisdom of leaving home and he was full of self-doubt. Tomorrow he would try to locate the recording studios, where he hoped they would take him on as a session guitarist. He had no idea if they would let him audition if he just showed up. Suddenly, the pot of gold at the end of the rainbow seemed as elusive as ever. He felt lonely and he missed Uncle Bart and Bobby. He especially missed Grace's body. He picked up his guitar and strummed a blues song which made him feel much better. The blues became his friend for the night and his comfort blanket. He got himself a coffee from the machine in the lobby, and as he sipped the bitter liquid he remembered that he'd driven past an auto repair shop just before he turned into the motel. There was a large sign saying, *'Help Wanted, mechanic.'* Chet had slowed down as he went past but he didn't stop. At the time, he was more concerned about finding somewhere to stay, but the auto shop was a possibility as he knew a little about fixing cars, but he didn't have any qualifications. This was the first night he'd ever spent away from his home town. His life had fallen apart, and it was time to put it back together again, but at least he was now in Memphis, where he wanted to be.

Chapter 7

Next morning Chet went down to the motel reception. The girl on the desk looked like she'd had a late night, she'd got bags under her eyes and her make up looked like it was put on in the dark.

'Where's good for breakfast?' said Chet.

'Most people go to I Hop.' The girl answered with a bored look on her badly painted face. No thought of a smile.

'Is it far?'

'Couple of blocks.'

'Know where Sun Record Studios is at?'

'No, sir.'

Chet realized he wouldn't get a lot of help from her, but he went with the girl's recommendation for breakfast. One large stack of pancakes later he decided to go exploring. He was anxious to find the recording studios, but his priority had to be to get a job, so he went back to the motel to use the pay phone to call some of the places in the want ads. There was a half-page advert for a driver and he dialed the number.

'Calling about the ad in the paper for a delivery driver,' said Chet when he got through.

'We're interviewing all this week; can you get down to our office today?'

'Sure.'

'Got any driving experience?'

'Been a driver for my uncle's business.'

'Bring some references, along with your resume.'

'Ain't got a resume.' Chet replied.

'Just bring your references, then.'

Chet felt the frustration boiling up inside, 'Ain't got them either.'

'You got any written testimonials?'

'No, but you can call my uncle, he'll vouch for my driving.'

The expression in the girl's voice became more monotone 'We need written references, as soon as you get them call me back.'

Chet called several other places wanting drivers but they all required references. Some asked for proof of his high school graduation and that was another diploma that he didn't have. Feeling deflated he decided to go find the recording studios. He discovered the address in the directory and got directions from a man he met in the hotel lobby. Chet entered the building and went up to the pretty receptionist.

'Hi, name's Chet Carter. I sing, and play guitar and I'd like to audition to become a session guitarist, I also write my own songs.'

She lifted her reading glasses and looked up at Chet. 'You got a demo tape?'

'No, but I got my guitar in the car and I'm prepared to play a couple of tunes.'

'We really need to hear a demo tape first. If my boss likes what he hears then we can set up an audition.'

'How about I make a demo tape in your recording studio?'

'It's fifty dollars an hour.'

'Can't afford that.'

'Well, if you make your own it'll be cheaper.'

'Maybe I'll just wait until your boss has ten minutes to spare then play him a couple of songs?'

The receptionist looked down at her paperwork, 'He doesn't have any free time. His appointment book is full all week and in any case…'

'I know he don't do auditions without hearing a demo tape first.'

'You got it,' she replied.

Chet was aware that the interview was fast coming to an end. He leaned forward on the desk. 'How about you and me going on a date? I'm new in town so you can show me around.'

'I already got a boyfriend.'

'Too bad, I'll call back when I got that tape.'

Chet decided to drive around and orientate himself. He found an employment agency and the lady on reception was polite and helpful, but she said the same things as all the others, references, resume, high school diploma. Every place he went was the same. Chet didn't have any way to prove that he was a hard worker. After a frustrating day, he went to get something to eat in a diner. It looked cheap which was how he liked it. As he sat eating his food a bum came up to the table, cap in hand.

'Got any change?'

Chet looked at the man in his scruffy jacket. He looked thin and dirty, hungry and homeless. The vagrant looked a little like his Uncle Bart, same bad teeth and dirty, uncombed hair, and Chet wondered what Bart was doing now. He thought back to when he moved in with his uncle at the tender age of fifteen and inevitably joined the family business. As far as Chet was concerned he was a courier, plain and simple, he didn't know, or care, what he was carrying. It soon became clear that his uncle was an illegal bookmaker, as well as a bootlegger. The contents of an envelope would make someone's day, or a losing bet might have the opposite effect. Bart made good money from all his rackets, or his portfolio as he preferred to call it. However, this was not always the case. One of the punters had told Chet about a time that he had won big, when his horses had all came in, and Bart had to beg, borrow and steal to pay him off. Chet realized that must have been the day that Bart had visited his father for a loan.

Chet took some comfort in seeing someone who was worse off than him, and gave the bum a dollar. If he couldn't find work and his money ran out, maybe Chet would end up just like the vagrant. This had not turned out to be a very productive first day in Memphis, all that remained was for him to go back to the motel and play the blues.

Chapter 8

Bobby was in Guthrie's chalking his cue. His eyes nearly popped out, and his mouth opened like a fish, as Grace walked in, arm in arm, with Carl Morgan. He nudged Rita. 'Didn't take her long to hook up with a new beau.'

'Do you think she'd got him lined up before she finished with Chet?' Rita asked.

'Who knows, Rita.'

'Still can't believe Chet is gone. Was it the bar fight, or his break up with Grace, that did it?'

Bobby lined up his next shot. 'More likely the fight, Chet's always had girls hanging off of him like fleas on a dog.'

'Is that why you always hung with him, so some of them fleas might drop onto you?'

Bobby had known that hanging around with Chet could get him into trouble, but he had thought that it was well worth the risk. Chet was popular with the girls and Bobby had wanted some of that charm to rub off on him. He missed his shot by a long way and glanced over at his girlfriend. 'Yeah, that's how I got you, Rita?'

Rita put her arm around Bobby. 'I used to have a crush on Chet, but that all changed when you came along.'

She gave her boyfriend a big smile and pecked him on the cheek. Bobby didn't flinch and seemed unimpressed by the compliment. 'Your shot, Rita.'

Rita bent over the pool table leaning over her cue with her cute little ass sticking in the air, and Bobby remembered why he liked having Rita as his girl.

'Bet you wouldn't have shown any interest in me if I wasn't Chet's buddy,' said Bobby.

'Hanging with Chet may have put you more in the spotlight, but it's always been your kind and generous nature that attracted me.'

'You're full of shit, Rita, but I like you being my girl. I just wish you were better at shooting pool.' Bobby smirked. He guessed that Rita was lying to make him feel good, but he didn't really care. He patted her backside happy in the knowledge that she gave him what he needed. When he put down the black, all Rita's balls were still on the table. He looked over at Grace and Carl who were standing at the bar. Grace saw him stacking the balls and wandered over. 'Heard anything from Chet?'

Bobby looked at the tip of his cue as he answered. 'Ain't expecting to for a while.'

'Know where he's at?' Grace remarked as she casually put on some lip gloss,

'Wouldn't tell you if I did, Grace.'

Grace thrust the lip gloss back in her purse and stared hard at Bobby. 'Why not? I ain't to blame for how things turned out. Chet and me came to a natural end.'

Bobby carefully took the triangle from around the balls and stared back at Grace. 'From where I'm standing it looks like you dumped him for Carl.'

'Look Bobby, I know you'll always take Chet's side, but he's an accident waiting to happen. When I first met Chet, I loved his rebellious nature, he reminded me of James Dean and we had some crazy times, but he's like a coiled spring wound so tight he can snap open at any time.'

'That's as maybe, Grace, but you better not start bad mouthing Chet in front of me. Chet don't take crap from nobody, he don't ever back down, and he stands up for his friends. That's why I've always admired him.'

Rita put her arm around her boyfriend and directed her gaze at Grace.

'Bobby's right, Chet did okay by you Grace. Reckon you don't know a good thing when it's staring you in the face.'

'We all know you got a thing for Chet, Rita.'

'I did have until you took him from me, but I lucked out when I got Bobby, and now you got Carl running after you like a love-sick puppy.'

Rita put her arm around Bobby's waist and the two girls snarled at each other, until Grace curled her lips and turned away. She didn't have to wait long before Carl came back from the bar and handed her a cocktail. Bobby knew exactly what Grace saw in Carl, as his daddy was manager of the biggest insurance company in the state. He'd recently appointed Carl a junior executive and the job came with a brand, new Chevy, unlike the old piece of junk that Bobby was struggling to keep on the road. Last weekend he had spent hours fixing the brakes. He thought of all the happy times he spent with Chet working on old cars. They didn't mind getting their hands dirty and enjoyed servicing their own automobiles. Not so long ago they had tuned up Chet's station wagon. Bobby watched Grace link her arm in Carl's like she used to do to with Chet and he felt like slapping the bitch. He didn't blame Carl as he was just taking advantage of the situation. By all accounts Grace was a good lay and now she was available.

Bobby thought back to how eager Carl had been to hang out with him and Chet. He may have been from a rich family, but he had desperately wanted to be thought of as a regular guy. He'd got the air of superiority that came with being a rich kid, but when he hung with Chet he got the street credibility he craved.

Bobby remembered the time when they had gone to see a band in the next town. Carl had a flash automobile with a tank full of gas and he didn't mind being the designated driver. When the band finished they left the auditorium and walked back to the car. Carl, who had been on coke all night, kept glancing behind as he realized that they were being followed by some local rednecks. As they got back to the car one of the rednecks accused Carl of staring at his girl. Carl held up his hands to show that he didn't want any trouble, but the youth took a kick at his car leaving a dent in the door. Chet grabbed the redneck by the collar and kicked his feet from under him.

As the guy hit the ground Chet stood on his neck, pushing it into the gravel. One of the local boy's friends pushed Chet off him allowing the boy on the ground to get up and trade blows with Chet until he was knocked down again. Chet jumped on top of him, straddling him, and pinned his arms to the ground, before asking him if he'd had enough. The boy nodded his agreement and the fight was over. Chet climbed off him and brushed the dirt off his clothes. They were both covered in blood and breathing heavy, but Chet had a smile on his face a mile wide. As the youths walked away Carl scratched his head as he surveyed Chet's bloody face and the dent in his car. 'Son of a bitch had no reason to do that.' Chet put his arm around his friend and told him that they could easily knock out the dent, but Carl said that he was more concerned about Chet's face than the auto. Chet had informed him that if it had been the other way around he'd be more worried about the dent.

Bobby now reflected that Carl had not only got the money, but he'd acquired the girl as well. He placed the triangle in its slot and looked over at the slime ball. 'Break up them balls, Carl, winner stays on and I just kicked Rita's butt, as usual.'

'Are you sure you don't wanna play Grace to improve the odds of keeping your winning streak going?'

'I'll play Grace after I've whooped your sorry ass.'

As he chalked his cue Bobby could see, out of the corner of his eye, Carl winking at Grace. There was something about Carl that caused Bobby not to trust him.

Chapter 9

Aaron sat on the stool in the corner of the ring, adrenalin pumping, his heart beating rapidly, as his trainer wiped his brow.

'More of the same, Aaron, you definitely won the round. Jab and move, jab and move.'

Aaron kept nodding his head. He already knew that the round was his and that the jab was working well. Everything was going according to plan, left jab to the head, dodge and back away. Not all his punches struck home as he sometimes hit his opponent's guard, but the jab got through, and found its target, enough times to win him the round. His opponent's head sent backwards time and again. He looked across the ring, the soldier he was fighting was a black man, a couple of inches shorter than Aaron but stockier with massive biceps and very strong. He caught Aaron once in the first round with a left cross, and it hurt, so Aaron had kept dodging and working the jab. His trainer had told him to wait for the right opportunity to use his combination left, right, left. Aaron had seized his chance when his opponent missed with a roundhouse and he had quickly slammed a left, right combination into the boxer's head. His third punch was a glancing blow as his opponent composed himself and countered with a hook to the side of the head, which didn't hurt as much as the earlier right cross. Aaron brought himself back to the present, his trainer was still talking. 'Don't get in close, this guy's dangerous. Keep out of his reach, jab and move, get in and get out. If you try mixing it with this guy, you'll lose.'

Aaron kept nodding his head. He knew his opponent had won his previous two fights, stopping both boxers in the early rounds. Looking across the ring he could see the soldier's bottom lip was bleeding which showed the effectiveness of the constant, stabbing power of his jab. The bell sounded.

'Seconds away.'

Aaron quickly rose to his feet, eager to get on with the job.

'More of the same, Aaron, jab and move,' his trainer prompted.

His opponent rushed in with a flurry of punches and Aaron dodged and weaved. His well-constructed guard blocked what he couldn't avoid and the only punches that connected landed on his gloves. Aaron hit back with his jab, swerved away then hit him again. And so, it went on, jab and move, same as the first round. Aaron continued notching up points. It was getting near the end of the round and Aaron could see that the soldier was getting frustrated with his inability to land any decent punches. His right eye was starting to close in addition to his fat lip. In desperation, he launched a massive roundhouse punch which Aaron saw coming and dodged out of the way, watching his opponent stumble, completely off balance, as he hit fresh air. Aaron saw his opportunity and slammed a left, right, left into the boxer's head, then he stepped back, ready to get back into the jab and move mode, but he could see that his opponent was hurt. The combination had done some real damage. Instinctively, Aaron stepped in with a body shot and another combination of punches to the head, the only response from the soldier was a feeble punch that connected but lacked any power. Aaron went for the kill, an uppercut followed by a solid right to the soldier's stomach, doubling him up in pain. Aaron went to work again, two left jabs followed by another big right and the soldier hit the canvas. Momentarily, Aaron stood over him, but the referee jumped in, quickly pushing him away, and started the count. The soldier lay on his back, clearly dazed, not moving for a couple of seconds. Then he tried to lever himself up, but he didn't have the strength and collapsed back on the canvas.

'Six, seven.'

The man looked up at Aaron with an expression of desperation in his eyes. Aaron had seen that look before and he knew that the contest was over. Even if his opponent made the count he was going down again. The only thing that could save him was the bell and Aaron wondered how long was left to the end of round. He waited, ready to pounce, hungry to continue where he'd left off.

'Eight, nine.'

The soldier was resting on his elbow, sweat dripping from his face. One last push to lever himself up. Did he have enough strength left in his arms? Had he got the will to carry on? He collapsed again, accepting the inevitable.

'Ten.'

The referee raised Aaron's arm aloft and the crowd cheered. His trainer smiled and slapped him on the back. The last time Aaron had felt like this was when, as a quarterback, he'd thrown the ball into the hands of the receiver in the end zone for a winning touchdown. Only this was even better. He looked at the wildly applauding crowd and saw, on the second row, a smiling Sergeant Hammond who winked knowingly at Aaron.

Chapter 10

Chet spent another miserable night wondering why he'd left the quite familiarity of the Smokies for an unknown city. He'd abandoned friends and family for loneliness, and a steady job for unemployment. His daddy and Bart had fallen out before Chet was even born. He wondered about his dysfunctional family. According to Uncle Bart, when they were youngsters Jethroe and him were full of brotherly love. According to Jethroe, Bart was a lazy, good for nothing, street wise, chancer, operating outside the law. Luke, the youngest of the brothers, joined Bart in the moonshine operation, but moved away long ago and Chet never knew him.

Next day Chet woke up determined to remain positive and he remembered the auto repair shop with the sign. It was probably as good a prospect as anything he'd seen in the newspaper. He'd seen the board just before he found the motel, so it wasn't far, and he was pretty sure he'd be able to find it again. Job vacancies had a habit of getting filled quickly so he decided to set off early. It suited his impulsive nature to act quickly. He figured he'd got nothing to lose and he'd give it his best shot, he just hoped the man doing the hiring wasn't hung up on qualifications.

Fortunately, the "help wanted" sign was still hanging outside the auto repair shop. A bell on top of the door rang as Chet walked into the office. At first no one seemed to be around then a man in dirty overalls, wiping his hands on a rag, came into the office from a door adjoining the work shop. Presumably the business wasn't big enough to have a girl at the desk. He said, 'Sorry to keep you waiting, son. What can I do for you today?'

'Come about the job,' Chet replied.

The owner of the business looked Chet up and down 'You a mechanic?'

'No but I know how to fix automobiles.'

The man put the rag in a pocket in the front of his coverall. 'What training and qualifications you got?'

'Keep that rusty old station wagon of mine, that's sitting outside, in good working order. Spent more hours than I care to recall fixing my uncle's pick up and my best friend's Ford.'

'I take it you ain't got any formal training, or qualifications, then?'

'No, sir.'

Chet kept looking the owner in the eye. He wanted to appear confident and to look away, or look down at his feet, would give the wrong impression. The man looked about fifty. He wasn't big but nor was he scrawny.

'The name's Bill Sanders and I own this business. Started fixing cars myself when I was about your age. Worked under some first-rate mechanics before deciding to buy this place and go it alone. Had two other mechanics but one's just upped and left. That means there's only Danny and me and he's gonna be in later as he's taking his wife to hospital. We're snowed under with work. I was about to give this Chevy truck a full service, but now I'm gonna ask you to do it and I'm gonna sit here and watch. If I like what I see you get the job. How's that sound?'

'Sounds fair to me, Mr. Sanders.'

'What's your name?

'Chet Carter.'

Chet followed Mr. Sanders into the work shop where a Chevy truck was high in the air on ramps. Bill asked Chet to outline what he would include in a full service and Chet went through all the jobs from changing the oil and filter to greasing all the bearings.

'So far so good, Chet. Go ahead and do what you just told me. You can use them tools over there and I'll fetch any parts you need.'

Bill pointed to a metal cantilever box full of wrenches of every description. Chet nodded his head and went to work. An hour later he'd finished the service and he looked Bill square in the face as he wiped his hands on an old rag.

'How'd I do?'

'There's a few things you missed but over all you done good, Chet.'

Chet beamed like a head light. He waited a few seconds then asked the million-dollar question. 'Do I get the job?'

'Mechanics working here also have to keep an eye on the office and pick up the phone. If we can't get to it in time we let the machine take the message. You okay with that?'

'Sure.'

'Okay, I'll give you a try. You will be on a month's probation and I expect you to listen and learn as much as you can from me.'

'When do I start?'

'Guess you already have, son. Pick up that coverall hanging over there and you can work alongside me for the rest of the day. Tomorrow we start at 8.00 am and finish at 5.00 pm, sometimes we stay later if need be. You get thirty minutes for lunch. Take it whenever it fits with the work.'

'Why didn't I get to wear this coverall before I serviced the Chevy. I could have kept my shirt and pants clean?'

'You weren't on the payroll an hour ago.'

Chet burst out laughing. 'You mean I don't get paid for that service I just did, either?'

Bill looked hard at the boy. 'You remind me of myself thirty years ago. I like the way you're prepared to speak up for yourself. If I'm satisfied with your work at the end of the week I'll pay you from the minute you walked in the shop.'

'Sounds good to me.'

'You ain't asked about the pay.'

'Figured you'd pay me the going rate.'

'You figured right, Chet.'

At a little after 5.15 pm Bill told Chet to go wash up as they were finished for the day. While they were drying their hands, Bill asked Chet where he lived.

‘I’m new in town, staying at the motel six a couple of miles from here. What about you?’

‘See that house over there?’ Bill pointed to a dwelling no more than a hundred yards away.

‘The one painted grey and white?’said Chet.

‘Yeah, that’s my home, although the wife reckons I spend more time here. The house came with the business. We’ve lived here for twenty-three years and raised two girls. Both have already flown the nest.’

‘Living that close to work is mighty convenient.’

‘Be here 8.00 am tomorrow, and don’t be late.’

‘I won’t.’

Chapter 11

Chet was servicing an old Buick. As he worked his mind drifted back to his family, remembering how close they all were when he was little. He pictured his mother cooking in the kitchen, his daddy working hard in the fields and Aaron and him playing in the yard. It was a while now since he'd seen Aaron and he missed his big brother a lot. He thought back to how Aaron had teased him when they played basketball in the yard. Aaron was three years older and much taller and he would hold the ball as high as he could. As Chet jumped up to try and knock the ball out of his hands he would move his hands and laugh as Chet hit fresh air. One day when Aaron had been performing his usual trick, Chet's face had banged into Aaron's elbow real hard, resulting in Chet's first black eye. Later, Aaron had bought him a popsicle to compensate. It was impossible to stay mad at Aaron for long and if Chet lost his temper, as he invariably did, Aaron would ruffle his hair and make a joke. Chet soon calmed down and that mischievous smile magically appeared on his face. Aaron often took Chet along with him when he was meeting his friends. They used to ask why he'd brought his kid brother along and Aaron replied, 'Asked him if he wanted to come along and he said yes. That's good enough for me.'

Chet had always felt a sense of pride hanging with his big brother and he decided now was a good time to write to Aaron as he'd got some good news for a change. He'd also be able to tell Bobby about his new job next time he called him. Chet was still day dreaming when he suddenly realized that Bill was asking him a question.

'Sorry Mr. Sanders, was thinking about my brother, Aaron.'

'Call me Bill. You getting home sick?'

'Not really, Bill, my brother's in the army.'

'My wife, Jean was wondering if you'd like to come for supper tomorrow night. She always cooks more than we can eat so it's no problem.'

'Wouldn't wanna impose, Bill.'

'You wouldn't be. My wife's a good cook, she loves entertaining and she enjoys meeting new people. Jean's home cooking is far better than the fast food you get across the street. Besides I need to make sure my workers are well fed.'

'Well if it ain't no trouble,' Chet replied.

'It ain't.'

'Guess I'd be stupid to turn down a home cooked meal. I've been eating a whole load of junk lately.'

'That settles it, I'll speak to Jean. She'll probably make meatloaf, it's her specialty.'

'Sounds good to me, Bill.'

'That's becoming your catch phrase, son.'

Chet picked up a wrench and started taking the wheel lugs off the Buick. He had taken to Bill Sanders in the same way he got along with his Uncle Bart, which wasn't too surprising as Chet made friends easily, but he didn't have any difficulty making enemies either. When Bill went into the office Danny, who was working in the next bay, shouted over. 'How's it going, Chet?'

'Pretty good,' Chet replied.

'Bill seems to have taken a liking to you.'

'He's a great guy.'

'You got a girl, Chet?'

'Not yet, I recently split up with my girl, but I'll probably go looking one night this week. You wanna come?'

Danny stood with his hands on his hips. 'You gotta be kidding, got a wife and three kids with one more on the way.'

'Shit, you don't look no older than me.'

'Married young, we we're at high school when Genie got pregnant,' said Danny.

Chet said, 'Had my share of girlfriends at high school but none of them got caught. Did you graduate?'

'Hell no, had to leave high school to get a job, only diploma I got is my marriage license. Shotgun wedding, but I ain't complaining.'

Chet said, 'I finished school early to go work for my uncle, never really fitted in at high school.'

'Why not?'

'Always in trouble, I had a fist fight my first week.'

Bill came back, and the guys ended their conversation and carried on working. He looked at Chet and said, 'Just been talking to Jean on the phone and were all set for supper.'

Chet replied, 'I'm looking forward to it, Bill.'

Chapter 12

Bart was loading up the Dodge, but he put the crate of moonshine on the ground as Bobby pulled into the yard.

'You heard from Chet yet, Bobby. His note said he'd call soon as he got settled.'

Bobby said, 'Chet called a few days ago and asked me to help you out at weekends. During the week, I got my own job to go to.'

'That's mighty good of you, Bobby. Finding it tough without Chet. Ain't as fit as I used to be.'

'You got some more hooch to run?'

'Six drop offs, got two more crates to put in the Dodge. I'd appreciate it if you load them, as my back's giving me some grief. You been friends with Chet since grade school ain't ya?'

'Yeah, we were on the same little league baseball team. I was only a bench warmer, as I was an overweight kid. Chet was the star batter in the team. Remember once during a game when I had been standing in the outfield and a low ball came my way. It had looked like a possible catch, but it bounced just in front of me and I missed it completely. The coach threw his cap into the dirt in disgust. Later in the same game I had been standing in line to bat when the coach tapped me on the shoulder and said, "If you weren't carrying so much blubber you'd have caught that ball." I told him it was a ground ball that had hit the turf before it reached me, but he said, "I say you should have caught it, fat boy." My chin dropped to my chest and I stared into the dirt, but Chet stuck up for me and said to the coach, "Don't believe it helps any, getting onto Bobby's case, coach?" The coach replied, "Don't remember asking for your opinion, Carter?" Chet retorted, "You got it anyhow." Coach Watson put Chet at the back of the batting line and had told him that he would regret speaking out against him. Chet had told him he'd regret putting him last to bat.'

Bobby was now grinning as he remembered the incidence, but Bart scratched his head and said, 'Are you trying to claim that Chet got the better of the exchange?'

Bobby replied, 'I thought he did at the time, but Chet always batted at the bottom of the line after that, and he never played the following season.'

Bart spat into the dirt and put his cap back on his head, 'That's what happens when you go up against authority.'

Bobby said, 'What it proved to me was Chet's prepared to stand up for his friends.'

'Same way he did against Sullivan,' said Bart.

'Yeah, reckon I owe him one for that too. I've loaded the Dodge. You got a list of customers?'

'You'll find the list and the address book on the passenger seat. While you're doing the run, I'll be able to make a few calls. I'll pay you when you get back.'

Bobby climbed into the Dodge and wound down the window, 'Appreciate the money, Mr. Carter, but I'm really helping as a favor to Chet.'

'Everyone needs money, son.'

'Without Chet around you're gonna need some regular help.'

'You're damn right, know anyone who could use a little extra cash?'

Bobby knew it would be difficult to find help for an illegal enterprise. He believed the local cops were turning a blind eye to Bart's venture, but he still felt uneasy talking about it.

'Can't say as I do, Mr. Carter. I'll keep coming over at weekends, but I don't think it's wise to be lifting too many of them crates at your age.'

Bart took off his baseball cap, smoothed his hair, and put it back on his head which was a habit of his when he'd got something on his mind. Bobby knew that Bart was concerned that Chet might not be coming back. He said to Bart, 'The news going around town is that Sullivan was wanted by the cops for illegal activities. If he goes to jail maybe Chet will be off the hook,'

Bart said, 'There's a cop that goes for a beer in Guthrie's and Maurice has a habit of listening in on conversations. Might take a trip into town for a few beers.'

Bobby pulled out of the yard, the mason jars rattling in the crates as he turned the corner. Bart went into the house and poured himself some moonshine, sipping it slowly. After a while he was asleep on the couch with Duke lying on the floor beside him.

Chapter 13

'Want some more, Chet?'

'Don't mind if I do Mrs. Sanders.'

'Call me Jean, and help yourself, there's plenty left.'

The meat loaf was tasty, so Chet didn't need asking twice. He spooned another large helping onto his plate. Bill wasn't joking about how tired he would feel at the end of a long day working in the shop. After supper, they talked for a while. Jean was a lovely lady and he could tell by the way that Bill looked at her, and she smiled back at him, that they were a devoted couple. Chet didn't want to linger too long as he planned to spend the evening exploring a few bars, but first he wanted to call Bobby. He thanked the couple for their hospitality and drove back to the motel where he located a pay phone. He was sure that Bill would have let him use the one at the house, but he'd already done him enough favors, and Chet didn't want to take advantage of his generosity. He called Bobby first, 'What's going on, Bobby?'

'Boy am I pleased you called, Chet.'

'Has something happened?'

'I'm worried about your Uncle Bart. I helped him out on Saturday, like you asked me to, but I really think he's struggling to carry those crates of hooch. When he straightens up, after loading the Dodge, his face seems racked with pain.'

'His back's been troubling him for a while. Guess he's getting too old to be doing too much manual labor.'

'Reckon he's hoping you'll be back when things have settled down.'

'Might have to disappoint him there, Bobby. I'm staying here a while longer. I'm working in this auto repair shop, earning good money and the owner treats me like family. Bart needs to find some help, or give up the moonshine racket.'

'If you're planning on being there a while maybe I ought to come visit.'

Chet wasn't ready to entertain Bobby. 'I'd like that, but Uncle Bart needs you more than me. Besides I don't even now the best places to go, yet. I'm gonna check out some bars tonight. How's Rita?'

'Rita's good.'

'You seen Grace?'

'Yeah, seen her in Guthrie's.'

'On her own?'

'No, she's seeing Carl now.'

'How about that, Grace and Carl. Come to think of it, they make a good match.'

'You ain't mad about Grace hanging with Carl?'

'Hell no, I didn't expect Grace to be on her own for long. I'll be looking for some female company, tonight.'

'I don't imagine you'll be on your own for long.'

'Me neither. Give my regards to Uncle Bart. I really appreciate you helping him out, Bobby.'

'He pays good, anyhow.'

'That's why I joined the family business, my good friend.' Chet felt relieved that Bobby seemed unaware of the little rendezvous with Rita. Nothing happened but it still bothered him. He was also anxious about Uncle Bart and felt bad about leaving him on his own. He didn't feel like it was the right time to inform him that he wasn't coming back any time soon. He decided he'd leave calling him for now.

Chapter 14

Bart shuffled into Guthrie's and slid into a seat at the bar, his plan was to find out if Chet was in the clear. Maurice wandered over to serve him.

'Get me a beer, Maurice. I've earned a drink this week.'

'Any news from Chet? said Maurice.'

'Not yet. Have you seen that cop that comes in here, lately?'

'Yeah, he was here yesterday.'

'Did he mention the fight?'

'No but I got some news about Sullivan. Seems the big guy's a trucker working for a family owned haulage business in Kentucky. He's been in no end of trouble but he ain't been convicted of anything. Look like witnesses always suffer from a loss of memory.'

'How'd you find that out? Cops don't divulge that sort of information.'

Maurice put his hands on the bar, leaned in closer, and lowered his voice, 'Truck driver from a rival company gave me the low down. We get a shit load of truckers in here being so close to the interstate off ramp.'

Bart ordered a beer and when Maurice put it on the bar he asked, 'Do you know if the big guy is out of hospital?'

'Yeah, I believe the feds came and collected him soon as he was fit enough to be moved.'

'Is he pressing charges for assault?'

'The cop didn't say.'

'Ask him next time you see him, Maurice?'

Maurice pointed to the door, 'Why don't you ask him yourself, he just walked in.'

Maurice nodded to the newcomer and went over to serve him. After he handed the cop his drink he pointed towards Bart who was looking towards the cop. The cop picked up his beer and wandered over to sit next to him. ‘You wanna speak to me?’

‘I was interested in the condition of the guy that got beat up in here a while back,’ said Bart.

‘What about him?’

‘Is he okay?’

‘Yeah.’

‘Is he pressing charges against the boy that hit him?’

The cop stared hard at Bart, ‘Why do you wanna know?’

‘Just curious.’

The cop leaned forward. ‘I know why you wanna know, it was your nephew, Chet, that done it. You heard from him?’

Bart raised his eyebrows, then looked away. ‘No, he’s skipped town.’

‘Well, soon as he gets in touch tell him we need to speak to him.’

‘You ain’t answered my question about pressing charges.’

‘Can’t give you that information,’ said the cop.

‘Guess our conversation’s over then.’

Bart turned away from the cop and sipped his beer. The cop pulled him around by his shoulder. ‘Just get Chet to contact us?’

Bart was never comfortable in the presence of cops, but he didn’t want any trouble either. He just wanted to get away as he felt like a raccoon standing too close to the rear end of a skunk. He stood up and supped the last of his beer. ‘So long, officer.’

Bart tugged the peak of his cap and slowly slouched out.

Chapter 15

The room was dimly lit, and Chet was standing at the bar with a beer in his hand. This was the second place he'd been in. The first one was too busy with a rowdy crowd playing pool which brought back bad memories. This bar was quieter, and he spotted a pretty girl and smiled at her. She returned the grin even though she was with a lanky youth who gave Chet a dirty look, which Chet assumed was a warning to keep away. Chet was not in the mood to get in a fight on his first night out in Memphis. He looked away and avoided making any more eye contact with the boy's good-looking girlfriend. There didn't seem to be any available, cute looking, girls in the bar. After spending the last few nights playing his guitar in his room he wanted to socialize tonight. As he sipped his beer he turned to a guy standing nearby. 'I'm new in town. Where's all the pretty, single girls?'

'Not in this bar,' the youth replied.

'You know a better place?'

'There's a Country and Western joint nearby that pulls in all the single ladies. The beer is more expensive, though.'

'Are you going there?' Chet figured he was as he wore a checkered, smart shirt, pressed jeans and cowboy boots.

'After I down this beer.'

Chet smiled at the youth, 'Okay if I tag along?'

'Hell no, I'll introduce you to my buddies.'

Chet said, 'You from around here?'

'Yeah, what about you?'

'I just moved from a small-town east of here and I got hired on as a mechanic.'

The youth swirled the beer around his less than half full glass. 'Do you have family here?'

'No, I don't know anyone.'

'That's tough.'

Chet scratched his ear as he spoke, 'Yeah, like starting at high school.'

'It was scary starting high school, but at least I knew a few kids from back in grade school.'

Chet grinned, 'Yeah, me too, it's probably not that similar.'

The youth chortled back, 'Are you ready to get out of here?'

'Sure, my name's Chet.'

'Pleased to make your acquaintance, Chet, I'm Richie.'

The boys shook hands. Chet felt fortunate to be have found a friendly local guy who could show him around. The boys finished their beers and Chet followed Richie to the Country and Western bar. The parking lot was full of fancy pickups. Inside it was cowboy hats, lace ties, smart shirts and boots. Plastic cowboys out to lasso a cow girl. Chet had never seen such a huge dance floor. There was an abundance of couples, gliding smoothly across the floor, doing the two-step mostly. There was no shortage of girls sitting together at tables. Chet wondered if any of the cowgirls were looking for a regular guy. The newly acquainted friends walked towards a very long bar. At one end were a group of four fillies and Chet met their stare head on and smiled at them. Richie ignored the girls and walked to the other end of the bar where two boys were standing drinking Budweiser's out of the bottle. Chet followed Richie, but he kept his focus on the girls until he'd walked past them.

Richie said, 'These are my buddies Randy and Matt.'

Chet said, 'Good to meet you, guys.' He shook hands with the guys.

Randy lifted his beer as he looked at Chet, 'What are you drinking, Chet?'

'Coors,' Chet replied.

Randy ordered beers for Chet and Richie. Chet decided to drink it out of the bottle as he often did, which would fit nicely with his new acquaintances. The boys quizzed Chet about his background and he gave short, clipped answers. His mind was on the girls at the other end of the bar who didn't seem to be with any guys. They were laughing and joking as if the alcohol was having the desired effect. Chet wondered what the boys were waiting for. He did the math and the numbers matched up perfectly. He was getting twitchy with impatience and said, 'How about moving to the other end of the bar, the scenery seems a lot better.'

Richie said, 'You wanna hit on those girls?'

Chet winked at Richie, with a cheeky smile on his face, 'Seems like a plan to me. Any of you guys know those young ladies?'

'Seen them before, but never took the opportunity to get into a conversation,' Richie replied.

'Don't you think it's time to put that omission right, Richie boy?' said Chet.

Randy explained, 'They play hard to get, I seen plenty of guys get blown out.'

Chet stood up, 'I see that as a challenge. What we got to lose?'

Richie replied, 'We reckon those girls seem a little out of our league.'

'Never think like that, Richie. Don't know about you guys but I've recently split up with my sweetheart, so I'm badly in need of female companionship.'

'Only Matt has a regular girl, Randy and I are in the same boat as you,' said Richie.

'Know one thing for sure, going home tonight with one of those fillies will lift my spirits. If you boys are a little shy I don't mind breaking the ice.'

Randy joined the conversation, 'That seems like another way of saying you get first pick.'

'Now that you mention it, Randy. I do have my eye on one girl, but as I'm the new boy in town I won't be too selective.'

Matt had been very quiet up until now. The way he looked at Chet was how Chet looked at a second-hand car dealer trying to sell him a lemon. Obviously, a man of few words he decided it was time to butt in. ‘You seem pretty sure of yourself?’

Chet replied, ‘I’ve never been shy when it comes to the ladies.’

Richie stood up and tapped Chet on the shoulder. ‘Go ahead, Chet, we’re right behind you.’

As the boys approached, the girls pretended to ignore them, but Chet was smiling at them as if he was a long, lost friend. ‘My buddies and I would like to buy you young ladies a drink.’

The prettiest girl with big blue eyes and a pony tail replied. ‘We’re drinking cocktails.’

Chet said, ‘I’ll take that as a yes.’ He caught the attention of the waiter and beckoned him over. ‘I’m buying, state your poison, girls.’

The girls ordered their cocktails and Chet asked the waiter to start him a tab. Richie wiped his brow. Chet didn’t know why he seemed so uncomfortable. Maybe he was shy, or perhaps he was just relieved that Chet was footing the bill. Chet couldn’t take his eyes off the girl with the pony tail. Whatever he said earlier he wasn’t about to let the others move in on her first. ‘What’s your name, sweetheart?

She replied, ‘Rosalie, what’s yours?’

‘I’m Chet and these are my buddies, Richie, Matt and Randy.’

Rosalie had a radiant smile that lit up her pretty face. Chet asked her to dance mainly to get her on her own, away from the others. He was an okay dancer and he knew how to two-step. He took her arm as they walked towards the dance floor.

‘Can’t believe my luck, first night out in Memphis and I’m dancing with the prettiest girl in the city.’

Rosalie blushed, ‘What brings you to Memphis?’

Chet replied, ‘I’m looking for a new sweetheart and it seems like I’ve found her.’

‘You don’t waste time getting to the point.’

‘I know what I like.’

Rosalie tilted her head backward a little, ‘Bet you got a girlfriend back in your home town.’

'Did have, but we broke up and now I'm living here.'

'Are you running away because she broke your heart?'

Chet smiled, 'It was more a jolt to the ego than a tug at the heart strings. Grace was a lovely girl, but she was plain compared to you.'

'You're such a smooth talker, Chet. I bet you got women all over the state.'

'Don't make a habit of moving, Rosalie. This is the first time I've left home, although I've been thinking about breaking loose for a while.'

'Why Memphis?'

'I want to be a musician and I thought there might be more opportunities here.'

'What do you play?'

'Country and blues guitar, some rock and roll and I like to serenade beautiful girls like you.'

'You ever quit with the compliments?'

'Only just getting started but I'll take a break when we kiss.'

Chet moved his lips towards Rosalie, but she turned away.

'You're mighty sure of yourself, Chet.'

'I got a good feeling about you, Rosalie.'

They danced one more song then went back to join the others. There was precious little conversation around the table and the girls looked bored. Matt stood up and offered his hand to Rosalie. 'Believe it's my turn to dance.'

Rosalie said, 'I'm gonna sit this one out, thanks.'

She looked across at Chet whose eyes had narrowed warning Matt to back off, but he stared right back at Chet. Richie stood up, 'Why don't we all get up and dance?'

He offered his hand to one of the girls who smiled back at him as she took it. Another girl by the name of Laura grabbed Chet by the arm. 'Come on Chet.'

Chet reluctantly accompanied Laura onto the dance floor, Richie and Randy escorted the other two girls, leaving Matt and Rosalie sitting alone at the table. While Chet danced with Laura he kept glancing over her shoulder at Matt and Rosalie.

Laura took hold of his face and turned it towards her, 'Hey, you're dancing with me.'

Chet looked at Laura, 'Sorry.'

'You've hardly taken your eyes off Rosalie since you got here.'

'You spotted that?'

'I think everyone has figured that out.'

'You're pretty too, Laura.'

She smiled at Chet, 'Thanks, Chet, but I reckon you're set on Rosalie.'

Chet maneuvered Laura around a couple that nearly collided with them. Laura glared at them, but they were oblivious. Chet brought her attention back to Rosalie, 'Does she have a boyfriend?'

'No.'

'I find that hard to believe.'

'She's not short on offers.'

'Maybe she ain't met the right one until tonight.'

After the dance, they went back to the table and Chet sat across from Rosalie. Her conversation with Matt seemed to have stalled and first chance he got he asked Rosalie to dance. She accepted, and he held her arm lightly as he guided her to the dance floor. He looked into her eyes, 'I wanted to get you away from Matt.'

'I think he only asked me to dance with him to antagonize you. He told me he's got a girlfriend,' said Rosalie.

'Yeah, I reckon Matt don't like me.'

'I thought you were friends?'

'Only just met him, but I know he's jealous because I'm dancing with the sweetest girl I ever did see.'

'I'm not used to guys fighting over me.'

'If he wants to act like a jerk let him go ahead.'

'I don't want any trouble, so please don't start anything?'

'I'm gonna save all my energy for you.'

'That's reassuring.'

Chet pulled her in a little close and said, 'You think you can handle my undivided attention?'

'Depends.'

'On what?'

'On whether you can keep me interested.'

Chet kissed her and this time she didn't pull away.

'How am I doing so far?' he said.

'Pretty good.'

The song finished but they stayed on the dance floor and continued talking. Chet said, 'If you're lucky I'll even give you a ride home at the end of the night.'

'We're getting picked up, besides you've probably had too much to drink to drive home.'

'I'm gonna drink coke from now on. Next time I take you out I'll be the designated driver and keep off the alcohol.'

Rosalie playfully, pushed him backwards and said, 'What makes you think I wanna go out with you?'

'Your smile gives it away.'

Rosalie's smile widened which he took as confirmation of his statement. They went back to the table. The others seemed engrossed in their own conversations and Chet slid his chair closer to Rosalie. She whispered in his ear, 'I don't date guys I've only just met, and I barely know you, Chet.'

'That's okay because we can spend the next few weeks getting to know each other. How about exchanging phone numbers? You got a pen in your purse?'

'Yeah.'

Rosalie fished out a pen from her sleek, white purse and gave it to Chet. He wrote his name, and the auto shop phone number, on a napkin and presented it to her. He picked up another napkin and offered it to her, 'Now you.'

Rosalie hesitated and stared at Chet. He felt a warm glow inside. The band put down their instruments and appeared to be finished for the night, but the crowd whistled and cheered for an encore. Chet and Rosalie continued to gaze deep into each other eyes, oblivious to what was happening around them. The musicians decided to play one more song. Rosalie took the napkin and wrote down her phone number. Chet smiled as he put it in his pocket.

Soon after the band left the stage folks streamed outside and couples walked hand in hand to their automobiles. Richie, Matt and Randy said so long to Rosalie's friends who stood waiting for their ride. Chet and Rosalie used the time to make out and they were still kissing when one of the girl's parents pulled up in a station wagon. It was new version of Chet's auto. The girls climbed in, Rosalie blew Chet a kiss and they drove off leaving him staring at the car until it was out of sight. He thought that the girls seemed a little old to be getting a ride home from their parents. Maybe teenagers were treated different in Memphis.

Chapter 16

Aaron arrived at the bar early to pay the bar fine. Two hundred baht meant that Choi could take the night off. Her beaming smile showed that she was pleased see him. 'Hi, soldier boy.'

'Hey Choi, you eaten yet.'

'No.'

'Let's go to your favorite restaurant?'

Choi nodded, picked up her purse and they headed for the door. 'We walk, it not far.'

Ten minutes later they went into a small restaurant. The waiters seemed to know Choi and they smiled and bowed as they showed her to a table. Aaron looked around, paintings of men working in paddy fields hung on plain, cream colored walls. Bare wooden tables and chairs were tightly spaced on the tiled floor.

'My uncle is cook. Food very good,' said Choi.

'I'll let you pick for me.'

The Thai curry was spicy, and Aaron wiped the sweat of his brow with a napkin.

Choi said, 'It too hot?'

'No, it's fine,' Aaron replied.

'You like Thai food?'

'So far so good.'

Aaron found it hard to stop staring at Choi's delicate features. Her hands were so graceful that he could imagine her playing piano and he watched her delicate mouth as she ate. She was the prettiest woman he'd seen for a long time.

'Why you join army?'

'To visit new places and get to meet beautiful women.'

Choi kept the same neutral expression on her face even though Aaron had a huge grin on his. 'You like Thai girls?'

'I like you.'

'You not have pretty girls in America?'

'We have some but I ain't seen any as lovely as you.'

Choi blushed.

'I come from the state of Tennessee, live in a town in the foothills of the Smokey Mountains.'

'Smokey like smokey cigarette?'

Choi pretended to take a drag of an imaginary cigarette and blow out the smoke. Aaron smiled as he tried to explain. 'There's a mist hanging over the mountains in the early morning. It just looks like smoke.'

Choi screwed up her eyes and Aaron thought she might be having difficulty understanding, but he continued, 'The Smokies are pretty as a picture, forests of spruce and pines enveloped by that natural fog. It's a wonderful playground for folks to go hunt and fish.'

'You like to hunt?' said Choi.

'Occasionally I'd go hunting racoon.'

'Me not know racoon.'

'A racoon is like a fox. We also have black bears in the mountains, but you rarely see them.'

Choi screwed up her eyes. 'Bears scary, can kill you.'

'That's one reason my daddy taught us to shoot.'

'The army not teach how to shoot?'

'I could shoot pretty good before I enlisted. Me and my little brother used to spend most of our summer vacations hunting, or fishing.'

Aaron remembered sitting next to Chet on the banks of the river. He could visualize the crystal, clear water cascading over rocks. 'If we caught any good-sized fish we took them home to cook. My daddy owns a farm and there's always lots to do. It's hard physical work.'

'You no like hard work?'

Aaron drank his glass of water and wiped his brow with his napkin to cool himself down from the spicy food. 'I like it right enough, but I wanted to try something different. College opened my eyes and made me want to see more of the world.'

'That why you join army and come to Thailand.'

'Pretty much sums it up. You get to see some interesting places when you're in the army.'

Choi put down her chop sticks to take a drink. 'You not worried you get hurt fighting?'

'That's what I'm trained for. Not seen much action lately.'

'Only fighting in bar.'

'That was unfortunate. We've never had any trouble before. Those jerks picked on the wrong guys.'

'You good fighter?'

'I better be, I joined the army boxing team. My plan, when I left school, had been to be a lawyer. I wanted to stand up for the little guy and put the world to right. Studying law at college changed all that. I spent too much time with my head stuck in books, memorizing case studies. By the end of the semester I was pining for the great outdoors.'

'You wanna be in Smokey forest?'

'You got it. I had seen an army poster which said, "*make something of yourself and see the world,*" you know the kinda thing. As soon as I finished college I went along to the recruitment office and signed on the dotted line. What about you? What do you wanna do with your life?'

Choi put her elbows on the table and cradled her face in her hands as she scrutinized Aaron before answering. 'Same as any Thai girl. Marry rich American and have better life.'

Aaron copied Choi's pose and said, 'That lets me out of the equation then. I ain't got a heap of money.'

Choi pouted, and Aaron touched her face gently and grinned. 'You gonna use and abuse me until I'm shipped off elsewhere, then find some other man to wine and dine you.'

Aaron's feeble attempt at a joke didn't amuse Choi as she had a frown on her face.

'What else is there for me, soldier boy? One day you gone, I still be here working in bar.'

Aaron changed his grin to a sympathetic smile. He was determined to keep positive and enjoy every moment with Choi. The future would take care of itself. He felt relaxed with

Choi, which is probably why he was prepared to open up to her. They had both finished eating and Aaron caught the waiter's attention by raising his hand indicating that he wanted the check. He couldn't believe the tiny bill. Everything was so cheap in Thailand. He left a generous tip and looked into Choi's eyes longingly. 'You want leave now?'

Her coy smile showed Aaron that she was ready to continue the encounter at home and that she knew what he wanted. Choi said, 'We go back to my place.'

'Okay,' Aaron replied.

'It not far.'

Choi linked arms with Aaron as they left the restaurant.

Chapter 17

Chet walked into the workshop with an extra spring in his step. Danny was already working hard underneath the ramp. He'd taken a few days off sick and Chet presumed he got in early to make up for it. Bill noticed Chet's jaunty step and the smile on his face. 'You just found a quarter on the sidewalk?'

Chet put on his coveralls as he replied. 'Met this beautiful girl, last night.'

Bill said, 'She must be a looker, you're grinning like you just won the lottery.'

'She sure is. I ain't ever been with a prettier girl.'

'Seeing her again?'

'Every chance I get.'

Chet could hardly wait to call Rosalie. Just hearing her sweet voice would be enough to lift his spirits.

'You better get to work, you're gonna need heaps of money now you got a new girl to take out.'

A frown appeared on Chet's face as he thought about meeting Rosalie's parents when he went to her house to pick her up. He had a feeling they were probably quite affluent, and he was more used to mixing with blue collar stock. 'You hit on something there, Bill.'

'What's that?'

'I reckon Rosalie's parents might think I ain't in their daughter's league.'

'Just because you're a mechanic?'

'I'm just a country boy from common stock. The only reason my brother, Aaron, went to college was because he was the star quarter back at high school.'

Bill put his arm around Aaron's shoulders. 'Your daddy owns a farm so don't sell yourself short, son. My Jean's been singing your praises from the rafters. She called you an amiable young man and believe me that's high praise from my wife. If you behave like you did at my house when you meet these people, you'll be fine.'

'Don't know why I'm feeling so nervous.'

'Just goes to show how much you like the girl. You say her name's Rosalie?'

'Yeah.'

Chet usually kept his feelings to himself. He rarely opened up like he was doing with Bill. He picked up the first set of keys from the rack for the next auto to be worked on. They belonged to a Buick that was in the lot outside and he drove it into the bay next to where Danny was working. He pressed the button raising the Buick into a position where he could stand underneath. Chet thought it would be good to get to know Danny a little better.

'How long you been working here, Danny.'

'About four years,' Danny replied.

'You must like it.'

'Pays the bills and I ain't qualified for anything else.'

'Me neither.'

'You missing your folks, Chet?'

Chet immediately felt guilty about how he was letting down his Uncle Bart and he turned his thoughts to Aaron, instead.

'Missing my brother.'

'You think highly of him, don't you?'

'Everyone does.'

'What's he doing now?'

'He's in the army fighting for his country.'

Bill was listening in on the conversation and decided to join in. I hated being drafted. Couldn't wait to get home. Does Aaron like the army?'

A big smile formed on Chet's face. 'Guess so, he's always been a tough son of a gun.'

Bill raised his eyebrows, 'What's the joke?'

'Just remembering the time when me and Aaron had gotten into a fight. It was a hot summers day and we had been fishing in the river. We sat sweltering on the bank, but we were happy because we'd caught a few fish. They were a decent size, so we'd put them in the keep net. A bunch of youths came walking past. They were about the same age as Aaron, except one who was about my age. The boy that looked like he was the leader pointed at the net and asked if we'd caught anything. I told him we'd got three good sized cat fish and he said. "Mind if I take a look?" But he didn't wait for an answer and lifted the net with the fish wriggling and squirming. Before Aaron, or me, could say anything. He turned the net upside down releasing the fish back into the river. I leapt to my feet to punch the son of a bitch when Aaron put his hand on top of my shoulders and told me to leave it. I shouted, "That asshole's thrown away our catch." And the youth said, "What you going to do about it?" He was baiting us, and his friends were laughing as if he'd just told a funny joke. Aaron just said that we were gonna throw them back anyhow. I couldn't believe that he was gonna let them get away with it. Then one of the other boys kicked over our box of bait. Again, I wanted to jump up and kick him in the balls, but Aaron held me back. The boy said, "Seems like this one's a feisty little fella, but the big guy's as yellow as a banana." Still Aaron didn't move a muscle. He just sat there, saying nothing, while them boys stood looking down at us. I kept waiting for Aaron to get up and smash his fist into that boy's face. I was itching for a fight. Eventually they moved off flapping their arms like wings and making chicken noises. I remonstrated with Aaron and he told me that the odds were two against six and he didn't want to take me home to Jethroe battered and bruised. I told him that I'd rather go home covered in blood than humiliated. He had laughed and lightly punched the side of my face, but for once he couldn't cheer me up. About two weeks later Aaron and me were cycling back from the lake when Aaron suddenly slammed on the brakes, jumped off his bike and ran towards two boys walking along the road. I quickly followed. Aaron stood in the way of the boys that had threw away our catch. The biggest of the two said "Get out of the way yellow belly.

Aaron gave the youth an opportunity to apologize, but he wasn't about to oblige and spat in the dirt. Aaron hit him hard in the face and I heard a cracking sound. The boy dropped to his knees and I leapt at the other boy and traded punches. He backed off and stood next to his brother who was still on the ground holding his face, making no attempt to get up. Aaron stood over him with his fists bunched and kicked him in the ribs. He jumped to his feet and punched Aaron in the face. Aaron grinned at his weak effort and hit him again and again. The boy staggered, and Aaron grabbed him by his collar ready to hit him again, but he said he was sorry and Aaron threw him into the dirt. He lay there whimpering like a puppy that had been locked outside. I wanted to continue fighting the younger boy as I'd barely hit him before he'd backed off, but Aaron had grabbed my arm and said, "Let's go," We had climbed back on our bikes and cycled home.'

Bill and Danny had kept quiet while Chet told the story. Now Bill stroked his chin with his hand, as he had a habit of doing when he was thinking.

'Seems like you got retribution.'

'They'd got what was coming to them. You mess with the Carters, you better look out. We look after our own.'

'Nothing wrong with that. But you don't always have to settle things with your fists, Chet. Sometimes it's better to resolve problems peacefully. Being tough ain't always enough,' said Bill.

'What's that supposed to mean?'

'There are times when fighting makes the situation worse. Both parties can end up getting hurt, yet the problem persists. Listening and talking is often a better option.'

Chet had his hand on his hips and his chin was jutting out, 'That may be so, but there comes a time when the talking stops and the fighting begins.'

'All I'm saying is the next time you wanna punch someone in the mouth, think twice. Sometimes it's better to walk away.'

Chet scratched his head. 'I'll bear that in mind but I ain't in the habit of backing down, Bill.'

'Anyhow, enough talking about getting into fights. I got a proposition for you. When we first bought the house, money was tight. It was before we got a supply of regular customers bringing in their cars to be serviced. The house has four bedrooms, so we rented one of them to help pay the bills. That was before we had children and needed all the bedrooms. Jean suggested you could move into our spare room. It would be better than living in a motel and closer to work.'

'That's real generous, Bill, but I wouldn't wanna impose.'

'You wouldn't be son. Jean's taken a shine to you and I think you could be okay with a bit of work.'

Chet knew he would have to find an apartment anyway as he couldn't afford to stay in the motel. Moving in with Bill seemed like a no-brainer.

'In that case when can I move in?'

'Any time you want,' Bill replied.

Chet held out his hand and shook hands with Bill. 'If it's okay I'll get my things from the motel and move in tomorrow?'

'Sure. I'll ask Jean to clean out the room, tonight.'

'Appreciate everything you're doing for me, Bill.'

'Just keep working hard like you've done so far.'

Bill punched Chet playfully on the shoulder. The bell on the office door rang and Bill scooted off to deal with the customer. Danny looked out from under the ramp. 'Seems like Bill's taken a shine to you. He'll treat you right, as long as you don't let him down.'

'Reckon so, Danny, and the feeling's mutual.'

'Bill Sanders is a good man. Then he's not so agreeable.'

Chet wondered if Danny was speaking from experience.

Chapter 18

Rosalie had selected a fancy Italian restaurant for dinner. Chet rubbed his hand across his brow as he looked at the menu. He only recognized pizza but he didn't want to let on that he was a little out of his comfort zone. 'What's good here?'

'I usually have the rigatoni but the tagliatelle carbonara is good,' said Rosalie.

Chet took another look at the menu and screwed his eyes. 'I'll let you order for me as you know what's good.'

'Okay I'll get the rigatoni for you and tagliatelle for me. You can try both and see which you like best.'

'Sounds good to me.'

Chet was happy to go with whatever Rosalie ordered. Otherwise, he'd have chosen what was most familiar, pizza. They started with Prosciutto di Parma Con Le Pere. According to the menu, finest slivers of Parma ham and poached pears, served on a bed of rocket salad with crumbled gorgonzola and toasted walnuts. Chet's translation was extremely thinly cut, ham salad. When the main course was brought out Chet liked the rigatoni best. It was described as rigatoni pollo Spinach, whole-wheat rigatoni with sliced chicken breast, field mushrooms and baby spinach in a creamy gorgonzola sauce.

'What do you think, Chet?'

'Good. I like pasta.'

'I think Italian is my favourite,' said Rosalie

'Only really had pizza and spaghetti before,' said Chet.

'I love pizza, too.'

The waiter cleared away the plates and asked them if they wanted dessert. Chet looked apprehensively at Rosalie and she took the hint.

'I'm stuffed,' she said.

When the bill arrived, Chet stroked his eyebrow with his fore finger as he checked out the total. It was a lot more than he expected. Take away pizza and a few beers would've cost a lot less. Rosalie noticed his unease. 'Wanna split the bill, Chet?'

'No, this is my treat,' Chet replied.

On the way home Chet wanted to drive to someplace quiet to fool around, but Rosalie had said she didn't want to get back too late. When they arrived at her parents' house, Chet leaned over and they kissed passionately for a while before Rosalie pulled away.

'I better go in now before mom and dad start looking out of the window,' she said

'When am I gonna see you again?'

'Friday would work best for me.'

'Pick you up at eight, but I'll call you tomorrow. I can't wait until Friday to hear your beautiful voice.'

Rosalie smiled, 'You throw compliments around like confetti.'

Chet said, 'Now there's a thought, me and you standing hand in hand with confetti in our hair.'

Rosalie blushed. She gave him one last kiss, ran up the drive to the house and waved goodbye as she turned the key in the door. While driving home Chet thought about the implications of what he'd just said and wondered where that had come from? Weddings were normally not on his radar. Rosalie was getting to him like no one else ever had.

Chapter 19

A smile appeared on Jethroe's face as he read the letter from Aaron saying that he'd be arriving back home next weekend. It was a short and sweet response to Jethroe's own hastily written letter asking his son when he was due to visit. Jethroe couldn't wait to spread the word around in the Rustler. Army homecoming were a big thing in this town and when Aaron got back everyone would wanna say howdy. Jethroe decided to organize a get together so he dropped in on Thelma to ask her to help.

'Who you gonna invite?' she said.

'Only got a hand full of friends worth a can of beans,' Jethroe replied.

'I need to know how many I got to cater for. Are you inviting your brother and your other son?'

'Bart and me ain't talked for years and I don't know how to get hold of Chet.'

'Don't you think it's about time you and your brother started speaking again?'

Jethroe went quiet as he thought about his acrimonious relationship with Bart and how irritated he was when Chet moved in with him. He had come to feel reassured that Bart was looking after the boy and he had to admit that Chet's disposition had improved under Bart's tutelage. A guy Jethroe had met in the Rustler told him that Chet had run chores for his family when he'd been sick. He'd also heard reports that Chet helped some old folks who needed to be driven to the doctor, or the hospital. Jethroe guessed that they were Bart's customers who had gotten blind drunk. Depending on who you talked to opinions about Chet varied from head strong to good natured.

When Jethroe's parents had died the farm passed to him and his brothers. Bart had been more interested in making moonshine than farming. By then Luke had left town so

Jethroe took on the farm himself. It had irritated him that he was toiling hard on the land while his brother was making easy money selling moonshine. The last time Jethroe ran into him in town he noticed how old and tired Bart was looking. Jethroe had thought about chewing the cud but a nod of recognition and a brief howdy was all he could manage in response to Bart's smile. His animosity to Bart and Chet had dissipated over time and Jethroe recognized that in some ways Chet was taking care of his brother, rather than the other way around. When folks grew old it was expected that it was a son's responsibility to take care of their older kin, especially if they started to suffer ill health. Jethroe was still strong as an ox but even he struggled to do some of the jobs on the farm that he used to find easy. Thankfully, his hired hands helped considerably with the heavy work. He wasn't getting rich from farming, but he was able to pay the bills which was all he cared about. He wondered if anyone would be around to look after him when he got old and feeble.

'I do believe you're right, Thelma. I'm gonna invite Bart to come to Aaron's homecoming.'

Chapter 20

Chet and Rosalie came out of the movie theatre hand in hand. Rosalie really enjoyed 'Death wish' and she was talking about it nonstop.

'Those guys had it coming to them,' she said.

Chet said, 'They sure did. An eye for an eye is what I say.

Rosalie re-enacted the scene from the movie, pretending to swing the make-believe sock full of billiard balls, at Chet who played right along and ducked. He thought how beautiful she looked when she was excited. Eventually they reached Chet's automobile. It wasn't easy to find in the massive parking lot. Chet politely opened the passenger door for Rosalie and she gracefully eased herself into the seat. Chet figured they'd finished the discussion about the movie and changed the subject. 'Got a surprise for you back in my room.'

'What is it?'

'Can't tell you, that would spoil the surprise.'

Rosalie pushed him lightly. 'You just want to entice me into your bedroom.'

'Ain't gonna deny that, but I do have a surprise.'

'Really?'

'You betta believe it.'

Chet had cleared it with Bill earlier, but he felt a little awkward bringing Rosalie back to the house. He wasn't sure how private it would be in his bedroom. Luckily it was down the corridor from the master bedroom.

When the youngsters arrived at Bill's place he was watching TV with Jean in the family room. Chet introduced the couple. 'Rosalie, this is Jean and Bill.'

'We've heard a lot about you, young lady. All good, of course,' said Bill

Rosalie blushed and smiled at Chet.

‘You guys want some coffee?’ interjected Jean.

Chet was going to decline the offer, but Rosalie said yes before he could reply. He noticed that Bill had a mischievous look on his face.

‘You gonna serenade Rosalie with your guitar, Chet?’

‘You just about gave away my surprise, Bill.’

‘Sorry Chet, I was just fooling around.’

‘Fact is I’ve composed a love song for Rosalie.’

‘Well, go get your guitar so we can all hear it,’ said Bill sitting forward in his chair.

Jean reprimanded her husband. ‘Perhaps, Chet wants to sing to Rosalie in the privacy of his room.’

‘That was the plan, but I guess I don’t mind if you and Bill hear it too.’

Chet hurried upstairs and returned from his room with his guitar. He sat on a stool, tuning his guitar. Eventually he looked up at his audience and sang his new arrangement.

I think about you night and day

I dream about you too

I long to see your smiling eyes

I wanna be with you.

Following your every move

watching what you do

waiting for that easy smile

I wanna be with you.

Telling you my daily thoughts

every word is true

hanging on your every word

I wanna be with you.

Holding hands in the movies

sharing candy too

feeling the tension in the air

I wanna be with you.

Walking with you hand in hand

contentment washing through

my head, my body and my heart

I wanna be with you.

I don’t care what the future holds

I only wish I knew

But what I know for certain is

I wanna be with you.

I want to see you,

hear you,

smell you,

touch you,

kiss you,

taste you,

hold you,

love you,

I wanna be with you.

Chet rested his hand on the strings of his guitar and looked up at his audience of three, who clapped loudly.

Rosalie was beaming, 'That was beautiful, Chet.'

'Wrote it especially for you, Rosalie.'

'You got real talent, Chet. I know a man who works for a record company. He's a friend of the family and I'll introduce you to him. Maybe he'll give you an audition.'

'That would be great, I ain't ever played in front of anyone in the music business.'

Bill said, 'Hey, I don't want to lose my new mechanic before I've even finished training him.'

'No need to worry, Bill, I ain't planning on leaving any time soon.'

Bill said, 'Play something else.'

'How about 'Ring of Fire' by Johnny Cash,' Chet replied.

This was one of Chet's favorites and when he'd finished he got another round of applause and Bill even whistled.

'You got any more country songs?'

'If you don't mind, Bill I'd like spend a little time with Rosalie in my room.'

Jean slapped Bill on the leg and said, 'Off course you do. You don't want to spend the whole evening with a pair of old fools like us.'

'You speak for yourself, Jean. I still feel like a young colt.'

'More like an old mule,' Jean replied.

Chet and Rosalie laughed at the joke and even Bill joined in. As soon as Chet entered his bedroom he put on a Johnny Cash record. They sat on the bed and started kissing, Chet gently eased Rosalie down until they were lying side by side. He whispered in her ear. 'Now for that surprise.'

Rosalie laughed. 'I thought your song was the surprise?'

'The song was my way of letting you know how I feel about. It's your turn to show me a little love and affection.'

Rosalie moved her lips towards his and they kissed. Chet's hands explored her body and it wasn't long before Chet started to unbutton her dress. Rosalie helped him off with his clothes. They were mindful of trying not to make too much noise while making love.

Later, Chet lay back on the bed thinking life couldn't get any better than this. They both put on their clothes and Chet drove his girlfriend home. He would've liked her to stay the night, but he knew that she'd promised her parents she'd get back before the curfew. Chet hoped that they would, eventually, be able to sleep together for the whole night. For now, he could only contemplate what it would be like to wake up lying next to Rosalie. He imagined looking at her while she was sleeping with her beautiful hair cascading over the pillow. He'd never felt so content in his entire life as he watched her skip up the drive to her front door. She looked back and blew him a kiss. Chet saw the curtain move. It seemed at least one of her parents had been waiting up for her.

Chapter 21

It was quite a while since Aaron had been back home. He was looking forward to telling Chet and Jethroe about how he had won his first fight in the light heavy weight division so convincingly. He had met Choi soon after the fight and she gasped when she saw his swollen eye and fat lip. He didn't remember taking many punches but the ones that had got through his guard had spoilt his good looks a little. However, his bruised lip did not stop him kissing her. He intended to see her every time he'd got some leave. That was the downside of his homecoming trip. He would miss Choi. The realization that she'd be seeing other men when he wasn't around troubled him a little. They never talked about how she earned a living, but all the GI's knew the score. Moreover, the army made sure that soldiers were aware of the need to use protection. Aaron knew that he was getting too attached to his delicate, china doll. She inevitably occupied his thoughts on the flight back to the States.

At high school, he had a crush on a tall, skinny girl called Sally. She had long black hair and full red lips and boys used to sing '*Long Tall Sally*' to tease her. Every time Aaron heard that song he thought about his childhood crush. Last time he saw her she'd grown into a fine-looking woman and was married with a kid. No longer skinny but well-proportioned in every way. Pity he had never summoned up the courage to ask her on a date. At college, he had a girlfriend for a while, but he knew nothing would come of it. He liked spending time with her, but he didn't love her. It was different with Choi. He felt that she was special, and she had got to him. Aaron would have liked to confide in someone about Choi, but his family weren't the kind to have heart to heart talks. She would have to remain his guilty secret. He wanted her to be more than that.

Aaron knew that if Chet was in his shoes he wouldn't be fretting about Choi. His younger brother found it easy to pick up girls and he liked to play the field. Even after he took up with Grace he still had the roving eye, so the rumors went. He could never see Chet settling down. He treated girls the same way he looked after his cars. He loved them when they were shiny and new and took good care of them while he was running them in. Then a new model would come along, and it was time for a change. Grace was sassy, outspoken and as loud as an IndyCar.

Chapter 22

Bart couldn't believe his eyes when he saw Jethroe's truck pull into the yard. He whistled, took off his baseball cap to scratch his head, and walked towards the car. By the time his brother parked and climbed out, Bart was standing by the car door facing him. Duke had been fast asleep on the porch. He stretched and ambled over to greet the visitor and sat by his master's side.

Bart said, 'If you've come debt collecting you might as well turn right back around.'

'Never expected to get that money back, Bart. Think of it as a gift for looking after my unruly son over the years.'

'Chet's kin and it's been a pleasure have him here.'

'Seems like you and Chet hit it off from the get go, not entirely sure why but he's always irked me.'

'I believe I know the reason.'

Jethroe snapped, 'What's that?'

Bart spat into the dust. 'Maybe one day we can have that talk, but not now. I got mason jars to fill.'

'Will that be the same day you return the money I lent you?' Jethroe bristled.

Bart narrowed his eyes, 'Thought you'd called off the debt.'

He was about to blow his top until he saw the grin on brother's face. Jethroe put his arm around his brother. 'I gave you the money because you're kin and you always will be. I ain't gonna sit back and watch you suffer for your sins.'

'The way I earn a living has been good to me.' Bart wiped the spittle from the side of his mouth that had oozed out as he tried to talk and chew tobacco at the same time. 'Occasionally the punters get lucky, is all. Hope you ain't forgotten a third of that farm belongs to me.'

Jethroe grimaced, 'I'll leave it you in my will.'

Bart said, ‘You think I’m gonna out live you?’

‘Hard work will probably do for me while you’re sitting around supping and chewing tobacco all day long.’

Bart spat tobacco juice into the dust as if to prove Jethroe’s point, just missing Duke’s leg. The mutt never flinched. ‘It ain’t easy supplying half the county with the beverage of choice in these parts. Anyway, let’s cut to the quick, what’s the purpose of this visit? You planning on marrying Thelma and need me to be your best man, again?’ Bart laughed and slapped his thigh.

Jethroe smiled back at the old rogue. ‘You did an okay job last time.’

Bart kicked the dirt. Dust flew up and Duke moved further away out of harm’s way. ‘Chrissie was a lovely woman. You were the luckiest son of a gun in town when you married her, and the unluckiest when she died.’

‘You ain’t ever said a truer word, brother, I still miss her sorely.’

‘No doubting that.’

‘Aaron’s home on leave next weekend. We’re having a get together for him at the farm and Thelma’s fixing some food. She wants to get some idea of the numbers’

‘You want me to bring along some moonshine?’

‘You don’t need to bring anything except yourself.’

‘I’ll be there, brother.’

‘You best wash up and wear your best clothes, if you have any.’

‘Got that suit I wore at your wedding. Ain’t worn it since but it still fits.’

‘Wear what you like but try and find something better than what you’ve got on now.’

Bart looked down at his dirty jeans and torn check shirt with half the buttons missing. ‘Guess you got a point. What you doing about Chet?’

‘Why are you asking me about the prodigal son?’ said Jethroe.

‘Thought you might have heard from him.’ Bart replied.

'I was gonna ask you the same question? Last time I heard from him was when he visited me before he left town and we had a fight.'

'No surprise there.'

Jethroe ignored the remark and carried on impassively. 'Chet knows Aaron's planning a visit, but he probably don't know when.'

'Bobby's the only one he's in touch with. He ain't called me, yet.' Bart lowered his head to hide the disappointment in his face. 'I was hoping he'd be back by now.'

'You're getting too old to be making that poison. The Revenue's gonna catch up with you one day. Why don't you give it up?'

'Wouldn't wanna let my loyal customers down. Besides, moonshine puts bread on the table and pays the bills.'

'If you need some help you only need to holler.'

Bart raised his eyebrows, 'You wanna drop off some moonshine on your way home?'

'Ain't offering to be your delivery boy but if you ever need hard cash let me know.'

Bart leaned forward and placed his palm on Jethroe's forehead. 'You feeling okay?'

Jethroe brushed away Bart's hand and sighed. 'Just make sure Bobby lets Chet know about the party. He wouldn't want to miss seeing his brother.'

Bart was taken back by his brother's amiable manner. He hadn't seen him so relaxed and happy for years. Their banter reminded him of the way they had made each other laugh when they were kids. He remembered when the brotherly love had ended. Jethroe had kept spouting on about the evils of alcohol, after he'd given up drinking. It was as if he'd joined the temperance society. They always say an ex-addict is the worst when it comes to preaching, but Jethroe was never an alcoholic like their other brother, Luke. Jethroe took no pleasure when his prophecy about the dangers of alcohol came to pass. They had known about Luke's heavy drinking. He moved to Illinois and his brothers rarely saw him after he left. One day he veered off the road, while drunk, and went headlong into a tree. At the funeral, Jethroe implied that Bart was to blame for Luke's drinking problem and he got so angry that he swore he wouldn't set foot on Bart's property until he stopped making moonshine. Bart told him to go to hell and since that day they avoided each other. It was the hardest thing that Bart had ever done when he had visited Jethroe to borrow money.

Bart brought his mind back to the here and now and thought how stupid they had been. 'I'll make sure Bobby passes on the invite to Chet.'

Jethroe said, 'See you at the party,'

He drove off and Bart went into the house with Duke walking stiffly behind him. Bart wasn't the only one that was getting old.

Chapter 23

Chet parked his car on the drive of the house in the upscale neighborhood. His old station wagon seemed out of place with all the new, or nearly new, models parked throughout the sub division. He surveyed the large, newly painted, sky blue house with its double garage, then pushed the doorbell. Rosalie opened the door with a big smile on her face and invited him in. 'Mom, this is Chet.'

An elegantly dressed middle aged woman, with immaculately coiffured hair and thickly applied make up, held out her hand. Chet shook it lightly.

'Pleased to make your acquaintance Mrs. Tully.'

Chet was hoping that Rosalie would be ready to go so that they could leave right away.

'Delighted to meet you, Chet. Rosalie has told us so little about you, we feel somewhat in the dark.'

'We're still getting to know each other, mom.'

Chet wanted to speak up for himself as was his custom. 'There ain't much to tell, Mrs. Tully.'

'All we know so far is you're new in town and you're a mechanic.'

Rosalie was grimacing. She knew how direct her mother could be.

'I'm from a small place in the Smokey Mountains. I figured moving to the city would give me more opportunities.'

'Are you looking to improve your situation?'

'Yes, mam.'

'Where are you taking my daughter, tonight?'

'We're gonna get something to eat.'

'I don't want her home too late.'

'Don't worry Mrs. Tully, I'll get her home before eleven.'

'We'll be disappointed if you don't keep your word, young man.'

Chet opened the car door for Rosalie just like a gentleman should, aware that her mom was watching, and drove off waving goodbye. He turned to Rosalie. 'Wasn't expecting that, the way she was talking I'd have thought you were sixteen, not twenty-one.'

'Think yourself lucky my dad wasn't there, he's even more protective of his daughter. They might come over as a little haughty but they're not so bad when you get to know them. They're hard working and ambitious and they want the best for their only daughter. Mom's in real estate and dad works in finance.'

'We know where to come for advice when we want to buy a house.'

Chet had made another Freudian slip, assuming that Rosalie and him were destined to be together. Rosalie smiled. 'Where're we going?'

'Gonna pick up some pizza and beer and head over to Bill's place.'

Chet hoped that Rosalie wasn't expecting dinner in a fancy restaurant again. 'You okay with that?'

'Sure, I like Bill and Jean.'

Chet slowed as he approached the stop sign. 'I landed on my feet the day I walked into Bill Sander's auto shop.'

'He must like you to let you stay in his house as well as offering you a job.'

'He's like the father I never had.'

'What's your real father like?'

'You don't wanna know. Me and him just don't get along. Since my mom died he's done nothing but bad mouth me. He thinks the sun shines out of my brother's fanny, but I'm his worst nightmare.'

Rosalie frowned, 'Why?'

'Don't rightly know. Guess my brother's kinda special and I just don't match up. Ain't as bright as him, ain't as strong as him, ain't as hard working, or diligent as him, according to my pa, anyways. Every time I got in trouble at school he'd take off his belt and say, "*I don't need this aggravation after working hard all day*."

Rosalie gasped, 'Did he beat you?'

'Just a few lashes with the strap. The humiliation was worse than the pain. It stopped when I was sixteen.'

'What happened?'

Chet pulled into the Pizza Hut parking lot. 'I stood up to him and he backed off. Then he kicked me out of the house which is why I went to live with my uncle Bart.'

They climbed out of the car. Rosalie held Chet's hand and she touched his cheek lightly with her other hand. They walked into the pizza shop and Chet ordered a large pizza and a six pack of beer. He looked at Rosalie, 'Beer okay for you?'

'I prefer wine, but beer's good.'

Chet had forgotten she liked wine and cocktails. The girls he usually dated drank beer. He was aware of the disparity in upbringing and the fact that he was from more humble stock. At least he had the ability to make her smile, and the sight of her smiling face was all reassurance he required. She made him feel special and the world seemed a better place with Rosalie in his life. He knew Rosalie liked him, but when it came to choosing a husband she might be looking for someone smarter, someone more like her.

Chapter 24

Chet was still on cloud nine as he walked into the auto shop the following day and picked up the keys of a corvette. He sat in the driver's seat, with the top down, imagining himself driving on the interstate with Rosalie in the passenger seat next to him, her hair blowing in the wind. The corvette was a white convertible, low and sleek, stylish and fast. Bill had an errand to run and he left Chet in charge. Danny had gone to the hospital for a checkup. Chet was under instructions to service the corvette first, as the owner was coming to collect it around lunch time. He'd just finished the service and was sitting there day dreaming when a man in his late twenties walked in.

'What the hell are you doing sitting in my car in your filthy overalls?'

Chet climbed out of the car leaving a grease mark on the side of the door as he closed it. 'Just finished servicing the car and I put a cover on the seat so it don't get dirty, sir.'

'You've just got grease on the door panel,' the man insinuated.

'Sorry sir, I'll clean that off immediately. By the way the name's Chet, I'm the new mechanic. I assume you're the owner of this beautiful automobile, ain't had the privilege of making your acquaintance.'

Chet held out his greasy hand and the man looked down at it as if it was contaminated. Chet wiped it with the rag and offered it again, but he knew the customer wouldn't shake hands, so he put it back by his side.

'I brought the corvette here to be serviced by Mr. Sanders, or Danny. Bill Sanders is a trusted family friend and an excellent mechanic. I certainly wasn't expecting a stranger to be sitting in my car. It's a very expensive model.'

'Bill had to go out for a little while. He got me to do the service because he wanted to make sure it was ready for you to collect at lunch time.'

Chet had raised his voice slightly and his fists were starting to clench. He wanted to smash this arrogant bastard in the face. The man was staring at him as if he'd just crawled out from under a rock. Chet stared back at him with steel in his eyes.

'I'm surprised Bill Sanders has hired an impudent son of a bitch like you.'

'I'm a good worker, and I've given your corvette a first-rate service,' said Chet.

They continued to stare at each other. It was like a wild west standoff. The door swung open and Bill walked in. He looked at the demeanor of the two young men and said, 'What's going on?'

Chet could see that Bill was worried about a confrontation with the customer and he realized that Bill had arrived back in the nick of time. The customer answered. 'When I got here he was sitting in my car in his dirty overalls. He got grease over the door handle and his attitude is disrespectful.'

'Chet's a hard worker and very reliable, Andrew. He's gonna be an excellent mechanic.'

Chet smiled at Bill sticking up for him.

Andrew said, 'My father rates you highly as a mechanic and trusts you implicitly which is why we count on you to personally look after our automobiles.'

'Well you should trust my judgement then, Andrew. All your cars get excellent treatment whether it's from me or my staff. In fact, Chet is so meticulous he likes to finish off a service by buffing the paintwork. So, you don't need to worry about any grease marks?'

Both men looked over at Chet who momentarily raised his eyebrows. The only polishing he was thinking about doing was removing the sneer from Andrew's face with his fists, but he took the hint from Bill's comment.

'Nothing would please me more than to buff up the paintwork of this beauty.'

Chet got to work applying polish to the corvette. Bill put his arm around the customer. 'Come in the office, Andrew, we'll sort out the paperwork and have some coffee while Chet's finishing the car.'

The men went into the office and Andrew sat down while Bill fetched the coffee. Andrew continued his gripe as Bill sat behind his desk writing the invoice. 'I'd appreciate it if in future you service the car yourself, Mr. Sanders.'

Bill put down his pen and stared at Andrew. The smile had disappeared from his face. 'I've known your father for nearly thirty years, Andrew. In all that time, I've never told him how to run his business and I don't expect you to tell me how to run mine. My work carries a warranty and if you're ever dissatisfied you know you can bring the auto back and I'll sort it out. If you want me to speak to Henry about how we take care of your family's autos, I'll call him right now.'

'That won't be necessary, Bill, my father's too busy to concern himself with my corvette. The new boy took me by surprise, is all.'

Ten minutes later Chet knocked on the office door. 'The corvette's shining like a super nova.'

'Good, drive it into the holding area, Chet, then give Mr. Jennings the keys.'

As soon as he left the office Chet's false smile turned sour as if he'd been sucking on a lemon. He wiped his hands with a clean rag, being careful not to leave any marks as he opened the car door. After he parked the corvette he removed the covers that had kept the seats clean. Jennings and Bill came outside prompting Chet to force a smile back on his face as he made eye contact with Andrew Jennings.

'Keys are in the ignition.'

There was no thank you from Jennings who didn't even acknowledge him as he climbed into his precious motor. Chet continued talking anyway. 'You got a beautiful car. I've tuned her up real good, so she'll be purring like a pussy cat when you hit the highway.'

Jennings gave Chet another dirty look and accelerated away as if he was on the starting grid at Indianapolis. Bill put an arm around Chet affectionately. 'You did good, Chet.'

'I wanted to punch that arrogant son of a bitch's lights out.'

'I know you did, son. I could tell you were seething inside. You did good to hold yourself in check. His father should have knocked the arrogance out of him long ago. Henry Jennings is a good customer, him and me go back a long way, so it was important you stayed calm.'

'I felt humiliated, polishing his car and all.'

'It's all part of the service, Chet.'

'Since when?'

'Since Jennings complained about grease on his car.'

Chet had his hands on his hips, looking uptight, confusion across his face. Bill continued, 'Folk like Andrew Jennings expect that little extra, so I gave it to him and added another ten dollars onto the bill. You didn't polish it for nothing.'

Chet slapped his thigh and started to laugh. 'Suddenly I feel a whole lot better, Bill.'

'Sometimes it pays to be accommodating, Chet.'

Chapter 25

Jethroe was like a man whose wife had just given birth. The news was spreading like wild fire and everyone in town knew about Aaron's trip. He still didn't know about Chet, so he decided to speak to Bobby himself. He might even get some new information about his youngest son. Jethroe went into the obvious place. Bobby was in Guthrie's sipping a beer. He took the bottle from his lips and he nearly fell off his stool when Jethroe came striding towards him.

'Ain't ever seen you in here before, Mr. Carter.'

'Not gonna make a habit of it either, Bobby. Are you okay?'

'Yeah, missing Chet though.'

'I'd like to thank you for helping out my brother in Chet's absence.'

'No problem, Mr. Carter.'

Jethroe sat next to Bobby but he ignored Maurice when he came over, as he had no intention of buying a drink. 'You heard from Chet, lately?'

'I spoke to him last week,' Bobby replied.

'Where is he?'

'I don't rightly know.'

Jethroe narrowed his eyes. 'He must have told you where he was going.'

Bobby said, 'He headed for Memphis.'

Jethroe put his hands on his thighs and leant forward, 'Memphis is a big place. You wanna narrow that down some?'

Bobby scratched his ear. 'That's as much as I know, Jethroe.'

'Got a number for him?'

Jethroe took a small notepad out of his inside pocket. Maurice came over and Jethroe presumed that he wanted him to order something, so he waved him away.

Bobby said, 'No, he calls me.'

Jethroe put the notepad back in his pocket. 'You ain't giving much away, son?'

'He don't tell me everything, Jethroe.'

'Getting information from you is like trying to keep my sow's feet clean when she's eating swill. It ain't gonna happen. Next time you speak to Chet tell him Aaron's back in town and we're having a get together on Saturday at my place. It would please me a great deal if he can make it.'

'I'll be sure to pass on the message,' said Bobby.

Jethroe stood up. 'Times pressing so you better get on stick, Bobby.'

As he walked towards the door. Bobby hollered. 'Good luck with keeping that sow clean.'

Bobby was laughing like a drunken teenager. Jethroe turned and shook his head in dismay. As soon as Jethroe left the premises Bobby went to the pay phone, dialed a number and waited.

'Sander's auto repairs.'

Bobby recognized Chet's voice.

'Chet, it's Bobby.'

'I told you only to call me here in an emergency.' Chet looked left and right but Bill was not in earshot.

'Got some important news.' Bobby continued, 'Aaron's home on leave on Saturday, Jethroe's having a party at his place and he's inviting you.'

'Last time I saw Jethroe he tried to break my nose.'

'He seems to have mellowed some.'

Chet said, 'Guess I ought to be there, but I got a regular girl now and I see her at weekends. She's as pretty as a movie star, and I get a warm feeling inside every time I look at her.'

'Seems like you got it bad. What are you gonna do?'

'It's a long drive, I'm gonna give it some thought.'

'What do you want me to tell, Jethroe?'

'Nothing. Leave the old man guessing. Are you still helping Bart with the moonshine run?'

'Every weekend since you left.'

'Is he okay?'

'He could do with more help, but it ain't the kind of job you can advertise. 'You still enjoying working on autos?'

'It's hard work but my boss has been good to me and his wife treats me like the one of the family. Guess I landed on my feet, Bobby.'

Bill Sanders hollered at Chet. 'You gonna be on that call all day, Chet?'

Chet put his hand over the mouthpiece and turned his head towards Bill. 'I'll end the call now, Mr. Sanders.' He put the phone back to his mouth. 'Bobby, I gotta go. Talk to you later.'

'So long, Chet.'

Chet went back to work on the car he was servicing. Bill looked at him and Chet realized that he wanted to know who was on the other end of the line. 'That was my best friend, Bobby. He told me my brother's home on leave this weekend.'

'Are you gonna visit?' said Bill.

'I'd like to, I ain't seen him in a while. It's a long trip in that old station wagon of mine. It would be more comfortable in a car like this, Bill.'

Chet pointed at the sedan he was working on.

'The man who owns this car runs the diner just off the interstate. We went to the same grade school. He had dated Jean for a while, until she dumped him for a humble mechanic. Guess she preferred a man who don't mind getting his hands dirty to a white-collar businessman. He was cut up about it at the time, but he eventually found himself a good woman. Anyways he gets a real kick out of driving his swanky car into my shop. He's showing off hoping Jean might see him and regret rebuffing him. His daddy is one of them assertive, ambitious types who owns a chain of restaurants. He got everything given to him on a plate. He ain't had to build up a business from scratch, but I'm sure his daddy is pleased that his son is following in his father's footsteps.'

'Why do fathers want their sons to be like them?' said Chet.

'They just want to do what's best for their kids, Chet.'

'Can't rightly say my daddy wants what's best for me. He wanted to break me like a wild bronco, but I'm too mulish.'

'Sometimes fathers think what's good for them, must be good for their sons.'

'My daddy plain don't like me. After my ma died all he ever did was chastise me.'

'You must have some fond memories of your pappy?'

'I remember one time when I felt proud of Jethroe. We had been at home when there was a knock on the door. Jethroe opened it and a man stood there with his boy by his side. As calm as a lawyer Jethroe invited him into the house. His piece of shit son pointed straight at Aaron accusing him of beating him up for no reason. He was the boy that Aaron hit for throwing our fish back into the river and refusing to apologize. The man started shouting and alleged that Aaron had broken his son's nose and loosened a few of his teeth. He said that when his son got his teeth fixed he was gonna give the bill to Jethroe. Then he threatened to go to the cops and get Aaron charged with assault. Jethroe had hardly said a word but he suddenly grabbed the man by the scruff of the neck and frog marched him to the door. He threw him outside so violently that he ended up rolling over and over like tumbleweed. He told him that if he ever come near any of his family again, he'd have a bill for his own medical expenses. The man got up and charged at Jethroe with his head down like a bull. He was aiming to slam Jethroe into the wall. Jethroe stood aside like a matador and chopped him on the top of the neck, knocking him to the ground. As he went to get up Jethroe kicked him hard, knocking him back down. He grabbed him by the hair with one hand and by his collar with the other hand and dragged him all the way to his car. He told the man's boy to open the car door. The boy quickly obliged, and we watched Jethroe throw the man into the passenger seat of the car. I thought the man was going to get out of the car and continue the fight, but his son pushed him over onto the driving seat, slid in beside him and said, 'Let's go pa.' He drove off, cursing Jethroe and we went back into the house. I was grinning like I'd just hit a home run. Jethroe looked at me like he always did with those disapproving eyes and said, 'What are you laughing at?' I looked over at Aaron who just shrugged his shoulders. I looked down at my feet to avoid Jethroe's glare. No one said a word after that. I could tell Aaron wanted to smirk like I did, but he kept a blank face. We should have been slapping each other on the back, hugs all round for the Carters, but it never happened. That was the last time I had felt good about my daddy and even then, he ruined it.'

Chet looked at Bill anticipating a reaction. Bill was frowning. 'Did you ever hear any more from that family?'

'I believe the man did go to the cops, but nothing came of it. I saw them boys once, or twice, but they knew not to mess with the Carter boys.'

'Did your pa say anything to Aaron about the fight?'

'Not as far as I know. He probably thought that kid got what was coming to him.'

Chapter 26

Bart was drinking a beer in Guthrie's when the stranger walked in. Maurice, who was tending the bar, did a double take. Bart figured that Maurice had seen that face before. The stranger sat on a bar stool and ordered a whisky. He swiveled around on the seat surveying the room as if he was looking for someone. Maurice brought over his drink but didn't say a word. The stranger took out his bill fold to pay. 'Have one yourself.'

'Thanks,' said Maurice seemingly not wanting to refuse to drink with the stranger.

'I'm looking for a local boy, name of Chet Carter.'

Bart was sitting in earshot and he looked across at the man. When their eyes met Bart took a sip of his beer and looked away. The stranger turned back to Maurice who answered, 'He ain't been in here for a while.'

'Do you know where he lives?'

Maurice glanced over at Bart, who was pretending not to listen, before he replied, 'Can't say as I do'

The stranger continued, 'A few months back there was a fight in here. A man got hit with a pool cue and was lucky his skull wasn't split open. That man is my brother. My name's Michael Sullivan.'

Maurice kept a deadpan, poker face, but it was obvious to Bart that Maurice had already made the connection. Maurice opened his mouth in surprise, 'You don't say.'

Sullivan put both his hands on the bar and leaned forward aggressively. 'I do say, and I believe you know more than you're letting on.'

Maurice stuttered, 'I remember the guy that got hurt. He got the same piercing eyes and jaw as you, but he was younger and taller. Your hair is longer, but the resemblance is unmistakable. I ain't seen any sign of the kid since the fight,'

Sullivan lit a cigarette and deliberately blew the smoke in Maurice's face. 'What about his friends? There was another youth and a couple of girls?'

'Can't recall who else was present that night.'

Sullivan grabbed Maurice by the collar, 'Can't or won't?'

Maurice spluttered, 'Sorry I ain't able to help.'

Sullivan let him go and took another drag of his cigarette. 'Seems you don't know shit from meatballs.' He looked at Maurice through gritted teeth, the snarl on his face made him look as if he'd been chewing leather all day. Maurice straightened his collar and went off to serve another customer. Sullivan put his cigarette in an ashtray and took out his bill fold. He peeled off some twenties, then hollered at Maurice, 'So far you ain't been very accommodating. If your memory improves some I'll show my gratitude.'

Maurice saw the money on the bar but paid no heed to Sullivan, concentrating on pouring a beer for another customer. Sullivan turned to Bart. 'What about you, old timer? You know this Chet Carter?'

'Can't say I do,' Bart replied.

'Is that all you people can say?'

Bart swallowed some more of his beer. Suddenly it tasted bitter. He wanted to gulp it down and leave, but it seemed wise to stay a while longer. Sullivan suddenly got off his stool and climbed onto a nearby table. He'd already started to attract attention by the sound of his raised voice. Now everyone in the bar was focused on him. Assured that he had an audience he shouted, 'Anyone here know Chet Carter? Sixty dollars is waiting on the bar for the first person who gives me some information.'

Even though all eyes were fixed on Sullivan no one moved. It was like a minute silence for someone who'd passed away. A few feet shuffled restlessly.

'I'm increasing the offer to one hundred dollars.'

Sullivan jumped onto the floor, took out his bill fold and peeled off two more twenties, slamming the money onto the bar. There was still no response.

'I'm staying in the motel on the edge of town, anyone suddenly recollect something come pay me a visit. I'm in room 23.'

He swallowed the last of his whisky and placed the glass down hard on the bar. Not exactly a slam but a defiant gesture showing he meant business. He looked around at the assembled onlookers. Some averted their eyes indicating they were scared shitless, other more resilient types met his gaze, but no one seemed prepared to engage with the outsider. Sullivan picked up the cash he'd left on the bar and waved it in air before returning it to his bill fold. Then with long steps he strode out of the bar.

Chapter 27

The saloon was quiet, as it was mid-week and folks had to go to work the next day. Rosalie and Chet were sitting in a booth, chitchatting like two love birds, seemingly engrossed in each other, blissfully unaware of anyone else in the place. Rosalie said, 'On Saturday, my girlfriend is having a birthday party, do you wanna come?'

'I'd love to, but my brother is coming home on leave from the army, so I'm planning a family reunion this weekend.'

Chet had mentioned Aaron many times so Rosalie knew how close they were.

'Yeah, you need to be at your brother's homecoming.'

Chet said, 'I hope to get back in time to see you on Sunday night.'

'Whatever works best, but there's no need to cut your trip short on my behalf.'

'Couldn't go the whole weekend without seeing you, Rosalie. I'd be like a drug addict craving a fix.'

'Not sure I like being compared to a drug.'

'I'm no junkie but I'll have withdrawal symptoms if I don't get to see your beautiful face over the weekend.'

Rosalie smiled. 'You're such a sweet talker, Chet Carter. I bet you use the same lines with all the girls.'

Chet moved a little closer, staring deep into Rosalie's eyes. 'Only telling it like it is. You know you drive me crazy.'

Rosalie pushed him away playfully. She was blushing as she always did when Chet teased her. She'd never been short of admirers and Chet was not her first boyfriend, but there was something different about him. A warm feeling washed through her veins when he put his arm around her. She liked his arrogant playfulness. He was rough round the edges but behind his tough veneer she sensed a gentle, softer side.

'I guess crazy is better than getting too serious,' she said.

'Perhaps, but when you want something bad enough you gotta make it happen and I want you.'

'How do I know you won't be shacking up with one of your old girlfriends over the weekend?'

'I ain't interested in anyone else.'

Chet put his arm around Rosalie pulling her in closer and they kissed. They came up for air and Rosalie looked at her watch. 'Time to go, we both got work tomorrow.'

As they drove away from the bar Rosalie wondered how much she would miss Chet this weekend. Chet turned off the engine when they arrived at Rosalie's house and they kissed for a while until Rosalie noticed the curtains being pulled aside and a face peering out.

'Looks like my father's watching us. I better go now, Chet.

'Okay, see you tomorrow at eight.'

Chet climbed out of the car and rushed around to the passenger side to open the door for Rosalie. He pecked her on the cheek as she stood on the doorstep searching in her purse for the key. Chet drove off with a big smile on his face.

Chapter 28

Next day at work Bill hollered at Chet. 'You gotta call from your friend, Bobby again.'

He handed the phone to Chet.

'Hey Bobby, what's up?'

'Got something important to tell you.'

'It betta be good. My boss don't approve of personal calls.' Chet looked over to see if Bill was listening. He wanted to keep the call brief, as he didn't want Bill to think that he was forever chit chatting on the phone when he should be working.

Bobby said, 'Everyone in Guthrie's has been talking about it.'

'About what? Spit it out, I ain't got all day.'

'The brute you hit over the head has a brother. Bart was in Guthrie's when he came in offering money to anyone who'd tell him about your whereabouts.'

'Sullivan's got a brother. Chet exclaimed.

'Yeah, his brother is older, but he's got a similar build and features. Rumor has it, Joe Sullivan is in prison.'

Chet looked up to the heavens. 'Shit, did anyone take him up on his offer?'

'Not in the bar, but he invited anyone who'd got information to visit his motel room and collect.'

'No one knows where I am, so he's wasting his money. Best keep out of his way, Bobby. He might be as free with his fists as his brother.'

'Yeah, I'm lying low. Wouldn't tell that thug anything anyhow.'

'I know that, Bobby.'

Chet wanted to end the call and try to process the information. If he went home at the weekend he might be walking right into a fight with another Sullivan.

Bobby said, 'You still coming back for the party?'

'Gonna have to give that some thought. I gotta go now.'

Chet ended the call and went back to work. He scratched his head and pondered the situation. This was now a whole new ball game. It might be wise not to go home at the weekend if Sullivan's brother was gonna be hanging around. Another incident could spoil Aaron's party. Maybe he'd go to Rosalie's friend's birthday party after all.

Chapter 29

The car that pulled into Bart's drive was a flashy Toyota. Bart had never seen it before. He'd just carried some empty mason jars into the barn and was walking back to the house, Duke at his heels as usual. He stopped dead in his tracks as the stranger from the bar stepped out of the car. Sullivan strode purposely up to Bart and grabbed him by the lapels with both hands.

'I do believe you lied to me old timer. Chet Carter lives with you.'

'He used to live here. I ain't seen him since the fight so get your fucking hands off me.'

Duke barked at the stranger, sensing trouble. Sullivan let go of Bart then, suddenly punched him hard in the stomach. Bart doubled up in pain and Duke growled and chewed on Sullivan's pants. He shook off the dog and kicked it hard, lifting it in the air. Duke yelped in pain as he landed hard on the dirt. Bart was down on one knee. He got up, grimacing in pain.

'I'll kill you if you kick my dog again.'

'Just tell me where Chet Carter's at, or I'll kick you and your mutt around the yard like a football.'

'Don't know where he's at and I wouldn't tell you even if I did.'

He'd barely finished his sentence when he felt the man's right fist pound his face. His head snapped back, and he fell to the ground. Bart wished he'd got his gun nearby. He knew he had no chance fighting off this younger, bigger and much stronger man. Lying on the ground he looked over at Duke who was shaking violently. Something was badly wrong with the hound. Sullivan put his boot on Bart's face and pushed down hard. Bart felt the grit of the dirt digging into his flesh.

'I'm waiting for some answers old man.'

Sullivan took his foot of his face. Bart didn't move or say anything then he lifted his head slightly and looked hard into the stranger's cruel eyes.

'Go to hell.'

The man kicked him hard in the stomach and then again in the head. Bart lay still waiting for the next kick, unable to get up. It dawned on him that if the assault continued the bastard might actual kill him.

'You're either stupid or senile, or maybe the kid didn't tell you where he went after all.'

Bart's head was spinning, and he retched. His stomach hurt like hell and he thought his ribs were probably broken. He strained to look over at Duke who was still twitching, like he sometimes did when he was having a dream. Bart was more worried about his dog than him own wellbeing.

'You ain't heard the last from me old man. When I find that boy it will be payback time. Nobody gets one over on the Sullivan's.'

Bart heard Sullivan's massive footsteps treading in the gravel. The car door opened and slammed shut, followed by a screeching of tires. He tried to move but the pain was excruciating. Nevertheless, he managed to crawl and drag himself until he was alongside Duke. The dog had stopped twitching and Bart's eyes welled up with tears. They began falling from his eyes like rain drops. He promised himself that one-day Michael Sullivan would pay dearly for this.

Chapter 30

Chet met Rosalie in the bar. It was supposed to be the last chance for him to see her before his weekend away. She beamed with delight when he told her he'd be coming to the party with her after all. She was able to reciprocate the good news. 'You'll never guess who's gonna be at the party.'

'Who?' said Chet.

'That music producer, friend of the family, I told you about. I'll be able to introduce you to him.'

'That's great.'

Chet put his bottle on the bar, so he could hug her. When she came out of the clinch, Rosalie raised her eyebrows. 'What about your brother's homecoming party?

Chet said, 'There could be trouble brewing. A guy's looking for me.'

'What for?'

'My best friend was about to take a beating from a drunken stranger in my local bar. I hit the guy with a pool cue and left him unconscious on the saloon floor. Paramedics took him to hospital and last I heard he'd recovered and was doing fine.'

Chet picked up his beer and paused for a reaction, but Rosalie stayed quiet, patiently waiting for him to continue the story. 'That was shortly before I left town and came here. It turns out the guy, name of Joe Sullivan, is wanted by the cops. Now it seems he's got a brother who's been asking after me in the bar.'

Rosalie shook her head. 'I understand you sticking up for your friend, but breaking a pool cue over the man's head is going too far.'

'It wasn't planned. I'd got the cue in my hand when Sullivan grabbed Bobby by the throat and took a swing at him. It was a reflex action.'

'Maybe to you but most people ain't that impulsive.'

Chet sighed. 'I ain't trying to justify what I done, Rosalie. Just saying I didn't start it, is all.'

'You sure finished it, though. Promise you won't react like that when you're out with me?'

'No need to fret. I'll think twice before retaliating in the future. I'm trying to be more laid back. That's why I ain't going back home this weekend. I wanna avoid getting into fights from now on. I'll be on my best behavior at the party.'

Chet was smiling but Rosalie looked pensive.

'I do hope so. Chet'

They arrived at the party early. Chet was wearing his best shirt, pants and a jacket. Rosalie had on very little make up, as usual, and was dressed modestly in a summer frock. Even so she was easily the prettiest girl in the place. When she smiled her face lit up the room. Chet looked around even though the chances of him knowing anyone were remote. He nervously flexed his fingers, and figured he needed a drink to calm him down but he'd promised to keep off the alcohol as he was driving. He desperately wanted to create a good impression with the record producer. Rosalie took his hand and they headed towards the birthday girl. She was busy meeting and greeting her guests, so Rosalie took a detour. A smile appeared on her face. She took Chet's arm and pointed. 'There he is.'

Chet followed her gaze and noticed a familiar face. He grimaced as he focused on his nemesis. Andrew Jennings spotted him at the same time. Jennings was standing next to a small brunette and they were talking to another couple. The brunette was petite, and her pale blue eye liner drew attention to her most attractive feature. Her tight dress accentuating her slim figure and firm breasts. Chet preferred Rosalie's natural beauty and more modest attire, but he found it difficult to take his eyes off the sassy brunette. Jennings put his hand lightly on her shoulder as if to show that she was his property, seemingly in response to Chet looking her up and down.

'Come along, Chet, I'll introduce you,' said Rosalie.

Chet felt like an ant that had just wandered into a hornet's nest as they approached the two couples. Was Andrew Jennings the record producer he was supposed to meet? If so he could forget any chance of becoming a session musician. Rosalie touched the other man, Chet didn't know, lightly on the arm. 'Clarence, I'd like you to meet my boyfriend, Chet.'

'Pleased to make your acquaintance, Chet,' said Clarence.

'Likewise,' Chet replied. He took a deep breath and relief flooded through his veins as he realized that Andrew Jennings was not the man that he was intended to meet. His forced grin changed to a genuine smile as he shook hands with Clarence.

Clarence said, 'This is my wife, Samantha.'

Chet nodded to Samantha. Rosalie touched Chet on the shoulder and indicated the other couple with an outstretched arm. 'And this is Andrew and Molly Jennings,'

Andrew said, 'We've already met.'

The sneer in his voice was unmistakable. He was a well-built man, at least six-foot-tall and his wife was a lot shorter. Chet offered his hand and Andrew reluctantly shook it. Chet expected him to attempt to assert his superiority by squeezing hard, but Jennings's grip was feeble, and Chet had to resist the temptation to crush his fingers.

Chet said, 'Yeah, Andrew brought in his corvette for a service, she's a little beauty.'

Chet was looking at Molly as he spoke. She flashed her eyes at him. Andrew's face became even more contorted and Rosalie interjected quickly. 'What a small world, Chet's only been in town a short while.'

Andrew continued to turn up his nose as he looked at Chet, while Rosalie tried to keep the conversation flowing. 'My father used to work with Andrew's father, Chet.'

'Really.' Chet didn't know what else to say.

Molly touched Rosalie's arm. 'You've certainly kept this handsome young man to yourself, Rosalie.'

'This is the first opportunity I've had to show him off, Molly. Tonight, we're going to mingle, but I particularly want

Chet to visit with Clarence as they have something in common.'

Andrew said, 'Surely not, Clarence is an executive and Chet's an assistant mechanic.'

Chet tightened his fists at Andrew's snide remark. He wanted to punch the limp wristed jerk, but he was determined not to break his promise to Rosalie. He kept reminding himself of Bill's words of wisdom, being tough ain't enough. Rosalie, apparently, sensed the tension. 'Music is the connection, Andrew. Chet sings and plays the guitar. He also writes his own songs.'

'Is that true, Chet?' Clarence's soft voice and calm demeanor showed Chet a warmth that was the opposite of Andrew's coldness.

Chet said, 'Yeah, been playing guitar since grade school.'

'What do you hope to do with your talent?'

'Just want to perform. Guess my dream would be to write a hit record and hear it played on the radio.'

Clarence said, 'Have you ever been in a band?'

'Occasionally, my uncle invited some of his friends around for a hillbilly shindig and I'd join in, but I mostly play solo. I used to play every week at the local bar in my home town.'

'Take my card and call my secretary to set up a meeting. Have you got a demo tape?'

'No, sir.'

'Bring your guitar to the meeting and you can play a couple of tunes. If I like what I hear you can come into the studio and record a demo tape. That way even if we don't have anything for you'll have something to take to other recording studios. I'm not promising anything, of course.'

'Not expecting anything, Clarence. Be good to get an opinion from someone in the business.'

Chet looked at the printed card Clarence had given him, *'Clarence Henderson, Record Producer, Sun Records.'* He looked up and saw Jennings still looking as if he'd swallowed something nasty. Rosalie whispered in Chet's ear. 'Let's get a drink.' She linked her arm in Chet's attempting to lead him away.

Chet looked bemused. 'Talk to you guys later.' He raised he eyebrows at Rosalie, but he understood that she was worried about a possible confrontation. When they were out of earshot of the others, he said, 'Everything okay?'

Rosalie said, 'It's probably wise to keep some distance from Andrew Jennings. He seems to be itching for an opportunity to cause a scene. I know him well, we went on a couple of dates before he met Molly. He's not my favorite person. He's very controlling and he's got a nasty streak. Molly's a good friend and deserves better than him. We can visit with Clarence and Samantha later.'

'Jennings gets my back up, too. The arrogant jerk put me down when he came to pick up his corvette. He made me feel small and it was deliberate. For two bits I'd put him on his back.'

Rosalie took hold of both Chet's hands. 'Bite your tongue and do whatever you gotta do to control your temper, please?'

'Don't worry, Rosalie. I ain't about to let Jennings get to me.'

Chet said this with a confidence he didn't feel. It was only a matter of a time until Andrew Jennings and himself came to blows, but not tonight. He didn't want to upset Rosalie, or blow his opportunity with Clarence. Rosalie waved at her birthday girl friend and she came over and spoke, 'Is this your new boyfriend?'

Rosalie said, 'Yeah, Chet this is Priscilla and she's twenty-one, today.'

Chet said, 'Happy birthday, Priscilla.'

'Nice to meet you, Chet. We'll have to sit down and visit with each other later, but I'm afraid I've got to circulate right now.'

Chet and Rosalie found another couple that Rosalie knew, and chit chatted for a while. Later, Chet went to the bar for refills. He ordered a coke and a glass of wine for Rosalie. He felt a tap on the shoulder and turned around to see Molly grinning up at him. 'You didn't stick around long after our introduction.'

Chet replied, 'Figured your husband doesn't like me.'

'Don't let that worry you. I like you.'

'That's good to hear. I'm surprised Andrew lets you get your own drinks.'

'I do what I please.'

She stood there twisting her torso from side to side, pointing her full breasts at him and fluttering her long eye lashes. Molly was a turn on and Chet felt a stirring in his loins.

'You look like a liberated woman.'

'You bet. I could show you how unconventional I am.

Chet wanted to pull her in close and feel the contours of her body pressing up against him. He was enjoying flirting with her, but he thought the conversation was getting a little too intimate. 'Not tonight.'

Molly said, 'Don't be such a party pooper.'

'If you've forgotten, I'm here with Rosalie.'

'I ain't forgotten, just thought you might occasionally like to play a different instrument, Mr. music man.'

'Tempting as that seems, I'll keep in harmony with what's familiar.'

Chet paid for the drinks. As he turned back around Molly touched him delicately on the arm. 'How about I give you my number? You can call me when it's more convenient.'

'Think I'll take a raincheck. You're married,' Chet replied.

'That's not what your eyes are telling me.'

Chet knew that was the truth. He couldn't stop looking her up and down. Molly moved in closer and whispered in Chet's ear. 'I think you and I want the same thing.'

Chet looked around conscious that someone might be watching and saw Jennings striding towards him.

'Stay away from my wife, red neck.'

'I ain't interested in your wife, I got my own girl.'

Andrew's fists were clenched. 'From where I was standing it looked like you were flirting with her.'

'Just enjoying the conversation. It was good talking to you, Molly. Betta get back to Rosalie with our drinks.'

Chet picked up the drinks from the bar and walked away. He'd only taken a couple of steps when Andrew pushed him hard in the back. Chet stumbled trying desperately not to spill the drinks, but he lost his balance and fell to the floor. The glasses broke, and the liquid splashed onto everything in the vicinity. Chet jumped to his feet. 'That does it, Jennings.'

'Chet.'

Rosalie's voice rang out and Chet turned his head to see her running towards him. His fists were bunched, teeth gritted, but the promise that he'd made to Rosalie was ringing in his ears. He looked at her imploring face. Then he looked back at Andrew who stood rigid, arms raised, fists clenched, ready to fight.

Andrew said, 'Go for it, grease monkey.'

Chet remained frozen, like a block of ice.

Andrew continued goading Chet 'What are you waiting for. You know you want to hit me, or are you chicken shit?'

All over the room eyes were focused on the pair waiting for the expected confrontation to begin. Chet ignored Jennings and turned on his heels back towards the bar.

'I need to re-order those drinks, barman. Seems like I had an accident.'

Molly put her hands on the bar reaching forward to attract the bar tender's attention. 'I'll pay for those drinks.'

Chet touched her hand. 'That's okay, Molly.'

Andrew pulled Chet around by the shoulder. His face was red, and his eyes glared like fireballs. 'Get your hand off her, slime ball, Molly get away from him.'

'You're behaving like an ass, Andrew, and I'm paying for those drinks.'

'Go to hell,' said Andrew.

'You make me sick. I can't even have a conversation with a guy without you acting like a jealous fool.'

Chet looked at the couple glaring at each other like boxers at the weigh in and realized that this wasn't just about him.

There were other issues here. He said. 'Let's just forget the whole thing. A few glasses got smashed. It's no big deal.'

Molly rested her hand on Chet's shoulder. 'No, Chet. Andrew caused you to drop those drinks. The least he can do is get some fresh ones.'

Andrew said, 'I thought I told you to keep away from my wife.'

Chet ignored the remark and turned back towards the bar, waiting for the barman to finish pouring the drinks. Andrew pulled him around by the shoulder again and threw a punch at him. Chet moved his head back taking some of the sting out of the blow. Rosalie quickly grabbed hold of Chet's hand, while Molly put herself between her husband and Chet. She glared at him as she pushed him backwards, out of Chet's reach.

'Don't shove me Molly.'

'Stop acting like a fool, Andrew.'

'Why don't you stop behaving like a slut?'

'You betta say sorry for speaking to me like that.'

'How about you apologizing for acting like a tramp?'

Molly pounded her fists against Andrew's chest, her head shaking from side to side like a maniac. Andrew grabbed hold of her wrists tightly to stop the bombardment and Molly kicked him in the shins. He winced but kept hold of her hands. A doorman appeared, as if from nowhere, and stood next to the grappling couple.

'Everything okay, folks?'

Andrew still had hold of Molly's wrists as he glared at the doorman. 'What's it got to do with you?'

'Nothing, but I suggest you start by letting go of the lady.'

'The lady's my wife and it's none of your business.'

'I might just make it my business if you're hell bent on causing a disturbance. If you don't settle down, I'm gonna have to ask you to leave.'

'We're going nowhere.'

'In that case why don't you both sit down and relax?'

'Or what?'

The doorman had been calm up to now. His neck was as thick as a tree trunk, his head shaven and he had a scar down one cheek. Although he was the same height as Andrew he was much bulkier, built like a prize fighter who regularly lifted weights. His clothes were a tight fit on his massive frame. The buttons on his white shirt were stretched to breaking point and the sleeves on his jacket would surely split if he had to throw a punch, but the menace in his voice was unmistakable as he stuck his face about six inches from Andrew's nose.

'I'm gonna give you one last chance. Either you go quietly back to your seats, or I'll throw your sorry ass out on the street.'

Chet wondered if Andrew was stupid, or drunk, enough to pick a fight with the doorman. Molly said, 'Let's sit down, Andrew.'

The futility of starting a fight with this man must have dawned on Andrew. He slowly, and deliberately, moved to a table where he pulled out a seat for Molly. The doorman watched him every step of the way, standing still as a statue. He continued to glare at Andrew until he sat down next to Molly. Chet and Rosalie returned to their table. Chet noticed that Rosalie was shaking slightly, and he could see from her eyes that she was close to tears.

'Let's finish our drinks and go,' she said.

'We shouldn't have to leave the party because of that ass hole, Rosalie.'

'I feel awkward, it's as if everyone is looking at us.'

'I stayed calm, didn't I?'

'Yeah, it's undoubtedly Andrew that's to blame. He's in a foul mood and it didn't help matters with Molly getting too familiar with you at the bar.'

'She was only being playful, Rosalie.'

'Maybe so, but I know Molly can be a flirt and you see how it affected Andrew. I really don't think it's wise to stay too long, Chet.'

'Okay.'

'You okay to drive home.'

'Yeah, I've been on coke all night.'

'You've done good, Chet.'

'At least if we leave the party early we can go back to my room for a while?'

'Are you sure you wouldn't prefer sex with Molly?'

Chet did a double take. He didn't want Rosalie to think that he had encouraged Molly, although he knew he was slightly guilty of that. 'What's that supposed to mean?'

'I've known Molly long enough to know when she's coming onto someone.'

'I'm not interested in Molly. She's a sassy little thing but I've already got the prettiest girl in the place. My heart belongs to you.'

'Prove it.'

'I will when we get back to my room. Let's get the hell out of Dodge.'

Chapter 31

When Jethroe pulled into the drive Bart was sitting in the dirt with Duke cradled in his lap. His tear stained face painted a picture of pure dejection. Somehow the old man had crawled to the phone and called his brother, then he must have dragged himself back to be with Duke. Jethroe had dialed 911 and drove to Bart's place as quick as he could. He sat down next to his brother and listened in silence as Bart described what had happened. Jethroe got to his feet when the paramedics arrived. Bart still hadn't moved a muscle.

'You need to let go of the dog, so we can check you out,' said the paramedic.

Bart gently placed Duke on the ground then he coughed and spat blood into the dirt.

'Take it easy old timer, keep still until we take a look at those injuries.'

Bart winced as the paramedic felt his stomach and ribs and said, 'We gotta get you to hospital.'

They put him on a stretcher and carried him to their vehicle. As they drove away. Jethroe rubbed his forehead in dismay wondering if his brother had got health insurance. He anticipated that Bart was going to receive good medical attention, either way, He wondered whether he ought to follow the ambulance to the hospital, Instead he stayed and buried Duke. Jethroe was better at providing practical help rather than giving moral support. He rubbed the back of his neck with apprehension at the prospect of having to tell his sons the bad news. Aaron's plane was due in a couple of days. The Sullivan's had now made themselves another enemy and as Bart wasn't able to do anything, Jethroe knew that he might have to step in on his behalf one day soon.

Chapter 32

Rosalie was sitting in the lounge sowing a button on a dress. For the last two years she'd been designing her own clothes. Although she loved making clothes she didn't enjoy mending them. She looked up and smiled as her father entered the room. He'd got a frown on his face showing he was in one of his serious moods. He sat in his favorite chair and opened his newspaper. Evidently not in the right frame of mind to read, he placed it on the coffee table.

'Your mom tells me you've got a new boyfriend?'

Rosalie looked up and stopped sowing, 'Yeah, his name's Chet'

'Where did you meet him?'

'In the country and western bar. He's new in town.'

'Where's he from?'

'A small town in the Smokies.'

Rosalie continued sewing focusing on her needle and thread rather than her father.

'Your mom said he seems full of himself, brusque and rough around the edges. Not the kind of boy you usually date.'

Rosalie put down her dress and the needle and thread. 'Mom said all that. She only met him once for a few minutes.'

Mr. Tully took a cigarette out of the packet and picked up his lighter. 'Your mom's very perceptive and I may have embellished things a little.'

'You mean you're jumping to conclusions.'

He lit the cigarette and took a drag. 'Are you sweet on him?'

Rosalie felt like a defendant being cross-examined, but she knew her father had her best interests at heart. 'We've only been seeing each other a few months, pop.'

'You've got a spring in your step and a twinkle in your eye, and that indicates it's serious. When can I visit with Chet?'

'You want me to invite him around, so you can interrogate him.'

'No need to be so dramatic, Rosalie. We just don't want you getting mixed up with the wrong sort. Next time he picks you up make sure you invite him in.'

Chapter 33

Jethroe drummed his fingers on the barrier as he waited for Aaron at the airport. He was really looking forward to seeing his eldest son, but he was sad about the news he had to tell him. All the same he was determined to enjoy the celebration on Saturday evening. Thelma had ordered all the food for the party and she was baking a cake. Jethroe had been put in charge of the BBQ. Passengers filed onto the concourse, eyes searching the waiting crowd for family, friends, or loved ones. Signs with people's names on were being held aloft. Jethroe looked at everyone who came through the concourse desperately hoping that Aaron's face would be next. Suddenly a man dressed in uniform appeared carrying an army bag. Jethroe waved his hands to catch Aaron's attention and his son held up his hand in acknowledgement. Aaron put his kit bag down and the two men put their arms around each other and hugged. When they broke from the embrace, Aaron was the first to speak. 'Long flight, pop. Got something to tell you. Don't look so worried, it's all good.'

'Pleased to hear it son, afraid my news ain't so good. Let's hear yours first.'

'I made the platoon boxing team.'

Jethroe raised his eyebrows. 'I remember you wrestling at high school, but mostly you played football. What made you take up boxing?'

'I was out with some of the GI's drinking in a local bar one night when some guys started causing trouble. We threw them out and Sergeant Hammond, who's an ex-boxer, was impressed by the way I handled myself. He invited me to train with the army boxing squad.'

'And you made the team?' said Jethroe.

'Yes, sir. Been training hard and I won my first fight.'

'I knew you could look after yourself, but never thought of you as a boxer.'

'So, what you think, pop?'

Jethroe shadow boxed but didn't actually throw a punch. 'I'm gonna enjoy telling folks we got the next Rocky Marciano in the family.'

Aaron shook his head. 'Not a chance. What's your news?'

'I'll tell you as we go. Let's get out of here.'

Jethroe started to walk towards the exit. Aaron picked up his luggage and got in step alongside him. Jethroe continued to fill Aaron in on the news. 'To start with, your little brother smashed a pool cue over a trucker's head in Guthrie's. The guy was hospitalized, and Chet skipped town when the cops came looking for him. Bobby promised to let Chet know you were coming home this weekend. No one else can get in touch with him. We're hoping he'll show up for the get-together, but we don't know either way.'

'Are we having a party?'

Jethroe playfully pushed Aaron on the shoulder with the palm of his hand. 'You bet your life we are. I'm in charge of the BBQ but Thelma doing the rest.' Jethroe lowered his head. 'There more to the trucker story. The guy that's in hospital has a brother who came looking for Chet. He showed up at Bart's place and broke your uncle's ribs. We had to bury Duke.'

Aaron clenched his teeth. 'Where's the bastard now?'

'Guess he's gone back to his watering hole. The word going around is that these Sullivan brothers are notorious bullies who are wanted for all manner of crimes in two states. I don't believe the cops have been able to pin anything on them. Witnesses have a habit of losing their memory.'

'I can't believe anyone would wanna hurt a likable old rogue like Bart. Always thought if he fell in a heap of shit he'd come out smelling sweet as a rose.'

'Seems like his luck ran out, son.'

'Sullivan's luck will run out when I get my hands on him.'

'You and me both, son. Anyone messes with the Carter family is gonna regret it. Your little brother started this but it's a family matter now. The trouble with Chet is he don't think before he acts. That Joe Sullivan, is a mean son of bitch who don't give a damn who he picks on. He only ended up in Guthrie's because he took the interstate off ramp for a rest stop. His brother, Michael, has the same mindset.

'Why did Chet hit Sullivan, anyways?'

'The brute went for Bobby.'

'I'd say that's good enough reason, Chet's always gonna back up his friend. We always look after our own, you know that, pop.'

Jethroe scratched his head. 'Guess so, but trouble follows Chet around like a faithful hound.'

'He's impulsive and head strong but his heart's in the right place. If them Sullivan brothers come back they'll wish they never set eyes on the Carters.'

Jethroe punched Aaron lightly on the arm and they climbed into the pickup. He glanced at his rifle on the back seat. 'You're darned right. My weapons are clean and fully loaded.'

Chapter 34

The party wasn't a big event, as Jethroe had predicted. Aaron kept Thelma's kids occupied playing horseshoes while Jethroe and Thelma took care of the catering. Mr. Thompson from the hardware store joined in the game, while Bobby, Rita and some of Aaron friends from high school drank beer. The talk was mainly about Bart who was still in hospital but desperate to come home. Jethroe had asked Bart to move in with him when he was discharged from the hospital. The family bonds that had previously been stretched and tattered had become tightened by the hostility shown by Michael Sullivan.

It was a warm evening, so the tables and chairs were set out in the yard. Thelma had covered the side dishes with cloth to stop flies getting on them. Jethroe heaped the cooked hotdogs and burgers from the BBQ onto a plate for the guests to help themselves. Aaron had been in high spirits when he stepped off the plane, but he seemed more subdued now. Thelma's eldest boy, Jessie, threw his horseshoe and narrowly missed the peg. Aaron ruffled his hair. 'Good shot. Way to go, Jessie.'

Brad Thompson was taking the game a little too seriously and he whooped with excitement as his horseshoe nestled against the peg. The ringing sound as it rattled, steel against steel, turned a few heads. When the game was over Aaron picked up a bottle of beer from the cooler and moseyed over to talk to Bobby and the others. Rita asked him about Thailand.

Aaron said, 'It's hot, Rita.'

'Do you like it?'

'It's okay, but I prefer the Smokies.'

Rita held her boyfriend's hand. 'It's about time Bobby and me did some travelling. We ain't been anywhere have we, Bobby?'

Bobby answered, 'Went to the Kentucky Derby with Chet once. Rich folk prancing around dressed like it was a wedding. Me and Chet always planned on going to Indianapolis to see the Indy 500, but we ain't made it yet.'

Aaron realized that most of the folks at the party had never left the United States. He said, 'Do you know where Chet's at, Bobby?'

'Somewhere in Memphis is all I know, Aaron. I told him about you coming back, the party, and all.'

Aaron looked hard at Bobby who was looking at his feet and kicking at the dirt. 'Did you tell him his uncle's in hospital?'

'Ain't spoke to him since that happened. Tried calling earlier today but no one picked up.'

Jethroe must have been listening in on the conversation. He took a swig from his glass of coke and said. 'I thought you said he only called you and that you couldn't contact him?'

Bobby eyes darted from Aaron to Jethroe and back. He shuffled his feet from side to side, like he wanted to pee. 'I can call him at his work place in an emergency. Seems like they don't pick up at the weekend.'

Jethroe spat in the dirt. Aaron could see that Jethroe was unable to hide his annoyance that Chet hadn't showed up.

Bobby continued. 'He's got a new life now, Jethroe.'

Jethroe stared hard at Bobby. 'Maybe so, but you don't forget your kin.'

Bobby nodded back in agreement. 'I told Chet about Sullivan's brother snooping around Guthrie's, asking folk about his whereabouts. Most likely he wanted to avoid trouble.'

Jethroe said, 'Probably scared Sullivan was gonna give him hell for what he did to his brother.'

Bobby stood tall and stared at Jethroe. 'Chet's no coward.'

'I expect you to take his side, but his uncle got beat up because of his actions and he ain't nowhere to be seen,'

Bobby held up his hand and tilted his head. 'I ain't arguing and Chet ain't here to put his side of the story.'

He put a burger in a bun, spread on some relish and bit into it, filling his mouth full of food. Thus, ending the conversation for a while at least.

Jethroe hadn't arranged any entertainment and folks were starting to leave. If Chet had been here he would have kept the party going by playing guitar, even if he only played the blues. Bart may have joined him on the fiddle. Aaron helped Jethroe clear away the empty plates. They left them in the kitchen sink. Eventually, all the guests disappeared, and Aaron sat in the lounge with Jethroe and sipped coffee. Rather than let food go to waste Thelma put the leftovers in the fridge. She set about washing the dishes. Normally Jethroe would dry, but as he was talking to Aaron, she left them to drain. She jumped when she heard a loud bang. Aaron and Jethroe sat up as the front door flew open. The sound Thelma heard was that of a large foot almost kicking the door off its hinges. The boot landed on the hardwood floor and the man who filled it continued to stride further into the room. Jethroe moved towards the rifle hanging on the wall.

The man said, 'Hold it right there.'

Jethroe froze as Michael Sullivan produced a pistol from his waist band. 'I'm looking for Chet Carter.'

'He ain't here,' Jethroe replied.

'Assume you're his pa?'

'Why do you wanna know?' Jethroe stared hard into the eyes of the man with the granite face that had violated his home.

Sullivan's stern expression showed that he was deadly serious. 'I'm your worst enemy, old timer. Your son put my brother in hospital. He's unavoidably detained, or he'd sort things out himself.'

Jethroe said, 'You mean he's looking at time in the state penitentiary.' Jethroe's stare was mainly fixed on Sullivan, but he intermittently glanced at the rifle hanging on the wall.

Sullivan followed his gaze. 'Bet you wish you had that rifle cocked and in your hand.'

Aaron pointed his finger at Sullivan. 'You're the bastard put my uncle in hospital. You're gonna wish you'd left town.'

Sullivan grinned. 'This is my party now. I'm the one holding the gun and I got a score to settle.'

'You think you're tough when you're fighting old men, or standing behind the barrel of a gun.' Aaron replied.

'Figure you're the older brother. Do you think you can take me, boy?'

'I know it.'

'I'd settle this man to man, but your old man would get hold of his rifle.'

Aaron said, 'Tie him up, there's rope in the barn.'

Sullivan was silent for a few seconds. Aaron guessed that he was mulling over the situation.

Sullivan said, 'Okay, let's go get it, nice and easy now.'

Thelma walked into the room. Sullivan turned the gun towards her, then quickly turned it back to Jethroe and Aaron. He snarled, 'Get over here, woman.'

Thelma still had on her apron and Sullivan frisked her to make sure she was unarmed. He said, 'We're going on a little trip to the barn, you betta come too.'

Jethroe put his arm around Thelma and led the way. Aaron followed with Sullivan close behind, the gun still pointing at them. The barn was huge. There was a large bay full of hay. A ladder was propped against a hay loft that provided further storage space above. Aaron picked up a bundle of rope from the corner of the barn. Sullivan looked around before pointing at a large wooden support. 'Tie your old man to that strut and the woman to the other one.'

Aaron said. 'I need a knife to cut the rope.'

Sullivan bent down, keeping his eyes straight ahead. He felt inside his left boot and took out a large knife. Like a circus act he hurled the weapon towards Aaron. It landed next to his feet, the blade imbedded deep into the saw dust. Aaron lifted his eyebrows in surprise at such an impressive throw. Sullivan's smirk emphasized that he'd done that trick many times. Aaron pulled the knife out of the ground admiring the shiny blade. He contemplated a return throw, but he knew that the response would be a speeding bullet. Besides Aaron was not known for his knife throwing ability. The sharp blade cut through the rope easily and he finished tying the knot that bound Jethroe tight to the strut. Sullivan was watching him like a hawk. He pointed at Thelma and Aaron tied her to another timber strut.

'Drop the knife and move to the corner of the barn.' Sullivan instructed.

Aaron moved away, and Sullivan picked up the knife replacing it back inside his boot. He looked over at the pitch fork nestling in the hay and made sure Jethroe and Thelma's bonds were well and truly tight. Aaron stood in his corner of the barn, thinking it a fitting arena to settle the score. He imagined himself in the boxing ring waiting for the bell. This was his domain and he was ready. When Sullivan slipped the gun back into his waist band Aaron smiled. Sullivan nodded. 'I'm gonna wipe that smile from your face. I was hoping to give your brother a beating, but you'll do fine. Older brother against older brother, seems fitting somehow.'

Aaron said, 'Give it your best shot, Sullivan.'

Sullivan strode slowly towards Aaron. When he was almost within touching distance he took an enormous swing hitting nothing but fresh air as Aaron dodged out of the way and swiveled, punching Sullivan hard on the side of the face. The big man touched his cheek as if he was wiping off some dirt, then he struck Aaron on the head with his other hand. Aaron was annoyed that he'd been caught off guard and he thought about his trainer '*jab and move, jab and move.*' Fuck that. He threw a massive right into Sullivan's face and the two men traded blows. Aaron bounced on his feet. He was in the zone. Sullivan's punches hurt but Aaron connected with three punches to every one he took. He dodged and weaved to avoid Sullivan's fiercest blows. When Sullivan missed again he looked worried for the first time. A combination followed by a roundhouse right hand rocked Sullivan's head back, and the big man dropped to the ground. As he hit the deck he deftly rolled away and reached into his waist band for his gun. This wasn't going the way he had planned. Aaron was too far away to do anything, but Sullivan was lying close to Jethroe who kicked the gun out of his hand. Sullivan scrambled after it, but Aaron ran up and kicked him in the head. Then he booted the gun away sending it spinning out of reach. Sullivan slipped his hand inside his boot and took out the knife. Aaron kicked at his arm and took a nasty cut to the shin, but he stamped down with his other foot on Sullivan's knife arm pinning it to the ground. Sullivan reached over to grab the knife with his other hand, but Aaron used his injured leg to kick him in the head. Then he stamped hard on Sullivan's hand loosening his grip on the knife. Sullivan rolled over and tried to get the knife again. Aaron kicked him hard in the ribs and the head. Then he kicked the knife away.

'Get up, Sullivan, I wanna finish you off with my fists.'

Aaron watched Sullivan force himself onto his knees, swaying from side to side like a drunk. His eyes no longer held the same menace and he was breathing heavily. Aaron's fists were raised in a boxer's stance. Sullivan took his time easing himself up, looking unsteady. Suddenly he leapt foreword wrapping his big arms around Aaron in a bear hug. It appeared he wasn't hurt as bad as he'd made out. Aaron knew Sullivan was making a last-ditch attempt by getting in close and grappling but he put a stop to the wrestling match by head butting him on the bridge of his nose. Sullivan loosened his grip and Aaron pushed him away to create enough space for a flurry of punches. Combinations and uppercuts slammed into Sullivan's face. Sullivan threw some week punches but was offering about as much resistance as a punch bag. His feet turned to jelly, and he started to fall but Aaron held him upright with one hand whilst pounding him with the other. He was not about to let up on Sullivan.

Jethroe said, 'That's enough, Aaron.'

Aaron paused to look over at Jethroe who continued. 'Let him be. It's over.'

Aaron let go and Sullivan crumpled to the ground. Aaron stood over him, the fire in his eyes burning holes in Sullivan's battered body. The hatred far from extinguished.

'Pick up the knife and cut me loose.'

Aaron did as Jethroe told him and the old man rubbed at his wrist where the rope had burned into it. Jethroe went over to Sullivan, who was still conscious, and bound his hands and feet together with the same rope, pulling it as tight as he could get it. He turned towards Aaron, who still had the knife in his hand. 'Don't forget Thelma?'

Aaron cut Thelma loose. She'd turned white with fear. Jethroe picked up the gun and put his other arm around her. 'You better call the cops.'

Thelma rushed into the house to make the call. Jethroe went over to his son whose body was still stiff with tension and took the knife out of his hand. When the local cops came Jethroe told them how Sullivan had burst into the house with a gun in his hand. He also told them about the previous assault on his brother, Bart. The cops handcuffed Sullivan and asked him if he'd got anything to say.

'I wanna speak to my lawyer,' he replied.

As he was being ushered into the cop car he looked back at Aaron and Jethroe standing in the porch. 'You ain't seen the last of the Sullivan brothers.'

Chapter 35

Chet was in the office listening on the telephone to Bobby describing the recent events. He couldn't believe what Bobby had just told him. Bart in hospital and Duke dead. He closed his eyes trying to shut out the pain. 'I presumed Sullivan would leave town when he found out that I wasn't around. I didn't expect him to assault Bart to even the score.'

'You couldn't foresee that, Chet. At least Aaron was around to put things right.'

Chet took solace in the fact that Aaron had given Michael Sullivan a thrashing, but he still felt bad. 'I should have been there, Bobby. I'm responsible for unleashing the fury of the Sullivan's. I'm gonna have to visit Uncle Bart.'

'Bart's still in hospital.'

'Guess, I'd betta make Jethroe my first stop. He can give me the low down on Bart.'

'Want me to tell Jethroe your coming back?'

'Not yet. I need to talk to my boss and arrange the time off work.'

As soon as Chet ended the call he put his head in his hands. Feelings of guilt welled up inside. For once in his life he was trying to avoid trouble, but it had backfired. Chet clenched his fist and pulled back his arm looking for something to punch. He settled for the palm of his other hand. A few moments ago, he was floating on air, about to tell Bobby about his invitation to audition at the recording studio. His elation was fast turning to misery. He walked back into the shop with his head lowered. He hoped work might take his mind off his uncle. Bill looked at him with his eyebrows raised. 'You okay, Chet?'

'Had some bad news, Bill. I'll tell you about it later.'

Chet wanted to tell Bill when he wasn't feeling so upset. He was silent for the rest of the day. After work, he called Rosalie and was relieved when she picked up rather than her folks.

'Hey Chet, what's up?'

'We need to talk. Something bad has happened to my uncle.'

'What is it?'

'I'll explain when I see you. Meet you at Callahan's at seven.'

'Okay.'

Chet went home and got cleaned up. Jean had made a pot roast, but Chet only picked at the food on his plate. Eventually he told them about his Uncle Bart.

Bill said, 'Are you gonna visit him?'

'I was hoping to leave on Friday.'

'You may as well take the rest of the week off. Me and Danny will be able to cope until Monday.'

'Appreciate that, Bill.'

Chapter 36

Rosalie looked at Chet, as he sat alone at the bar picking at his finger nails. His face looked drawn, his smile was missing.

'What's going on, Chet?'

'My uncle's been beat up and his dog's been killed all because of me.'

'How can it be your fault, you ain't been home since you moved here?'

Chet lowered his head. 'That's just it, I should've been there.'

'What happened?'

'Sullivan's brother showed up at Uncle Bart's place searching for me. As I wasn't around, he attacked my uncle, putting him in hospital, and he kicked Duke to death. Then he went looking for me at my brother's party where his luck ran out when he, foolishly, took on Aaron. I thought that by staying away I was avoiding trouble, seems like I got that wrong.'

Rosalie touched his hand, gently. 'If you'd been there, you might have been the one in hospital.'

'Maybe, but at least I could have protected my uncle.'

'Seems like Sullivan was hell bent on causing trouble whether you were there, or not.'

Chet leant forward. 'It should have been me in that show down. I need to go and check on my uncle.'

He had tears in his eyes. Rosalie put her arms around him. She could smell the alcohol on his breath indicating that he'd already downed a few beers.

Chet used his fingers to dry his eyes. 'I'm gonna miss that dog. We'd go tracking coons and be gone most of the day.' He continuously clenched and unclenched his fists. Occasionally he punched his right palm with his left hand.

Rosalie said, 'I've never seen you like this, Chet.'

'I feel like shit.'

They sat in silence for a while then Rosalie tried to lighten the mood by telling him about her day, but Chet didn't appear to be listening.

'It's no good, Rosalie. I ain't gonna be any fun, tonight. I just wanna get drunk.'

'We could go to the movies to take your mind off things?'

'I ain't in the mood for the movies.'

'My dad was hoping to meet you, tonight.'

'Better take a rain check. I ain't in the right frame of mind to be chit chatting with your pa.'

'Maybe you should get drunk then.'

Check took another slug of his beer. 'Right now, liquor seems like the only thing that's gonna make me feel better.'

'I'm not sure I wanna see you get drunk, Chet.'

'You don't need to hang around.'

'Okay, I'll go.'

Chet nodded his head. He needed to be alone to wallow in his guilt. Rosalie kissed him on the cheek and left. Chet ordered another beer. He was full of remorse. The more drunk he became the more uncomfortable the bar stool felt, and he very nearly fell off a couple of times. Looking around he noticed two empty chairs at a nearby table. He picked up his drink and slumped down in one the seats. After a while two young men walked up and stood looking at him.

'Hey guy, these seats are taken.'

'What?' Chet replied.

'You're sitting in my chair. Can't you see the drinks on the table?'

'What about them.'

'We've been to the rest room and we want our seats back, asshole.'

Chet grinned at the youths. 'You always go for a leak together.'

One of the youths put his hand on the back of Chet's chair and said. 'Don't be a smart ass, just get out of the fucking chair.'

'Seems to me you lost your seats when you went to the john.' Chet turned away and sipped at his beer.

'You ain't listening. Leaving them glasses of beer on the table meant we were coming back. They're the rules, country boy.'

'I don't see any rules.'

The youth pulled at the chair, but Chet stayed put. 'Just get the fuck out of my chair.'

Chet turned and stared at the youth. 'Or what?'

'Or I'll drag your redneck ass off of it.'

Chet stood up and the youth smiled. 'About time you started to see sense.'

The more vocal of the two went to sit in the chair and Chet slugged him in the side of the head. The guy didn't see it coming and clattered against the table. He leapt at Chet and they traded blows. Onlookers moved away to give the fighters more room. The other youth grabbed Chet from behind, pinning his arms. A woman shrieked as his friend slammed a fist into Chet's unguarded face. Chet wriggled and kicked, trying to get free. He kicked his heel, hard, into the shin of the youth, who let go of him. Two burly doormen came running in and one of them quickly took hold of the guy punching Chet, the other put Chet in a head lock. They manhandled the two youths towards the exit before throwing them into the parking lot. The other youth followed them out, raising his hands in surrender.

'You guys get off home,' said one of the doorman.

Chet was covered in blood, his cheeks already beginning to swell, and he started to feel dizzy as the fresh air hit him. The youth that did most of the fighting walked up to the doorman and pointed at Chet. 'He started it. We should be let back in.'

The doorman pushed him away hard. 'No way, you boys are out of here.' He continued to give them a stare like Clint Eastwood before he uttered the immortal line, '*make my day punk.*' The youths stared back at the doorman with insolent eyes. They didn't move, seemingly determined to hang around.

'That redneck stole our seats.'

On hearing this Chet ran at them, his fists flailing like windmills. The burly doorman intervened again, putting him in a full nelson. Chet went limp and stopped resisting, but the doorman was reluctant to let him loose.

'You need to go home, son. You're already in a bad way.'

'He's fucked up,' said the smart-aleck youth.

The boys were standing with their fists clenched ready to continue fighting. The other doorman pointed at them. 'This boy's taken enough punishment, tonight.'

'The jerk asked for it. He threw the first punch.'

The doorman pushed the lippy youth hard in the chest. 'I ain't gonna tell you again, go home.'

The boys must have figured that they weren't going to be allowed back in and they slouched off. Chet was a little unsteady on his feet and he knew he was out of it.

'You want us to call someone to come pick you up?' said the doorman.

'My car's in the lot.'

'We ain't about to let you drive, fella. Got any friends, or family, who can come and get you?'

'Only just moved here, got no kin in Memphis.'

The doorman examined Chet's bruised and swollen face, his hair was matted with blood. He held a finger in front of Chet's eyes. 'How many fingers do you see?'

'Two.'

'You might wanna visit the hospital.'

Chet licked blood from his lips. 'They're only flesh wounds.'

'If you ain't going to the hospital you need to go home. You got any money?'

Chet pulled a bunch of notes out of his pocket and some of them fell to the ground. The doorman picked them up and straightened out all the crumpled notes. They were mainly singles but there was a ten and two five-dollar bills. He looked at Chet. 'There's enough here for a cab, so we can get you home.'

Chet shrugged.

The other doorman went inside to make the call. When the cab arrived, the driver took one look at Chet and shook his head. 'This boy's gonna get blood on the seats. Most likely throw up, too.'

'Ain't you got some sort of cover for the seats?' said the doorman.

Chet ran the back of his hand across his nose and looked at the blood smeared on it. His eyes were sore, and his jaw hurt every time he moved it. His anger had dissipated, and he actually felt better than he did earlier. The pain of his injuries being preferable to the ache of a guilty heart. Now all he wanted was to go home and sleep, but he didn't really want Bill, or Jean, to see him like this. The taxi driver found an old sheet in the trunk and put it over the seat.

'You feel like throwing up, let me know and I'll stop the cab, so you can do it outside.'

Chet nodded and told the driver his address. The doorman settled the fare from the wad of notes and stuffed what remained in Chet's pocket. On the ride, home the taxi driver kept checking on Chet in his mirror. When they arrived at Bill's house he stopped, quickly opened the door, and rushed around to help Chet out. He seemed relieved that Chet hadn't been sick, or got blood on the upholstery. Chet staggered towards the house and fumbled in his pocket for his key. When he pushed open the door he was staring right into Bill's face.

'What the heck?'

'You should see the other guys.' Chet smiled at his weak attempt at a joke, but Bill wasn't laughing.

'What you been fighting about?'

'Sat in some guy's chair and he asked me to move. Didn't feel like obliging him.'

Bill said, 'You're gonna get yourself killed one day. Jean, come and help clean up Chet.'

Jean gasped as she looked at Chet's face. She went into the kitchen and filled a bowl with hot water, then she got some iodine from the medicine cabinet. 'Been a while since I used this. It's gonna sting.'

Chet winced as Jean cleaned him up. Bill made them all some hot chocolate and they sat in the kitchen. Chet placed his arms on the table and rested his head in them, his eyelids were beginning to droop. 'Guess, I'll get some shut eye.'

Bill grabbed hold of his shoulders. 'You need to wise up, Chet.'

Chet could see by the look on Bill's face that he was furious. He nodded in agreement while Bill just shook his head in despair. 'Go to bed. Jean will check out those cuts in the morning.'

Chapter 37

Chet pressed the doorbell on Rosalie's door, anxiously drumming his fingers on his leg as he waited. Although Jean had cleaned him up the best she could, he looked like something out of a horror movie. Both his eyes were swollen, and they were already starting to turn black and blue, or more accurately purple and yellow. Not quite the colors of the rainbow, but getting there. He felt his jaw which still ached whenever he talked. He wanted to see Rosalie before going to visit his folks but now he was wondering if that was a wise decision. When Rosalie's mom opened the door, she took a sharp intake of breath. 'Oh my god, Chet. Whatever happened to you?'

'It's nothing Mrs. Tully.'

'Your face looks like someone's been using you as a punch bag.'

Chet smiled, trying to relieve the tension. He'd called earlier so Rosalie was ready. She was putting on her coat as she came to the door. She grimaced as she surveyed his wounds. 'Are you okay?'

'It looks worse than it is.' Chet replied.

Rosalie's mom still held the door open. 'You wanna come in for a little while, Chet?'

'No mom, we're already late. Let's go, Chet.'

Rosalie took Chet's arm and shepherded him to the car. Chet whispered in her ear as they walked down the drive. 'Late for what?'

'Just get in the car. I don't want my dad to see you looking like this,' she replied.

'Why not?'

'You look like you been in a car wreck. Explaining to my father how you got into a bar fight is hardly likely to make a good impression.'

'It was only a disagreement. It's no big deal.'

Rosalie sat rigid and upright in the car, her face looking like a stern school teacher. 'Your eyes are swollen, you got a fat lip and you keep holding your jaw. I'd say that's more than a disagreement. What was the fight about?'

'Couple of guys said I was sitting in their seats and wanted me to move. Didn't feel like accommodating them.'

'You'd rather get in a fight than get out of a chair?'

'I was in no mood to be pushed around.'

'You were itching for a fight, more like.'

Chet shrugged his shoulders, 'Maybe.' He knew that Rosalie wasn't far off the mark.

Rosalie looked at him disapprovingly. Chet had seen that look many times before in Jethroe's face. He tried to put his arm around Rosalie, but she shrugged him off. 'This is the first fight I've been in since I moved to Memphis, I ain't about to make a habit of it, Rosalie.'

'I don't want a boyfriend who can't keep his cool.'

'No need to chastise me, Rosalie. I ain't a little kid. I was riled about not being able to prevent what occurred in my uncle's yard.'

'What happened to your uncle is no excuse for getting into a fight.'

'The bastard killed my uncle's dog, Rosalie.'

'That's no reason to get drunk and take out your anger on the first person who annoys you. You were like a time bomb waiting to go off and those guys lit the fuse. If you're going to overreact when things don't go the way they should, maybe you need to find another girlfriend.'

Chet thought about saying '*there a time for the talking to stop and the fighting to begin,*' but he knew that Rosalie wouldn't appreciate his maxim. He recognized that last night was typical of how he acted when he was despondent and full of beer, In Rosalie's world that was not normal behavior. It was senseless. He had to admit that in the sober light of day, it seemed ridiculous brawling over a chair. He was reminded of the time that Jethroe had challenged him about his show down with the baseball coach. Chet told Jethroe that him and coach Watson didn't see eye to eye. Jethroe had urged him to make his peace with the coach but Chet had said, 'I ain't about to go licking his boots.' Jethroe replied, 'You ain't gonna win an argument with the coach. He's the boss, plain and simple.' Chet said that he didn't give a shit and Jethroe had told him he ain't got a lick of sense.

He looked at Rosalie who was now glaring at him, still waiting for a response. Chet looked at his finger nails to see if there was any dirt he could pick out.

Rosalie said, 'You're gonna have to change your attitude, Chet?'

A grin appeared on Chet's face. 'Next time I'll drink slower and not talk to strangers.' He thought by making a joke he could gloss over the whole situation.

Rosalie pushed him in the chest. 'Do you think this is funny, Chet?'

'Guilty as charged.' Chet considered that he had been rebuked enough and the conversation had burnt itself out. He turned the ignition key to start up the car. 'Let's go.'

'I ain't going anywhere, Chet.'

Rosalie climbed out of the car and slammed the door shut. Without looking back, she walked up the drive and into the house. Chet thought that must be the shortest date he'd ever had. He sat for a while thinking he should go after Rosalie to apologize and promise it wouldn't happen again. Instead he drove off.

He turned into Bill's driveway hoping to go straight to his room, as he was in no mood for another reprimand. No such luck as Jean greeted him at the door. 'You're back soon?'

'Yeah, just had a disagreement with Rosalie.'

'Sorry to hear that, Chet. Do you wanna talk about it?'

Chet said, 'Not now, I just wanna finish packing and hit the road.' He started climbing the stairs.

Jean hollered. 'You take care, Chet.'

Chapter 38

The good thing about driving on the freeway was that you could just stay in your lane and get some thinking done. Before he left he had called Rosalie and had told her he would try and get back on Sunday to take her out. She had responded by telling him not to rush back on her account. Chet could tell she was still made with him. She had sounded remote and indifferent and he wondered if he'd blown his chance with her.

Chet checked to make sure he wasn't exceeding the speed limit. He had lots of thoughts swirling around in his head. He was apprehensive about seeing his Uncle Bart, knowing how upset he'd be about Duke. He wasn't looking forward to seeing Jethroe, as their last meeting ended in a fight. Moreover, he expected Jethroe to admonish him for not showing up for the party. On the other hand, at least he'd be able to visit with his brother and Bobby. He contemplated turning himself in to the cops and awaiting his fate.

An old Buick pulled in front of him cutting him up. He thought about sounding the horn, but he shook his head, instead. He heard a bang and the Buick slowed. Chet hit the brakes and tried to swerve out of the way, but he collided with the car's fender. Both cars pulled onto the shoulder. He noticed the Buick's blown out tire as he jumped out of the car and stomped up to speak to the driver. The old guy sat stiff as a corpse with his eyes open wide. The old woman sitting next to him was trembling with fear, as Chet spoke, 'You cut me up real bad.'

He driver replied, 'I checked in the mirror and thought I was clear. I was being tailgated by an impatient asshole and Martha wanted me to pull over.'

The old timer's wife dug her elbow into his ribs. Chet scratched his head. He felt sorry for the old boy as he visualized him in the fast lane, doing the speed limit, being pressured to pull over. 'You should have looked over your shoulder before changing lanes. I guess I was in your blind spot.'

The man nodded, 'I got a blown-out tire. That's why I hit the brakes.'

'Yeah, I know. I tried to avoid you, but I was too late. Are you okay?'

The old man looked at Chet's battered face. 'I'm a lot better than you by the look of your face.'

'Old flesh wounds, but I betta check out the motor.'

The old man climbed out of the car and they surveyed the damage to both autos. Chet's station wagon had come off worse. Broken headlight for starters. The Buick only seemed to have a dent in the fender and the old man scratched his head. 'Mine ain't too bad. I just need to change that wheel.'

Chet said, 'You got a spare?'

'Yeah.'

'Need a hand getting that wheel off?'

'I should be okay. I done it before.'

Chet went back to his car to take a closer look. The old man hollered to his wife. 'Martha, get a pen and some paper to give this young man our insurance information.'

Chet went to the passenger side off the Buick and watched the old lady fumbling in the glove box. She located a biro and a note pad, her hand shaking as she wrote. Then she tore of the sheet and handed the pad to Chet. 'Write down your name, address and insurance details, son.'

It was a yellow, lined pad probably purchased from Wal-Mart. Chet wrote down his details and handed the pad back to the woman. 'I work in the auto business, so I may fix mine myself.'

She looked up at Chet. 'These are our details including our phone number.'

He smiled down at her and for the first time the woman smiled back. Chet could only just make out the old girl's shaky writing. The old man's name was James Robertson. Chet folded the paper and put it in his pocket, then he went over to the old man who had already lifted the spare out of the trunk and had placed it next to the blown-out tire. He was breathing heavily, and he winced as he stood upright, then leaned back to stretch his back the other way. 'Guess my old muscles ain't as flexible as they used to be.'

'Sure, you don't want help with that wheel, Mr. Robertson?'

'Mighty kind of you, son. You can loosen them wheel lugs soon as I locate the wrench. My old back don't take kindly to too much bending nowadays.'

'No problem.' Chet replied.

The old man found the wrench in the trunk and handed it to Chet. He said, 'Martha was worried when she saw you walking over to the car. There are some angry people in this world, reckon she thought you might be one of them.'

'Looks like you caught me on a good day, grandpa. We've both got away lightly with this little mishap.'

Chet loosened the wheel lugs and Mr. Robertson showed him where to place the jack, although Chet had already figured that out for himself. After he put on the spare he turned to the old man whose face had got back its color. 'You okay to drive?'

'A little shaken up is all.'

'Maybe you oughta sit a while.'

'I'm gonna be fine, son.'

'In that case I'm gonna take off.'

'You got our phone number, so you can call if you need anything else.'

'Likewise, Mr. Robertson. My name's Chet and I've given you my uncle's address. That's where I'll be staying. You take care and remember to look over your shoulder before changing lanes.'

'That's sound advice, Chet. Have a safe journey.'

As Chet drove off he realized that his car was worse than he first thought. The front wheel was knocking a little. He might need to replace a wheel bearing. It seemed like lady luck was not on his side right now. He muttered a familiar turn of phrase to himself, *shit happens.*

There was no point going to Uncle Bart's place as Bobby said he'd be recuperating at Jethroe's house when he came out of hospital, so Chet pulled into his daddy's yard. The first thing he saw was Bart sitting in a rocking chair on the porch. His trepidation at meeting Jethroe dissipated some as he strode towards Bart. 'You okay, uncle?'

Bart screwed his eyes as he scrutinized his nephew. 'Better than you by the look of your face.'

'Sorry to hear about, Duke.'

'Miss him more than I can say.' Bart gritted his teeth. 'If I was a younger man Sullivan would be the one lying in a grave.'

Chet said, 'I should have been here to deal with him.'

Aaron came out when he heard Chet's voice. He threw his arms around his younger brother. Then stepped back to study his face. 'You still walking into fists?'

'How do you know I wasn't in an automobile accident?'

Aaron casually, punched Chet's shoulder. 'Because you drive better than you fight.'

'You ain't seen the other guys.'

'The smart thing is to avoid getting hit, little brother.'

Chet sighed, 'Only time I manage that, other people seem to get hurt.'

Chet looked over at his Uncle Bart who was still rocking in the chair, like a school boy on a swing in the park. Chet continued, 'Looks like you got a few marks on that handsome face of yours, Aaron'

'Had to deal with the bastard that beat on Bart. It seems like he was hell bent on revenge and any Carter would do.'

Chet said, 'Big mistake, taking on you.'

'Damn right.' Aaron replied.

'Do you know where he's at, now?'

'The cops took him away. He was shouting he'd be back, so we may not have seen the last of him.'

Bart abruptly stepped of the chair which continued rocking gently back and forth. 'If he comes here again I'll fill him full of lead.'

Chet tapped him lightly on the shoulder. 'You ain't in a fit enough state to handle a rifle, Uncle Bart.'

'Don't you believe it.' Bart replied.

Chet said, 'Heard you got broken ribs?'

Bart coughed and put his hand to his side as he winced in pain. He sat back in the rocker. 'Hairline crack is all.'

Aaron put his hand on the rocking chair, stopping his uncle rocking it. 'You're under orders to rest up, uncle.'

Jethroe came out to see what all the commotion was about. 'Well, what do you know? The boy that started all this shit comes home when it's all over.'

Chet replied, 'Figured if I wasn't around Sullivan would leave town.'

Jethroe sniffed. 'You got that wrong.'

'I would have been here if I thought Sullivan was gonna hurt Uncle Bart.'

'That offer of support has come a little too late, son. You messed with the wrong people this time, just like I told you.'

Bart grabbed Jethroe's sleeve. 'Leave the boy be. He ain't responsible for Michael Sullivan's actions.'

'Maybe not. But if he hadn't put Joe Sullivan in the hospital in the first place none of this would've happened and Duke would still be alive. Them Sullivan brother's ain't gonna let it be.'

Chet hoped that Jethroe was wrong, but he suspected that he probably wasn't. Bart tried to lighten the atmosphere. 'Sullivan didn't realize he was taking on a member of the United States army boxing team.'

Jethroe beamed with pride and Chet's eyes opened wider. 'You boxing for the army, Aaron?'

'You better believe it, Chet.'

'How'd you get into that?'

'Sergeant saw me sort out some trouble makers and thought I shaped up well as a fighter. Got me training with the battalion boxing team and before you know it I'm fighting in the light heavy weight division.'

'You had any fights yet?'

'Just one.'

'How did it go?'

'Knocked out my opponent in the second round.'

'Holy shit.' Chet bobbed and weaved and threw pretend punches at Aaron. 'Guess I need to take some boxing lessons.'

'Lesson one. Don't get into a brawl unless you got no other options. Were you fighting over a woman?'

'I was feeling like shit about old Duke getting killed and two cowboys were in the right place at the wrong time.' Chet was embarrassed about his latest bar fight and wanted to avoid having to explain himself further. 'Hey uncle, I got bruised ribs too.'

Bart grimaced as he leant forward. 'That ain't nothing to be proud of. Aaron's right you get into fights too readily. Only a fool goes looking for trouble. You think I ain't angry. For the last ten years Duke followed me like a shadow. Cracked ribs ain't nothing compared to the pain of not having him around.'

Chet had never seen his uncle looking so downcast. The smile that he perpetually wore on his face was missing. The old man seemed five years older than the last time he'd seen him. 'I miss him too, uncle.'

Bart stood up. 'I need to get back home. Got chickens to feed and moonshine to make. I can't afford to be moping around here.'

Jethroe stood in his way and put his hands on Bart's shoulders. 'You need to stay here until you're in better health.'

Bart knocked Jethroe's arms off him. 'I got customers to supply.' He tried to push past his brother but Jethroe stood firm like a rock.

'You think you can load up the Dodge in the state you're in?' said Jethroe.

Bart sat down again and sighed. He took off his cap and ruffled his hair. Aaron put his arm around his uncle's shoulder.

Chet said, 'Want me to deliver the weekly load, uncle.'

Bart sat forward. 'Are you staying?'

'Only for the weekend.'

Bart's shoulders slumped again. 'I'd sure appreciate some help, Chet. There's a truck load of hooch bottled and ready to deliver.'

'No problem, uncle. Only other thing I gotta do is fix my car. I got in a fender bender on the interstate.'

'Well the pick up's still purring like a baby.' Bart pulled a sheet of paper out of his pocket and gave a list of names to Chet. 'Lost a couple of customers since you've been gone, so the weekly load won't take as long. John Rutledge owes four weeks. He's been given time and now it's time for him to pay up. You know the script; *the Carter family don't wanna take this personally....'*

Chet said, 'Know it off by heart, uncle.'

Bart said, 'Jethroe wants me to move in here with him.'

'That makes sense, uncle.'

Jethroe smiled and put his arm around Chet. Bart shook his hcad in disbclicf. 'Never thought I'd see the day Jethroe and Chet agree about something. Seeing you too together is like watching a raccoon playing with a hound.'

Chet knew that Bart was right, He was usually at loggerheads with Jethroe. Moreover, it was a rare for both sets of brothers to be in the same place. If nothing else this business with the Sullivan's had brought the Carter's closer together. Jethroe put his other arm around Aaron.

Bart said, 'Wished I got my camera, seeing my brother with his arms around both his sons is a first.'

Jethroe fixed Bart in the eyes. 'You stay put until you're fighting fit, brother.'

Chet considered that was the last words on the subject, as far as Jethroe was concerned, anyway. His pa went into the kitchen, where Thelma was cooking supper. He sniffed the air. The sweet smell of roast chicken permeated the room.

Thelma said, 'You just had to start in on Chet, didn't you?'

Jethroe tilted his head to one side. 'Are you listening in on family conversations?'

'Couldn't help hear you bad mouthing the boy.'

'I do believe the conversation ended harmoniously, Thelma. I had my arms around both my sons.'

Thelma held both Jethroe's hands. 'I'm pleased to hear it. Don't forget you promised me you weren't gonna be so hard on the boy. Aaron and Bart are always happy to see Chet, but you always seem to spoil the moment.'

'Every time I look at him I get a sick feeling inside, Thelma.'

'There's something strange about that.'

'I can't look at him without thinking about the day we found Chrissie dead in the barn.'

'Well that ain't natural. You shouldn't associate that with the boy.'

Jethroe nodded and put his arm around Thelma. 'I'll try and cut him more slack. He does seem to be trying to turn his life around.'

Chapter 39

There was something comforting about driving the Dodge on his old route again, the mason jars rattling in the back. The first stop was the Routledge place as Chet wanted to get any potential confrontation out of the way, so he could chew the cud with the other customers the way he usually did. He knew they would be pleased to see him and delighted to get their weekly quota of moonshine. He'd always found John Routledge an agreeable man. It was a surprise to Chet that he was behind with his payment. He parked in the Routledge driveway and left the hooch in the back of the Dodge. He wasn't about to leave any liquor until Routledge paid up.

'I wasn't expecting you, Chet, I thought you'd skipped town. What happened to your face?'

'Back again like the prodigal son, John. You know me, I ain't ever been able to avoid a fight.' Chet saw the state of his face as an opportunity to get down to the crux of the matter. 'Talking about disagreements, Bart says you owe four weeks and he don't want it to spoil a long-standing friendship.'

'I'm having family problems right now. I need more time to get the money together.'

'That ain't possible, John, Bart wants you to settle up.'

John sat down and lowered his head. 'I just ain't got it, Chet.'

'The Carter family don't wanna take this personally, John. Think you know what's gonna happen if you don't pay.'

Rutledge looked up. 'You don't have to threaten me, Chet. I know all too well about the Carter's reputation.'

'Just giving you a friendly warning, John. You don't want to quarrel with the Carter's over sixty-nine dollars.'

'My wife, Jenny is an alcoholic, Chet. Not only is she drinking moonshine, she's buying bottles of Jack Daniels from the liquor store. I keep finding empty bottles stashed around and the money for paying bills has all gone on drink. Had to hide her car keys to stop her driving over to the store to get more. We're gonna have to cancel our order while I try and sober her up.'

'Sorry to hear about Mrs. Routledge, but that ain't the Carter's problem. Your biggest concern is paying the money you owe. You gotta make this your priority.'

Without saying a word Routledge walked out of the lounge into the kitchen. Chet followed wondering what his next move was going to be. You never could tell what a desperate man would do. If he had a gun Chet wanted to see it before he heard the speeding bullet heading his way. Routledge opened a cupboard and took out a screwdriver. He took a couple of paces towards Chet and stopped. Chet braced himself. Routledge bent and lifted a rug exposing bare wooden floor boards. He took out a couple of screws then pulled up a piece of board. He got up suddenly, spun around, and threw something towards Chet.

'Catch.'

Chet flinched and held out his hands at the missile flying towards him. He failed to catch the object and it hit his chest before clanking on the floor. He looked down at the key, picked it up, and raised his eyebrows. Routledge shrugged. 'You can take that old Ford out front in lieu of the debt.'

Chet moved to the window and saw a rusty looking blue Ford in the drive. 'Is it drivable?'

'Hell yes. Jenny's been driving that car for years. Milometer may be high, but I'd say it's worth more than sixty-nine dollars.'

'We usually only deal in cash but considering the circumstances I do believe this would be a fair exchange.'

'Like I said I've been hiding the car key, if you take the auto I won't have to worry about Jenny using it to replenish her stock of liquor. I certainly don't want any hassle with the Carters.'

Chet put the key in his pocket. 'We rarely get any aggravation from our customers, John. Only gotta mention the family name and folks find a way to pay.'

'Not surprising given your family history.'

'What's that supposed to mean?'

'I was referring to the Donnelly's.'

'Still none the wiser, John.'

'You've got to be shitting me?'

'I shit you not, John. I don't know what you're talking about.'

Routledge massaged his scalp. 'I find it hard to believe that neither Jethroe, or Bart, told you about the Donnelly's.'

Chet sat down in a chair showing that he was going nowhere until Routledge filled him in on the Donnelly's. 'How about you enlightening me?'

'Don't see what harm there is in it. A boy should know about his kin. Two families of Donnelly's lived on the outskirts of town, both had two sons, one had a daughter as well. Everyone knew the Donnelly's were white trash. The boys were feral. They were either stealing, or verbally abusing folk. Their pappies were no better. Jake Schneider operated the moonshine business back then and your uncles, Bart and Luke, used to help him. The Donnelly's liked to drink hooch. Liked it more than was good for them. One day a couple of Donnelly boys got inebriated but wanted more moonshine. They took a drive to the Schneider place to replenish their supplies, only they weren't about to pay. Jake told them to get the hell off his property, so they set upon him. Bart and Luke heard the commotion and came running. Bart tackled one of the Donnelly boys and they grappled in the dirt until Bart got on top. Luke picked up a piece of timber lying on the ground and hit the other Donnelly boy across the head. Killed him outright. Jake was badly beaten and shaken. The judge was aware that the Donnelly's were known trouble makers. He said Bart and Luke acted in self-defense. Everyone was fine with the verdict, but the Donnelly clan had other ideas and wanted retribution. All the male Donnelly's headed to the Carter property with weapons and flaming torches. Your grand pappy, Seth, and his brother Jed were standing on the front porch with rifles in their hands. Your grandma had been told to take the boys, Jethroe, Luke and Bart into the basement and she was happy to oblige. Seth hollered to the Donnelly's to go home while they were still able. That was the best advice ever offered but not taken. Within seconds of the first bullet being fired the six Donnelly's were dead on the ground. Seth Carter was the finest shot in the whole of Tennessee. His brother wasn't far behind him. Jed needed hospital treatment, but Seth only had flesh wounds. Rumor had it that one of the Donnelly boys didn't die straight off. Folks said that Jed stood over him and finished him off executioner style. Those who were acquainted with the Carters knew that Seth and Jed Carter hit where they aimed, and they were aiming to kill. The coroner only found one bullet hole in each of the Donnelly's bodies, so it was plain for all to see that it was self-defense. The Donnelly women claimed an injustice, but they were driven out of town by the townsfolk.'

Chet's mouth was now wide open in genuine surprise. 'Never heard that story before, John.'

'It's as true as I'm standing here. Seth and Jed were well liked in these parts. Their ability to fire a rifle was well known to everyone, except the Donnelly's, I guess. Shortly after the incident Jake Schneider had gone to live with his son. The beating he took from them Donnelly boys left him in a bad way. Jake said if it wasn't for Luke and Bart them Donnelly's would've killed him, so he let them have the business for a song. They paid Jake rent on the property until he died. In his will Jake left the deeds to Bart and Luke, but Luke had moved on by then. He had always felt bad about killing that Donnelly boy and some say that's why he took to drink.'

'No wonder whenever I mention the Carter family reputation, folks think back to the feud with the Donnelly's,' said Chet.

'Most people around here know the legend of Seth and Jed. They see the same steel in Bart and Jethroe. Aaron followed in their footprints and folks weren't surprised when you hit that trucker in Guthrie's.'

'I reacted instinctively, John. I didn't have any axe to grind against Joe Sullivan. I was standing up for my buddy, is all.'

'I see that as family trait.'

'Don't know how long I'll be around, but it won't do any harm to let folks know I'm back, John. I appreciate the car.'

He now understood about his family reputation. However, with Aaron in the army and Bart incapacitated, Chet didn't want anyone to assume that the Carter's were no longer a force to be reckoned with, especially with the Sullivan's poking around.

Chapter 40

Back at the house Bart peeked out the window as he heard a car pull into the drive. He was first to the door to greet Chet. 'How'd it go?'

'Good.' Chet replied.

'Everyone paid up?'

Chet handed Bart a roll of cash, 'Yeah.' He went into the family room with Bart close behind.

'What about John Routledge?'

Chet took a key from his pocket and held it up. 'He gave me the key to his wife's car in lieu of the money he owed. I thought me, and Bobby would go pick it up, later.'

Bart scratched his head. 'Things that bad with John Routledge?'

'His wife has a problem with alcohol. On top of drinking moonshine, she's buying bottles of Jack Daniels from town.'

Bart eased himself onto the easy chair. 'Some folk just don't have any sense of loyalty. We could've increased her supply.'

Chet held out his hands, palms up, and raised his voice showing exasperation. 'John's trying to sober her up. She's spending money on liquor that should be paying bills.'

'Well, there goes another good customer.'

Chet shook his head. 'John's in deep shit and all you're worried about is losing business?'

'Why you getting so uppity? I'm only joking. I can sympathize with John Routledge. Liquor's been the ruin of a many a good man, or woman. Is the auto any good?'

'It's seen better days, but John says it runs well.'

'You can keep it until you get your station wagon fixed.'

Chet slouched on the sofa. 'I was hoping you'd say that. I was planning on fixing her this weekend but I gotta get some parts. I'm gonna need some wheels for the trip back to Memphis.'

Bart slumped over. 'I was hoping you'd stay a little longer, Chet?'

'I got a job and a beautiful girlfriend waiting for me back in Memphis.'

Jethroe came into the room. Chet looked up expecting the cold, hard stare that he usually got from his daddy. 'I want a word with Chet in private,' he said.

Bart interjected. 'He's only just got here. Let him rest a while.'

Jethroe sat facing Chet. 'Just a few questions, is all. It won't take long.'

Bart shook his head and looked at Aaron who said, 'Let's go into the kitchen for a while, uncle.'

Jethroe waited until they both left the room and were out of ear shot. 'I want you to help persuade your uncle to give up the moonshine business. Now you're living in Memphis he ain't able to cope. Nor is he able to defend himself against any more intruders. The sheriff that comes into the Rustler has always turned a blind eye to Bart's moonshine operation. I believe Bart's paid him off. Trouble is he's retiring, and the new guy might not be so obliging. Overheard Bart say that he's losing customers, so the time's right for him to call it a day. I've got plenty of room, so he may as well move in here.'

'What about his chickens?'

'They can scrat around here just as well as at his place.'

'What if I decide to stay put and not go back to Memphis?'

'Thought you'd got a good job and a new sweetheart. Things seem to be looking up for you, son. Are you getting anywhere with your music?'

'Trying to set up an audition at Sun records. I already met one of the record producers.'

Jethroe sat forward. 'Sounds promising. Listen son, I know you think I've been hard on you but I'm mindful of that temper of yours. You've done right by your uncle and he's relied on you. Now it's time for you to do right by yourself. I don't know two hoots about music, but folks say you got talent. If you're aiming on being a musician then you should give it your best shot, or you may regret it for the rest of your life. Go back and pursue your goals. Be persistent and don't give up.'

Chet was amazed that Jethroe was giving him genuine fatherly advice. Since he'd been back he had a real feeling of family solidarity. 'I don't like letting uncle Bart down, pa.'

Aaron and Bart came in with drinks. Aaron gave a bottle of beer to Chet and Bart handed Jethroe a glass of water.

Bart said, 'I suppose you've been talking about me.'

Chet said, 'Jethroe thinks you should bring your chickens here and retire from the moonshine game, uncle.'

'I do believe there's life in this old man, yet.'

'You ain't able to manage on your own and I've got a new life waiting for me in Memphis.'

'If that's what you want, go for it, Chet. Wouldn't wanna hold you back.'

'You gonna move in with Jethroe?'

'Need to think hard about that. He's a miserable old critter, I'm not sure we could live under the same roof.'

Everyone smiled except Jethroe who put his hand on Bart's shoulder. 'It ain't as if we'd be under each other's feet.'

Bart sad, 'We only just started speaking and you want me to move in. You gone soft in the head?'

'We're all getting older, Bart. It ain't wise for you to be on your own without Chet looking out for you.'

Bart stood up with his hands on his hips, his chin jutting out. 'It's me been looking after Chet all these years, not the other way around.'

Jethroe said, 'That's as maybe, but you ain't getting any younger.'

'You go back to Memphis, Chet and don't fret about your uncle. I ain't ready for the scrap heap yet.'

'My boss has been real good to me and I wanna repay him for his generosity. I let him down badly when I got into that fight. His wife cleaned me up good, but I could see the disappointment in their faces. We got a full work load next week, so Bill's expecting me back in the shop on Monday morning.'

'Then you oughta go back and fulfil your obligation. Sanders is right you need to stop getting into fights before you really get hurt.'

Chet was getting tired of hearing the same advice from everyone, like a record stuck in the groove. He decided to change the subject and take the spotlight off himself. 'Talking about getting killed. How come nobody told me the tale of Grandpa Seth and the Donnelly's?'

Jethroe, Bart and Aaron looked at each other. Chet thought they looked like boys caught with their fingers in the pie. Jethroe was the first to speak. 'We didn't want to tell either of you, but Aaron heard the story from a kid at school and I told him not to let you in on it. We didn't know how you'd react, you being so headstrong.'

Chet said, 'A boy should know about his family history.'

Jethroe said, 'Didn't think you were mature enough to handle the fact that your grandpa and his brother killed six men.'

'So, when were you planning on telling me?'

'When you got older, but you left home before I got the opportunity.'

Bart touched Chet on the shoulder. 'Jethroe's right, it ain't easy to talk about something like that. Families often keep their skeletons in the closet.'

'What did you think I was gonna do, walk around like "Billy the Kid" and threaten to shoot anyone that I didn't like the look of?'

Jethroe said, 'Something like that.'

Bart's smirk started Aaron grinning, which made it difficult for Chet to keep a straight face.

Jethroe continued. 'The fact is, in those days justice was often self-served. Nowadays we call law enforcement officers to settle disputes.'

Chet nodded his assent. He was surprised at how cordial his pappy was being. It seemed like Jethroe was giving him years of parenting all in one go. Moreover, Jethroe was making a real effort to patch things up with Bart. He'd never seen the pair so brotherly and he put it down to Thelma's influence. She seemed to be playing a major role in changing Jethroe's attitude. 'I've been thinking about visiting with the cops before I go back to Memphis.'

Blank faces and silence greeted that statement. No one seemed to know how to respond. Chet was mindful that if he did turn himself in, the cops may find it necessary to detain him.

Chapter 41

Next day Bobby picked up Chet and they drove to the Routledge property. Chet gave Bobby the keys to the Ford while he went inside to collect the vehicle's documentation. Bobby ran his hand over the paint work then he looked inside. It needed valeting. He was checking the mileage when Chet came out of the house.

'What do you think, Bobby?'

'The body work ain't too good.'

'More interested in how she drives. Start her up, Bobby boy.'

Chet sat in the passenger seat as Bobby turned the ignition. It started it up first time.

Bobby said, 'Don't sound too bad.'

'Needs to be in good shape, its gotta get me to Memphis tonight. I won't be able to drive the station wagon until that wheel bearing's been replaced.'

Chet got out of the car and Bobby did likewise. 'You want me to fix it while you're gone.'

'I'd appreciate that Bobby.'

'Maybe I could bring it Memphis and you could show me around.'

Chet wanted Bobby to be around to help Bart and he wasn't ready for visitors. 'That could work but you might find yourself playing gooseberry when I'm out with Rosalie.'

Bobby scratched his nose and changed the subject. 'You gonna play guitar at Guthrie's, tonight?'

'I ain't got time. I still gotta go back to Uncle Bart's place, put away the empty jars, and feed the chickens. Wanna tag along?'

'Sure.'

Chet drove the Ford back to Jethroe's to pick up the Dodge. Bobby followed in his own car. Thirty minutes later the boys pulled into the Bart's yard. Chickens came running from all over as Chet scattered feed along the ground. They'd been scavenging for food all over the yard and they weren't about to turn down a free lunch. Bobby carried the empty bottles into the barn. 'Holy shit!'

Chet heard the exclamation and ran over. There were two snakes sliding around the barn. Chet scratched his head, 'They're only garter snakes.'

Bobby said, 'They made me jump.'

Chet said, 'Never seen snakes in the barn before. I guess old Duke would have kept them away.' The thought of Duke brought tears to Chet's eyes.

After they had put away the jars and tidied up, Bobby went home. Chet had one more thing to do before driving back to Memphis. He decided to go and visit the cops.

Chet felt uncomfortable walking into the station house. This was the first time he'd been here voluntarily, but he walked right up to the front desk. 'Name's Chet Carter. I was involved in a fight in Guthrie's bar a few months ago. I've come by to clear things up.'

The officer manning the desk looked up. 'Wait there while I get the officer that's handling that incident.'

Chet looked around while he waited. Grey walls, even greyer faces. After a few minutes, the man at the desk came back. 'Follow me.'

He took Chet to a small office and opened the door. 'Sit here, a detective will be with you shortly.'

There were two chairs either side of a table. Chet sat in one of them. When the detective came in he looked familiar, but Chet couldn't remember where he'd seen him before. He sat on the chair opposite Chet and said, 'Chet Carter?'

'Yes sir.'

'I'm detective Clarke, we've been looking for you in relation to the fight in Guthrie's.'

The officer was a tall man with a moustache and he had a deep voice. Chet was expecting an interrogation. 'That's why I come by.'

'We heard you left town.'

'Yes sir, just back for the weekend, visiting my folks.'

'Why did you run off? You should've turned yourself in. We need to hear your account of the fight before we decide whether to take any action.'

Chet was starting to get worried. He was beginning to regret dropping by. 'Nothing much to tell.'

'By the look of your face it seems like you're still getting into fights. Go ahead and tell me what happened at Guthrie's.'

'Sullivan was manhandling Rita, my buddy's girl, so my friend, Bobby, told him to butt out. Sullivan attacked him, and I backed up Bobby by hitting the big ape with a pool cue.'

The cop was taking notes. He looked up. 'Knocking him out cold.'

'Yes, sir.'

'Lucky shot?'

Chet shrugged and narrowed his eyes as he wasn't sure what the cop was inferring. 'I guess.'

'Not for Sullivan. You admit you assaulted him?'

'It was self-defense. You should be hauling him in for harassing Rita.'

'Had Sullivan threatened, or hit, you?'

'No, but he was about to beat the crap out of Bobby.'

'So, you decided to whack him in the head, first?'

'Yes, sir.'

The cop put down his pen. 'That's about the same account that we got from other witnesses.'

Chet started to think that he might be okay. 'That's how it went down, officer.'

'We asked Sullivan if he wanted to press charges.'

Chet sat forward. 'What did he say?'

'Said he sorted out his own disagreements.'

'So, what happens now?'

Officer Clarke folded his arms across his chest and waited for a few seconds before answering. 'In the circumstances, we'll issue you an official warning.'

'Am I free to go?'

'Yeah.'

Chet felt relief flooding through his veins. 'I'm planning on turning over a new leaf, officer Clarke.'

'What if Sullivan comes looking for retribution?'

'His brother already has. He beat up my uncle and killed his dog. You gonna charge him with that?'

'Your Uncle Bart didn't want to press charges, either. He said the Carters took care of their own business. Seems like the Sullivan's and the Carters have got the same tribal code of ethics. In the state of Tennessee, we got law enforcement officers to uphold the law. We ain't living in the wild west anymore. We handed Joseph Sullivan over to the Kentucky state police as they had a warrant out for him. Michael Sullivan's a free man but we advised him to keep away from Jackson County.'

Chet realized that the detective knew far more about him than he first thought. 'Sullivan promised he'd be back and I'm worried about my family. I'm trying to make a new life for myself in Memphis'

'Doing what?'

'I'm a mechanic, but I aim to be a musician.'

'I've heard you playing guitar in Guthrie's. You're damn good.'

'Thank you, sir.' Chet raised his eyebrows. 'When were you in Guthrie's?'

'I'm a member of a barber shop quartet. We've performed there a few times. I sing the bass.'

Chet snapped his fingers and pointed. 'That's where I seen you. I remember listening to you guys. Great harmony.'

'Thank you, Chet.'

'Are you gonna be watching out for Michael Sullivan?

Detective Clarke stood up and slid his chair under the table, 'We'll be doing our job, but he ain't likely to give us any advanced warning.'

Chet got up too and did the same with his chair. 'My pappy and uncle are getting old and they ain't capable of defending themselves against the Sullivan's. I'll be in Memphis and my brother's in the army.'

'Bart and Jethroe may be old timers but they can still fire a gun.'

Chet looked hard into Clarke's eyes. 'Thought you don't approve of folk taking the law into their own hands?'

'We don't, but neither do we expect them to lie down without a fight.'

Detective Clarke held open the door for Chet, who had the impression that the cop knew the Carter family and wondered if he knew about Seth and Jed. A vision flashed through Chet's mind of two men striding purposely onto the Carter property. But it wasn't Seth and Jed waiting with their rifles cocked. It was Jethroe and Bart. Chet snapped out of his reverie. 'Last thing the Carter's want is more bloodshed.'

'I sure hope so, son.'

They walked down the corridor and Chet shook hands with the detective before heading for the door. 'So long, officer Clarke.'

'Take care, Chet.'

Chapter 42

Rosalie was on Chet's mind as he drove the Ford back to Memphis. He'd never been in love before and he didn't want to lose her. He couldn't wait to see her beautiful face again. He glanced at his watch as he turned into the Sander's driveway. It was nine o'clock and the light was still on inside, which meant that Bill and Jean hadn't gone to bed. Chet walked into the lounge where Bill was sitting on his chair reading. He took off his reading glasses and looked up. 'Boy, am I pleased to see you. How was your trip?'

'Saw my brother, and my pappy was civil for a change.'

'How's your uncle?'

Chet sat on a chair next to Bill. 'He's recuperating at my pappy's house, but his ribs are still hurting some. How's work?'

'Busy, got a full docket tomorrow. Can you work late?'

'Sure.'

'Good we may need to stay until 7, or 8 pm, most of the week.'

'No problem, Bill. Can I use the phone to call Rosalie?'

'Go ahead.'

Chet went into the hall and dialed Rosalie's number. Usually her mom answered but this time Rosalie picked up. Chet was pleased to hear her voice. 'Hi honey.'

'When did you get back?'

'Just now. I always planned on getting back today. Gonna be working late all week, but I wanna meet up tomorrow after work to talk things over.'

'Okay'

'I didn't like leaving with you mad at me, and all.'

'Me neither.'

Chet smiled to himself. He was worried for nothing. Rosalie didn't seem to be mad with him, any more. He said, 'So, are we good, now?'

'I don't want you getting into any more fights, that's for sure.'

'I'm gonna steer clear of trouble from now on, Rosalie.'

'I got a message from Clarence Henderson.'

'No shit.'

'He's interested in hearing you play and if he likes what he hears he may have a proposition for you.'

Chet raised his fists in the air and shook them as if he'd just watched his team score a touchdown. 'That's great. What's he's got in mind?'

'He didn't say but it seems promising.'

'I ain't about to get my hopes up, he ain't even heard me play, yet. I'm relieved you ain't given up on me'

'You need to change your attitude.'

'From now on I'm gonna be more laid back. See you tomorrow?

'Okay, what time?'

'I'll aim to get to your place by eight thirty, but I'll be picking you up in a different auto.'

'You got a new car?'

'Station wagon's needs fixing, so I'm driving an old Ford until I get it back on the road. Different car, different attitude, but the same fun loving, passionate boyfriend.'

'Don't forget to call Clarence. You still got his card?'

'Yeah. I'll call him tomorrow.'

Chapter 43

Jethroe saw the sign for the airport and took the turn. The conversation had dried up and he wondered what Aaron was thinking. It had certainly been an eventful trip. 'How much longer do you envisage staying in the army?'

Aaron said, 'Not sure.'

Jethroe had seen precious little of his eldest son over the last few years. Having both his sons at home for a couple of days was a rarity and he liked it. He felt he'd mended some bridges with Chet. The quarrels that had kept Bart and him apart now seemed in the distant past. It saddened him when he thought of all the wasted years. He remembered the tragic death of his brother Luke. It was time to treasure his family and strengthen the ties that had loosened over the years. 'What you gonna do when you get discharged?'

'Don't rightly know.'

'You still interested in the legal profession?'

'No, being a lawyer ain't for me.'

'Professional boxer?'

'You gotta be kidding. I'm still hurting from those shots I took from Sullivan.'

'You ain't spoiled your good looks, any.'

'I've only had one fight so far, pa. There's gonna be fights where I take some big hits. That may be when I call it a day.'

Jethroe sighed, 'Wish Chet thought like that. I'm sick of seeing that boy's face smashed up.'

'He'll learn, pa.'

'How come he always gets into trouble and you come away a hero?'

'He ain't got a lick a sense when it comes to fighting. He just wades in without thinking of the consequences.'

Jethroe found a parking space and turned off the engine. 'Ain't that the truth. If you ain't gonna be a lawyer, or a boxer, how are you gonna put bread on the table when you quit the army?'

'Maybe I'll come home and work the farm.'

This was music to Jethroe's ears. 'I figured you'd had your fill of farming when you went off to college.'

Aaron collected his kitbag and lifted it onto his shoulder, 'Was itching to spread my wings, is all. I always enjoyed working on the land, pop.'

Jethroe smiled with pride at how effortlessly Aaron handled the heavy bag. He remembered how strong the boy was, and how he easily he coped with farm work. 'The farm will belong to you and Chet one day.'

'That's likely to be a long way off, considering how fit you are.'

'I may not want to run this place much longer.'

'What are you getting at?'

'If you did decide to settle down you could manage the farm. You done just about every task and you're a hard worker.'

They approached the check in desk and joined the line. Aaron put down his bag. 'What would you do?'

'Hunt, fish, sit back and relax. Maybe spend my time feeding the chickens like your Uncle Bart.'

'You know, pa, I've seen a lot of different places but there ain't anywhere as pretty as the Smokies.'

'There ain't no place like home as the saying goes. This farm started when your great, great, grandpa Sam Carter bought forty acres from the government. He got some livestock, planted enough corn and wheat to feed the family, and be self-sufficient. He didn't want to rely on folk. He didn't trust them. That's how it was with Sam.'

'Yeah, didn't he marry a Chickasaw squaw.'

'That's right. Prettiest girl he ever did see, raven black hair, beautiful big brown eyes. It was love at first sight. In them days folk were prejudice against Indians. Some individuals wouldn't speak to Sam after he took his bride. The only ones that ever insulted her, or showed any disrespect, were either very brave, or extremely foolhardy. Sam was a tough man, hard as granite. Anyone messed with him ended up counting their broken bones. This family is part Cherokee and damn proud of it.'

Aaron gritted his teeth. 'Anyone ever taunt me, or Chet, about our birthright would end up eating dirt.'

'The Carters always protect our own. I'd be proud if you took over the farm and continued the Carter tradition, son.'

Chapter 44

Sunday night started slowly at Guthrie's, but by the time the entertainment started, at nine, there was a decent crowd. Rita and Bobby were sitting at a table drinking beer when Grace walked in with Carl. They approached the table and Carl pulled out a chair for his girl. 'I hoped Chet might be here tonight.'

Bobby stared hard at Carl. 'Why you think that, Carl?'

Carl said, 'Heard he was back in town.'

'Who told you that?'

'He's been seen delivering hooch.'

'By who?'

Grace had her hand on Carl's thigh. She let go and leaned forward getting into Bobby's face. 'Why you getting so uppity, Bobby. Everyone knows Chet's gonna visit his brother.'

'What I wanna know, Grace, is why's Carl's suddenly so concerned about Chet?'

Grace shook her head in exasperation 'He just asked if he's gonna be here tonight, is all.' She rolled her eyes at Carl, who seemed determined to speak up for himself.

'Hell, Bobby, why wouldn't I be interested in Chet? We all hung out together, didn't we?'

Bobby wondered if he was making too much of this, as Carl was bound to be apprehensive about Chet's reappearance since he was now dating Grace. He said, 'Well, he ain't coming, Carl.'

Carl said, 'Has he left town again?'

'Maybe.'

Grace slammed her hands on the table. 'What's the big secret, Bobby?'

'None of your fucking business, Grace. Ain't about to tell you, or Carl, about Chet's whereabouts.'

Grace turned to Carl in frustration and he put his hand on top of hers to try and calm her down. 'Leave it be, Grace, Bobby thinks he's Chet's guardian angel.'

They sat in silence for a while waiting for Bobby to respond but he appeared to be done talking. The quiet was broken when Carl stood up, pushed his chair back, and snarled. 'I'm going to the bar.'

While he was gone Grace sat back in her chair trying to appear relaxed. The expression on her face softened and she lowered her voice as if was talking to a child about a sick relative. 'Is Chet okay?'

Bobby replied, 'Sure. Chet's always gonna land on his feet.'

'I really wanted to hear him play tonight.'

Bobby drank some beer. 'It ain't gonna happen, Grace.'

'Is he getting anywhere with his music?'

'Yeah.'

She waited for Bobby to elaborate, but he just took another swig of beer. 'You gonna tell us more?'

Rita said, 'Chet don't want Bobby telling his business, you need to respect that, Grace.'

'I do, Rita, I just don't see the need for all this secrecy.'

They all sat back focusing on the stage where a guy was doing a poor imitation of Elvis. His voice was out of key. Rita looked at Grace and they both laughed. Bobby said what they were all thinking. 'He sucks.'

Grace echoed Bobby's comment. 'You can say that again. He sounds like a coyote singing to its mate.'

Rita had her hands over her ears. 'You gotta admit, Chet was the best musician in Guthrie's, Grace.'

She replied, 'That ain't saying much, Rita.'

The girls laughed again, and the frown finally disappeared from Bobby's face. When Carl returned with the drinks everyone was smiling. The tension had dissipated. 'Someone told a joke?'

Grace said, 'This guy's singing is so bad it's funny.'

Carl put the beers on the table. 'He's ruining a good song.'

Grace lifted her glass. 'Let's toast the best singer in Guthrie's, Chet. Maybe he was too good for this place after all.'

They all raised their glasses and chinked them together. Bobby could see by the furrows on Carl's forehead that a question was forming in his mind. Carl said, 'Do you believe that Chet left town to improve his chances of becoming a musician, Bobby?'

'Mostly.'

'Is he in Memphis?'

Bobby slammed his glass down on the table. 'There you go again, Carl. Trying to ferret out information about Chet.'

'I'm just curious, Bobby.'

'You ain't gotta worry, Carl, Chet's got a new girl now, so he ain't interested in Grace no more.'

Carl said, 'You think I'm worried about that, Bobby?'

Bobby shrugged, then pointed at Carl. 'There's gotta be some reason for all the questions?'

Carl stood up. 'Anyone would think you've joined the CIA. I'm going for a leak.'

Bobby waited until he left the room then followed him. When he reached the door, he pushed it slightly ajar and peered into the hallway. Carl was using the pay phone, his back to Bobby making it hard to listen in on the conversation. He eased through the door and crept closer to the phone. Carl looked over his shoulder, then quickly ended the call.

Bobby said, 'Who you calling?'

'My father.'

'What about?'

Carl put his hand on his hips and pushed his chest forward. 'None of your fucking business. What is this, Bobby?'

'Someone's giving Sullivan information about Chet. It better not be you, Carl, or you're in big trouble.'

'With who?'

Bobby moved a step closer. 'With me for starters.'

The two friends squared up to each other, chest to chest. It was apparent no one wanted to make the first move.

'You wanna fight me, Bobby, go ahead and take a shot.'

Bobby realized that Chet would have already head butted the creep, or slammed a fist into his face, but Bobby wasn't like him and he didn't want to throw the first punch. If Carl struck him that would be a different matter. Even so he didn't want to back down. At least in that respect he was emulating Chet. 'You ain't worth it.'

'You mean you ain't so tough without Chet backing you up.'

'Think what you want but know this, Carl, I'm watching you closely and if you're giving information to Sullivan, god help you.'

Bobby turned and stomped back to the table. Rita and Grace raised their eyebrows in surprise at the stern look on Bobby's face. They knew that something must have happened.

Rita said, 'Everything okay, Bobby?'

'Sure, Rita.'

Carl went to the restroom before following Bobby back to the table. He'd got a worried look on his face too as sat down next to Grace.

Chapter 45

They were sitting in the parking lot of the movie theatre. Chet had enjoyed *'Rich man, poor man.'* It was his kind of movie, but he was unusually quiet. He was comparing himself with Tom, the unfortunate brother, who hadn't made it good. He had worry lines on his forehead. Rosalie said, 'What's up Chet?'

'I'm thinking about the audition, on Thursday.' Chet scratched his head. 'Not sure what songs to play?'

'Why not play one of your own?'

'Better to do something Clarence will know.'

'Play him one of your country songs.'

'What if he's more into rock and roll?'

Rosalie gently touched his hand, 'Whatever you play he'll be able to see you got talent.'

'I need to practice two or three of my best tunes, so I don't make any mistakes, or forget the words. Trouble is I'm real tired after the long hours we're doing at work, we're so busy.'

'Has Bill given you time off for the audition?'

'Yeah, but I'm gonna work Saturday morning to make up the time.'

'Don't fret, Chet, you'll blow Clarence away. You wanna go home and practice now?'

A big smile appeared on his face. 'I wanna go home with you to practice something else.'

He leant over and kissed her, breathing in the sweet smell of her hair. He cherished how good it felt to be with her again. Every time he kissed Rosalie's soft warm lips he felt a stirring in his loins. He slipped his hand underneath her top, behind her back, to unclasp her bra. He'd long ago mastered the art of unclipping a bra one handed, but tonight he was struggling. Finally released from their captivity he caressed one of her soft, warm breasts, the nipple was hard and standing to attention.

'Let's go somewhere more private, Chet?'

Chet didn't bother to reply. He quickly sat back in his seat, put on his seat belt, and started up the car while Rosalie readjusted her clothes. His anxiety was dissipating as he focused on his girlfriend. He couldn't wait to get back to his room and make love to her. He hoped that Rosalie's confidence about making an impression on Clarence, whatever songs he decided to play, was well-founded. He would practice for the audition tomorrow. Tonight, he would play a different kind of sweet music.

Chapter 46

Chet scrubbed his hands trying to remove the oil and grease. The grime was hard to shift. It was the one thing he hated about fixing cars. He liked his nails to be clean, especially when he was seeing his girlfriend. Today, he wanted clean hands for the audition. Clarence might not appreciate a guitar player with dirt under his finger nails.

Bill said, 'You knock him dead with that fancy guitar playing, Chet.'

'I'll give it my best shot, Bill.'

'Jean thinks you're gonna be the new Elvis.'

Chet grinned as he dried his hands on the towel. 'If only.'

Bill said, 'Think big, son.'

'Gotta keep my feet on the ground, Clarence ain't even heard me play yet.'

'Well me and Jean think you got what it takes.'

'Hope Clarence Henderson shares them sentiments. If not, I'll just have to be the best mechanic I can.'

'Fixing autos has served me well, but you need to see if you got what it takes to make it in the music because.'

Bill looked at his watch. 'You best get on a stick or you'll be late.'

The recording studios were at the same building Chet visited when he first arrived in Memphis. He walked up to the reception with his guitar in hand. The girl sitting at the desk was the sassy little thing that he'd flirted with before. Pretty, blue eyes and pony tails. She looked up from her paperwork and smiled. Her shiny white teeth were an ad man's dream. Chet propped his guitar against the wall, then he put his hands on the desk and leaned forward so that his face was close enough to smell the girl's peppermint breath. He had a big smirk on his face. 'I've got an appointment with Mr. Henderson. Remember me, I'm the one who ain't got a demo tape. I reckon he must be making an exception today.'

The girl smiled bashfully. 'Yeah, I recall you asking me for a date.'

'Turned me down if I remember rightly.'

The girl seemed younger, more vibrant, seemingly abandoning the formal tone she'd used when he called to schedule the meeting. She twirled one of her ponytails, indicating to Chet that she wanted to flirt.

'I had a boyfriend at the time, but I'm available now.'

'Too bad, because I got me a girl now.

She put one of her ponytails into her mouth. 'You look like the kinda guy who plays the field.'

Chet licked his lips and held her gaze. 'If things go well, I may wanna go for dinner to celebrate.'

'I'd like that,' she said.

Chet grinned. 'My girlfriend may not appreciate me bringing you along.'

The smile disappeared from the girl's face and she abruptly sat back in her chair. Chet was grinning like a cheerleader. 'If I didn't have a girlfriend you'd be top of my list, sweetheart.'

She looked down at her desk moving around some papers, seemingly trying to look professional again, before studying Chet's face. 'How long's that list?'

'Two names.'

There was electricity in the air as their eyes met and the playful grin returned to the girl's face. Chet kept his eyes on her as she stood up and made a show of smoothing down her short, tight skirt. She walked, as if she was on the runway, to one of the offices, her fanny rocking from side to side. Chet was enjoying the view. He would have liked nothing better than to follow her, turn her around and grab her tight little ass with both hands, then pull her sexy body tight against him. He envisaged planting his lips onto hers, before lifting her onto the desk, her skirt pulled back ready for action. However, he was here for business and that was a pleasure he would not be enjoying. As long as he was seeing Rosalie, he could only fantasize about the girl. She opened the door to the office, giving him a sultry look, before gesturing him to go inside. 'Take a chair. Mr. Henderson's will be with you soon.'

Chet picked up his guitar and headed for the office, his eyes still fixed on the girl, mentally undressing her. He pouted his lips as if he was going to cry. 'You gonna leave me in here all on my own?'

The girl was now the sophisticated, professional secretary again. 'Mr. Henderson will be right with you.'

She sauntered back to her desk. Chet adjusted his pants and he waited, as instructed. The walls of the office were covered with framed photographs of all the singers that recorded for the record label. He recognized Elvis, Buddy Holly, Johnny Cash, Carl Perkins and Roy Orbison. All big stars. Chet contemplated the day when there might be a signed picture of him on that wall. Clarence entered the room with his hand outstretched and Chet shook hands with the man that could fulfil his dreams. Clarence said, 'Delighted you could make it, Chet.'

'Good to see you again, Mr. Henderson.'

'Call me, Clarence. I see you've got your guitar with you. I'm a busy man so let's get right to it.'

He led the way, down a corridor, to one of the recording studios. The room was filled with instrumentation. Clarence sat behind a panel and fiddled with some controls. He said, 'Make yourself comfortable and show me what you got.'

Chet sat on a stool and quickly tuned his guitar. He had fine-tuned it before he left home, but he wanted to make sure it was still okay. He played an acoustic version of the Johnny Cash number, *'Ring of Fire,'* which had gone down so well at the Sander's house.

Clarence said, 'Pretty good tone to your voice and the guitar sounded fine. Do you know any rock and roll numbers?'

'Sure,' Chet replied. He decided to play *'That'll be the day.'* by Buddy Holly. It was a song he'd performed at Guthrie's a few times. When he finished he looked up expectantly, believing that he did a decent version of the song.

Clarence stared hard at him for a few moments, seemingly composing his thoughts. 'I've got a proposition for you, Chet. A band I manage is looking for a new lead guitarist.'

Chet scratched his head not knowing what to think. He'd always played solo, except for the ho downs in the den with Bart playing the fiddle and some other Tennessee mountain men on guitar and banjo. Those were wild times when moonshine flowed freely and the hillbilly's got more and more animated, the more they supped, stamping their feet to the lively rhythm. 'Only time I played in a band is at get-togethers at my uncle's place with a bunch of old timers.'

'These guys are young, like you. They call themselves the Revolvers and it's only a matter of time before they make it big. We've got a few gigs lined up. You can meet them if you want, they're in the other recording studio.'

'Okay.'

Clarence led him into another room where three guys dressed in white shirts and jeans, with slicked back hair, looked him over. Clarence said, 'I'd like to introduce you to Jimmy, Steve and Ryan. They've just parted company with their lead guitarist and I've suggested you as a possible replacement.'

Chet shook hands with the band members. Ryan said, 'We've been listening to you play, man. You're not bad.'

It was apparent that Ryan was the spokesman for the group. Chet looked around the room thinking that the speakers must be linked to the other room. Chet was intrigued by the band and wanted to know more. 'What kinda music do you play?'

Ryan said, 'Mostly rock and roll, Buddy Holly and Eddie Cochran, and we do a few of our own songs. We rehearse three times a week and we need a new lead guitarist, real quick, cos we don't wanna cancel any gigs. We ain't found anyone suitable yet. You wanna practice with us tomorrow night?'

'Guess so.'

Ryan frowned. 'You don't seem too excited?'

He sounded aggressive and Chet stared defiantly back at him. 'Why should I be? I ain't heard you play, yet.'

'Ain't you been listening to what Clarence said? We're gonna be the biggest thing to ever hit Memphis.'

Clarence said, 'You're getting carried away, Ryan. I think you're an up and coming band with prospects, but don't forget Chet's only just met you.'

Chet thought that the way Clarence looked at Ryan was like a father looked at his son when he was admonishing him, and Chet knew that look only too well. Ryan stood up waving his arms, as he became more and more animated. 'The Revolvers are about to explode onto the music scene whether he knows it, or not.'

'Calm down, Ryan,' said Clarence.

Ryan sat back down, tight lipped, with his arms folded tight against his chest. Chet lounged back in his chair like a student being disrespectful to a teacher. Clarence seemed a little dismayed at his couldn't care less attitude. He said, 'The Revolvers have already got a dedicated, local following, Chet, and the word's spreading fast. Tomorrow's practice is an opportunity to see if you fit in. Do you wanna give it a go?'

'Sure.'

'Show a little more enthusiasm, kid? This could be your big break,' said Clarence.

Chet sat more upright and nodded. 'Appreciate the offer, Mr. Henderson, and I'll give it my best shot. I'll liven up soon as we get playing.'

He turned away from Clarence and smiled at the band members. Jimmy and Steve grinned back, but Ryan's face looked stern. Chet had him down as one arrogant son of a bitch.

Ryan said, 'You're gonna need to learn quick because our standards are high and we're passionate about our music.'

'I'll echo that, Ryan.'

The two youths stared at each other like boxers at the weigh in.

Chapter 47

It felt good waking up with a beautiful woman lying by his side. On the flight, he thought about his conversation with Jethroe. He wasn't lying when he said that he didn't envisage a career in boxing, but he was disingenuous about not saying how much he enjoyed fighting. The long flight back to Thailand had given him plenty of thinking time. He recalled the thrill of pitting himself against his fellow man in the ring, determined to inflict pain rather than be hurt himself. It was that simple, him or me, winner take all. Glory, acclaim, and accolades to the victor, but nothing for the loser except pity, or sympathy, and these were sentiments he did not value. Army life involved team work and standing up for your compatriots. In the ring, you were on your own and the contest depended on strength, fitness, guile and determination. Aaron figured he had those attributes in spades. Farming also required some of those same qualities and Aaron felt destined to work on the farm, eventually. The more he thought about it the more he felt homesick. Thailand was too hot, and the air wasn't pure like back home. The only thing he'd missed while on leave was Choi. She stirred, smiling as she looked across at him. He kissed her tenderly. 'I could lie here all day but I gotta get back to base, Choi.'

'Okay.'

A frown formed on his face as he climbed out of bed and picked his briefs off the floor. This was always a difficult moment for him. He put on his pants and lifted out his bill fold to pay for services rendered. He didn't begrudge her the money. On the contrary, he was happy in the knowledge that he was helping her avoid a life of poverty, which was rife in this country. Nevertheless, it made the proceedings seem a little sordid. Choi was his friend and his lover, but it was her profession to sleep with men for money. Aaron really looked forward to the time they spent together. As far as he was concerned he was having a love affair with someone special who added spice to his life. He put twenty dollars on the night stand, which was the going rate. She preferred dollars to baht and her smile was the equivalent of thank you. She said, 'I happy you're back from your trip. You know you my favorite.'

Aaron said, 'I missed you, Choi.'

He gave her one last lingering kiss before walking out the door.

Chapter 48

Rosalie lay with her head on his chest. He could feel her warm breath on his skin. He was bathing in a sea of contentment, a wave of satisfaction washing over him. He was happier than he'd ever been in his life. He hoped Rosalie felt the same way about him. He thought she was asleep, so it startled him when she spoke. 'You excited about being in a band?'

'I'm a little anxious.'

He'd already told her about meeting the band and how the practices had been positive. Clarence had no hesitation about offering him the lead guitar position, although he was on trial. Ryan had taken a dislike to him and the feeling was mutual. The next gig was fast approaching, and he hoped he'd be ready. Rosalie stroked his chest. 'I'm sure it'll work out fine.'

'I'm burnt out with the over-time and now the band practices. You coming to the gig?'

Rosalie put the pillow behind her back as she sat up. 'Wouldn't miss it for the world.'

'Don't expect too much. I'll probably play a few wrong cords.'

'As if I'd notice.'

'We're playing a new song that was written especially for the Revolvers. It's got a catchy tune.'

'Are you singing?'

'Only the backing on the chorus, Ryan's the singer. He's good but he's a conceited ass hole.'

'Don't let him get to you.'

'I won't. He's the band's leader so I need to keep him on side.'

Chapter 49

Next day Chet hurried into the room. 'Sorry I'm late guys, I had to finish the brakes on a Chevy and it took longer than expected as I broke a brake pipe.'

Ryan's face looked like he'd just bitten into a lemon. 'We don't give a shit about your other job. If you wanna play in this band you gotta make rehearsal your priority.'

Chet wanted to wipe the sneer from the jerk's face, but he knew Bill Sanders would advise him to sit on his hands. 'Ain't in the habit of being late, Ryan. We're working like crazy in the shop this week. My boss was good enough to give me time off to go visit my folks, but I gotta make the time up. Hadn't figured on any band practice when I agreed to work late.'

Ryan turned his head to one side and put up his hand, dismissing him. 'We ain't interested in your excuses, let's get started.'

Chet decided not to react and concentrated on tuning his guitar. He was thinking to himself that this wasn't going to work if Ryan didn't let up on him. After a while Jimmy, the drummer, caught his attention. 'Ready, Chet?'

Chet had taken a liking to Jimmy. He was a lot more agreeable. 'Yeah.'

Jimmy said, 'We'll start with Peggy Sue. You okay with that, Chet?'

'You bet.'

Jimmy raised his drum sticks and started drumming. It was a favorite of his as it heavily, featured the drums, with its rolling back beat. Chet played rhythm while Ryan spat out the words. When it came to the small segment focusing the lead guitar, Chet really went for it. At the end of the song Jimmy looked at the others and nodded his head. 'Pretty good, but we need to get tighter. Let's go again.'

By the end of the practice Chet was drained, physically and mentally. Most of the tunes he knew, but he had to learn a new song for the gig. It was a song composed especially for the Revolvers by writers working for the studios. It was getting late when they decided to wrap it up. Jimmy was in charge of rehearsals in the absence of Clarence. 'Let's call it a day and go to the bar to unwind. Are you coming, Chet?'

Chet was putting his guitar in its bag. 'You got to be kidding, I'm dead on my feet. Gotta get up early for my day job so I need to get to bed, Jimmy.

Ryan sniggered, and Chet felt the need to comment. 'I gotta earn a living, Ryan. Who pays your bills?'

Ryan replied, 'We all got jobs.'

'Doing what?'

'Me and Steve are waiters and Jimmy's in sales. We met at Kentucky U. Where'd you go to college?'

'I went to work for my uncle, so I didn't finish high school.'

'Figures,' scoffed Ryan.

Chet zipped up his guitar bag. 'What are you getting at, Ryan?'

'Had you down as a high school dropout and I guess I was right.'

Chet put his bagged guitar down and stood up quickly. 'Figured you as an arrogant son of a bitch and I'm right on the money.'

Ryan got out of his chair and stood, fists bunched, inches away from Chet. They were so close Chet could smell the tobacco on Ryan's breath. Jimmy quickly got in between them and eased Chet away. 'Take it easy, guys.'

Steve had hold of Ryan who was pointing at Chet. 'I ain't about to take any more shit from this low life, Jimmy.'

Chet leaned around Jimmy, who was holding him back, and pointed back at Ryan. 'You better watch your mouth.'

'Yeah, or what?'

Jimmy spoke before Chet could answer. 'Just leave it, Ryan. We got a gig coming up and we're all stressed out. How about giving Chet a break? He's working hard to get in sync with the rest of us, and he already told you he's working his balls off during the day.'

Ryan said, 'He should be praying to God, thanking him for the chance we're giving him.'

Chet said, 'You want me get on my knees and kiss your feet?'

Ryan strained to get at Chet, but Steve still had him pinned. 'You'll get yours one day, Chet.'

'Any time you wanna try your luck, pretty boy,' said Chet.

Jimmy still had hold of Chet, but he was no longer struggling to get at Ryan. He'd got a huge grin on his face, as if he was enjoying the confrontation. Clarence came in and said, 'What's going on, Jimmy?'

'Ryan and Chet ain't getting along,' Jimmy replied.

'He's gotta realize it takes commitment to be in a band,' Ryan blurted out.

'Just get off my case, Ryan.'

Ryan pointed at Chet. 'How about you giving me some respect, you're the new kid on the block. We're about to hit the big time and I ain't about to let a jerk like you mess things up.'

Chet said, 'Do you think all your big talk impresses me?'

'I'm the leader of this group and you either ride my wave, or you get thrown overboard,' Ryan replied.

Clarence dropped his cigarette on the floor and stamped it out. 'You two can stop right there. I manage this band and I say what goes. Chet, you gotta remember you're still on probation. We've already lost one guitarist because of your attitude, Ryan, I suggest you cut Chet a little slack.'

Ryan said, 'If Chet shows the same dedication as the rest of us I won't have a problem.'

'I'll work as hard as anyone, just don't wind me up as I ain't the sort to let anyone push me around,' Chet replied.

Clarence said, 'It's time we put this argument to bed. You boys shake hands.'

Chet could tell that Clarence was unhappy about the tension that pervaded the room and that he had heard enough. 'That's fine by me, Clarence.'

Chet offered his hand, and Ryan went to shake it but pulled his hand away at the last second. A malicious grin appearing on his face, before he turned on his heels and walked off. Chet stood there with his hand still outstretched and shook his head in disbelief. He felt like going after the little shit and punching his baby face. Clarence put his arm around Chet's shoulder. 'I know Ryan can be a pain in the butt and I ain't asking you to suck up to him, but I want you turn a deaf ear to his intimidation.'

'That ain't gonna be easy, Clarence.'

'Try hard, son because Ryan's a key cog in this machine. Let's go to the bar and I'll get you a beer.'

'Not tonight, Clarence. I gotta be up early in the morning.'

'Okay, I'll talk to Ryan and make him understand that we're all in this together.'

On the drive home Chet resolved, for the sake of the band, to try and ignore Ryan's jibes. If the other guys held the jerk back nothing would happen, but he knew that if Ryan pushed too hard a showdown would be inevitable.

Chapter 50

'How do you find the defendant?'

The foreman of the Jury stood up in response to the judge's question. 'Not guilty.'

The prosecutor shook his head in disbelief and turned to his associate, speaking in a whisper. 'The witness has been got at again.'

The man in the suit whispered back in the prosecutor's ear. 'The old fella got scared. Before we came to court he swore he saw Sullivan threatening the victim.'

'His memory sure let him down when cross examined by the defense.'

The prosecutor's assistant nodded. 'Yeah, the jury had no alternative.'

They looked like they'd lost in a photo finish at the Kentucky Derby. In contrast, there were jubilant scenes on the defendant's bench with Sullivan's lawyer grinning like he'd just picked the winner of the same race, which in effect he had.

'One of these days we'll get enough on Sullivan for a conviction,' said the prosecutor.

Joe Sullivan's was smirking as if he'd just won the heavy weight title. All that was missing was his lawyer raising his arm aloft. In the gallery Michael Sullivan winked at his younger brother. As soon as they were outside the court room, Sullivan's mother hugged her youngest son, tightly. When she let go he touched his head and ran his finger along the length of the scar.

'Does your head still hurt, son?' she said.

'Occasional headache is all. Nothing to fret about.' Joe Sullivan replied.

It was raining so Sullivan's mother opened her umbrella. 'Don't know what you were doing in that godforsaken town, anyhow?'

'It was a stopover. I'd been on the road all day, ma.'

They walked quickly, in a hurry to get out of the rain. 'You know I used to live near there?'

Joe raised his eyebrows. 'When?'

She replied, 'Before you were born.' She crossed herself like the good catholic she was. 'Before I even met your father, god rest his soul.'

'You lived in that tin pot town?'

'I'll tell you all about it over coffee.'

She pointed to the diner which, luckily, was close to the courthouse. The diner was a railroad car, long and thin. Joe and his mom squeezed into one side of a booth and Michael sat opposite. They ordered, and the waitress brought over three cups of coffee and placed them on the table. 'Two black and one white, right.'

Joe said, 'You got it.' He slid over the coffee with cream and spooned sugar into his cup, stirring mechanically while his mother continued her story. Michael was listening intently, slowly sipping his black coffee. Suddenly he put the cup down abruptly. He sat with his mouth open in surprise and slowly shook his head from side to side, as if he couldn't believe what he was hearing. Joe slammed his fist on the table. 'Damm. If we didn't already have a score to settle, brother, we sure got one now. We gotta finish what was started long ago, Michael.'

'I ain't been able to locate the young Carter boy that hit you, but one of the locals is gonna let me know when he gets back in town.'

Joe said, 'You sure you can rely on them hicks?'

A grin appeared on Michael Sullivan's face as he rubbed his forefinger and thumb together. 'Money talks, brother.'

Chapter 51

The venue was packed to the rafters. Three bands were performing, and the Revolvers were the last band to play. The second band were still on stage. They had really got the crowd buzzing. The Revolvers were anxiously waiting in the wings. Chet paced nervously up and down. He'd never performed before so many people.

Jimmy said, 'You okay, Chet?'

'A little nervous, Jimmy. I'll be fine, soon as we get started.'

Jimmy held out a small white pill. 'Here, take one of these.'

Chet screwed up his eyes. 'What is it?'

'Just a little something to give you extra energy.'

'Not into drugs, Jimmy. The adrenalin rush is all I need to get me through the night.'

Jimmy shrugged and swallowed a pill, He washed it down with a swig of beer. Ryan held out his hand and Jimmy gave him his pick-me-up. He smiled at Chet for a few seconds before swallowing the stimulant. 'That baby's gonna keep me going all night. You ready to rock, Chet?'

'You bet.'

Ryan held up his hand for a high five. Chet expected him to pull it away like he did before, but he went for it anyway, and the two hands smacked together. Ryan looked hard into Chet's eyes. 'You sure you're okay, Chet.'

Chet nodded back and wondered if Ryan was warming to him. It was the first time he'd been the least bit agreeable since they met. Maybe he wasn't so bad after all. The crowd were shouting for an encore and the guys strained to hear the lead singer shouting above the din. 'Okay, one more.'

Jimmy put his hands on his hips, as the band started up again, and sighed impatiently. 'Looks like we gotta wait a while longer.'

Chet scanned the crowd looking for Rosalie and spotted her about six rows back. Ryan saw him peering into the audience and said, 'Is your girl out there?'

'Sure is. What about yours?' Chet replied.

'Different girl, every gig for me. Chicks are waiting in line to get picked up. Ain't no need to bring one.'

Chet didn't doubt him. Ryan looked like a rock star with his long, slicked back hair and baby faced, good looks. He oozed with the confidence of someone who expected to become a super-star. Chet was fine with Ryan being the pin up boy of the band, as long as he kept away from Rosalie. The crowd were still whistling and shouting for more as the band left the stage. Clarence told them to wait for a few minutes before going on, to build the suspense. All Chet wanted was to start playing his guitar to calm his nerves.

Clarence said, 'Okay guys. Go slay them.'

As soon as they walked on stage the audience went wild. There were obviously some Revolver fans out there. Chet felt like a phony for taking the applause for something that he'd not yet been a part. He saw Rosalie waving at him and held up his hand to acknowledge her. Ryan was gushing like a kid about to open his Christmas presents. This was, obviously, what he was born to do.

'Appreciate all you Revolver fans coming to see us tonight. You ready to rock.'

The crowd showed they were by shouting and whistling, with a few whoops thrown in for good measure. Ryan held up his hand to quiet the crowd, and spoke again. 'Let's get this show on the road. We're gonna start with an Eddie Cochran number. Ready guys. One, two, three.'

Steve strummed the base, Chet added the rhythm and Ryan blasted out the words. 'Ah well, c'mon everybody and let's get together tonight.'

It was a great song to start the show and the crowd were bopping and shaking to the beat. With barely a pause the Revolvers followed with Buddy Holly's, '*That'll be the day,*' the song that Chet had played at his audition. He wondered if it was fate that made him choose that song, demonstrating to Clarence that he'd fit right in with the Revolvers. Ryan introduced the next tune. 'We're gonna play our new song, *'See you later'*. We're hoping it's gonna be our first single.'

Judging by the applause it seemed to go down well. Chet was enjoying the gig. They had only planned on doing five songs and their next song was another Buddy Holly song, '*Heartbeat.*' When they finished, Ryan gestured to the guys and they walked off stage. As soon as they were out of sight of the crowd, they gave each other high fives. Clarence went around patting everyone on the back. The crowd were baying for more. Making the crowd wait for an encore, was a game they all played. They had another song ready to finish the set. Clarence held out his hand as if he was a traffic cop holding up a line of cars. 'Let them wait a while.'

The boys were focused on him, waiting for the go ahead. The delay seemed to last forever. Eventually, Clarence said, 'Okay, give them hell.'

They bounced back onto the stage to the roar of the crowd. The place was rocking, and Ryan held up his hand to hush the audience, so that he could be heard. 'You been a great crowd so we're gonna give you one more song. Before we do I want you to give a round of applause for our drummer, Jimmy.'

The audience shouted and clapped as Jimmy did a drum solo.

'On bass, Steve.'

Steve strummed his bass guitar and the cheering went up an octave. When he finished Ryan held up his arms. 'My name's Ryan, and we're gonna finish with another Eddie Cochran song, *Summertime Blues.*'

Ryan signaled to Chet and he started strumming the tune. The others joined in and Ryan gyrated his hips as he sang. A few minutes later they came to the end of the song. The audience were still shouting and screaming for more as they left the stage. The man hosting the show ran on the stage and said, 'Let's hear it for the Revolvers.' The audience hit the roof. In the wings Clarence gave Ryan a hug. 'Were out of here, boys. We're paid to do five songs. Leave them wanting more.'

As they walked down the passageway, Chet tapped Ryan on the shoulder. 'How come I never got introduced?'

Ryan ruffled Chet's hair 'You're still on trial.'

Chet shook his head in dismay as Ryan walked off. He wondered if Ryan had deliberately done it to aggravate him. He decided to let it go as he didn't want to cause a scene. Jimmy put his arm around him. 'You did good, Chet.'

'I hit a few bum notes.'

'You gotta expect a few mistakes on your first performance.'

Chet said, 'You think anyone noticed?'

'Not a chance.'

Chet felt relieved. Ryan came back with four beers and handed a bottle to each of the guys. Jimmy got the pills out of his pocket. Steve took one, swilling it down with a slug of beer. Ryan took two, throwing one in his mouth and offering the other to Chet. 'Here you go, Chet.'

Chet stared at the little white pill that Ryan held in his hand. 'Not for me, Ryan.'

Ryan said, 'Lighten up, you're a rock star now.'

'Don't want, or need it,' Chet replied.

Jimmy slapped him on the back and grinned. 'Don't you want this high to last?'

'I'm already as high as I wanna be.'

Ryan butted in. 'If you're gonna be a rock star you need to start acting like one.'

Ryan was back to his normal pushy self and he was starting to get Chet's back up. Chet said, 'All I wanna do is relax and sink a few beers with my girl.'

Ryan said, 'You gonna introduce us to the little lady?'

'Sure.'

Chet left the guys to go and look for Rosalie. He soon spotted her standing with another girl. Rosalie kissed him on the cheek, 'That was great.' She introduced him to her friend. 'Chet, this is Julie.'

'Hi, Julie,' said Chet.

Julie had a silly smile on her face and was blushing. She was a plain girl, with glasses and a straight up and down figure. When the guys in the band approached, Chet introduced them to the girls. Jimmy put his arm around Rosalie and looked into her eyes. 'What's it like having a boyfriend in a rock and roll band, honey?'

'Exciting,' Rosalie replied.

Jimmy patted Chet on the back. 'I reckon the new boy's got what it takes.'

Ryan turned towards Rosalie and her friend. 'Are you girls into Cochran and Buddy Holly?'

Julie beamed like a school girl on her first date. 'You better believe it.' She clearly had her eyes on Ryan, but Chet noticed that he was looking around for prettier devotees. A couple of girls were standing nearby, sniggering and whispering to each other. It was obvious they were talking about the Revolvers.

Ryan said, 'Looks like it's time to show some appreciation to our fans. Come on guys.'

He led the way, Steve and Jimmy played follow the leader. When they noticed that Chet was staying put they turned and waved. Chet could see the disappointment on Julie's face as she watched Ryan flirting with another girl. He knew that Ryan could have his pick of girls and that Julie had no chance. He'd been hoping one of the guys in the band would hang with Julie so that he could have Rosalie all to himself. It seemed like Julie didn't have the looks, or the body, to interest them. Chet thought they may as well mingle. He pointed to the guys in the band. 'Let's go on over.'

They joined the others who were soon surrounded by a swarm of star struck fans. Ryan was telling them how they started the group when they were at college. Chet tapped Steve on the shoulder and whispered in his ear. 'Hey Steve, Julie really digs the bass.'

Steve smiled awkwardly at Julie and said, 'Are you enjoying yourself, Julie?'

Chet wanted Steve to strike up a conversation with Julie and it appeared that he had got the message.

'Yeah. It was a great show,' Julie replied.

Steve said, 'What did you think of the other bands?'

'They were okay.'

'Not as good as the Revolvers, eh?'

Julie pulled at her earlobe. 'If I said they were better than the Revolvers would you be offended?'

Steve smiled. 'No, but I'd question your taste in music.'

Julie dug her elbow into Steve's ribs and gave him a cheeky smile 'The Revolvers are definitely better looking.'

Chet raised his eyebrows. Julie had got pluck. She was also exhibiting a confidence that made Chet think that she might just hit it off with Steve. He whispered to Rosalie. 'How about that. They fit together like a pair of comfortable trainers.'

Rosalie said, 'Julie's a popular girl, Chet.'

'Really?'

'Yeah, everyone likes her.'

Julie and Steve were laughing and flirting, and Chet hoped that Steve was settled for the night. Chet had been so busy concentrating on the performance that he hadn't given any thought to how the rest of the evening would pan out.

'How'd you get here?' he asked Rosalie.

'Julie gave me a ride, that's why she's not drinking alcohol.'

'I'm on water for the rest of the night,' Chet replied.

Chet was hoping Julie would take Steve home. He didn't know if Steve had a girlfriend, or even if that would make any difference.

Later he noticed Ryan and Jimmy slip away with a couple of girls. It seemed like the Revolver's success was about to continue late on into the night.

Chapter 52

Bobby was surprised to see a puppy running around the yard as he pulled into Bart's driveway. It jumped all over him as he stepped out of the car. Bart laughed like a drunken teenager as Bobby tried to push the hound away.

'Got yourself a new dog?'

'Customer of mine brought this critter around, seems his hound had a litter and he's anxious to find them all a home. Cost me a case of white lightening.'

'What are you calling him?'

'She a bitch, dumb ass. What do you think I'm gonna call her?'

Bobby scratched his head. 'Ain't got a clue.'

Bart cuffed him around the ear. 'Duchess, of course.'

Bobby crouched down and Duchess licked his face like he was a popsicle. Bobby didn't really need another wash, so he pushed her away. She bounded back, jumping up at him, thinking they were playing a game.

Bart said, 'Good thing you came around, Duchess needs a play mate. Them chickens are getting tired of being chased around the yard.'

'Okay by me, I prefer playing with Duchess to running moonshine.'

'Exercise Duchess then finish off loading the truck. That's what I pay you for. Playing you do out of the kindness of your heart.'

'You're a hard task master.'

'Only trying to utilize your talents to the full.'

Bart threw a ball to Bobby, but he didn't react quick enough and it hit him in the chest and rolled along the ground. Duchess was quick to scoop it up and run off, with her head high in the air, displaying her trophy. Bart looked at Bobby and shook his head. 'Hope you throw better than you catch.'

'You threw it before I was ready.'

'That's no excuse, I thought you played ball with Chet at high school?'

'I was an okay baseball player, but Chet was the star batter.'

Bart said, 'Spent most of my youth hunting and fishing. I'm gonna teach that puppy to track raccoon when she gets bigger. Meanwhile, you can run her ragged throwing that ball, if you ever get it back.'

Bobby said, 'I fixed Chet's station wagon. It's good to go.'

'You gonna call him to see when he can pick it up?'

'Sure.'

Bart stroked his chin. 'Spoke to him lately?'

'Last time we talked he told me he'd joined a rock and roll band.'

'I figured Chet to be more of a country singer, like Hank Williams.'

Duchess dropped the ball at Bobby's feet but as he stooped to pick it up she grabbed it again. He said, 'Kids play rock and roll these days.'

Bart bent down, took the ball from Duchess, and gave it to Bobby. 'Whatever tickles their belly. When you finish wearing out Duchess you best hit the road. My customers are getting thirsty.'

Chapter 53

Rosalie wanted to get back home early which suited Chet as he, too, had an early start in the morning. The Ford seemed a little sluggish on the drive to Rosalie's house. Chet made a mental note to check it out in his lunch break. He missed his reliable, old station wagon. Maybe it was time to invite Bobby to Memphis, so he could swap the Ford for his car. He didn't have time to go back himself. He walked Rosalie to the front door but before she had a chance to put her key in the lock, the door swung open and Rosalie's father was staring right at them.

'Pop, you spooked me.'

'Sorry honey, I didn't want Chet to go rushing off. I've been looking forward to meeting you, young man.'

Chet gave Rosalie a puzzled look. She raised her eyebrows and shrugged before taking hold of his hand and leading him inside.

Mr. Tully said, 'You guys want a drink? Something nonalcoholic for you Chet, as you're driving.'

Chet wanted to create a good impression. 'Coke would be good.'

'Rosalie would you get a coke for your boyfriend and something for yourself.'

Rosalie smiled weakly as she disappeared into the kitchen leaving Chet alone with her father. Mr. Tully showed Chet into the family room and offered him a seat. 'I hear you're in a band.'

'Yeah.'

Mr. Tully sat on a comfortable chair next to Chet. 'What sort of music do you play?'

'Rock and roll.'

'Are you hoping to make a living as a musician?'

'The band's ambitious but it's early days.'

Mr. Tully picked up a pack of Marlborough from the coffee table and pointed the pack towards his guest. Chet put up his hand, and shook his head at the same time, indicating that he didn't smoke. Tully lit a cigarette and took a drag, blowing the smoke high into the air. 'Rosalie's got her mind set on becoming a clothes designer. She's got an aptitude for it, I'm led to believe.'

Chet said, 'I don't know a thing about designing clothes, but if that's what she wants.'

'We wanted her to go to college. It came as a surprise when she went to work in a boutique.'

Rosalie came back into the room with the drinks and her father glanced up at her. 'We're just talking about you, sweetheart.'

'That's worrying.'

'I've just been telling Chet how disappointed we were that you didn't go to college.'

Rosalie frowned. 'I'm looking at courses in clothes design.'

Tully flicked ash onto an ash tray on the coffee table. 'We bought her a sewing machine for her birthday. Did you go to college, Chet?'

'No, Sir.'

'Well that's something you have in common. Of course, you don't need a college education to be a mechanic.'

'My boss is training me.' Chet replied.

'But you've set your sights on being a professional musician?'

Chet smiled. 'That'd be a dream come true.'

'What if the band doesn't make it. Are you going to be content working in the auto repair business?'

Chet took a sip of his Coke. 'Always enjoyed fixing cars but I never thought I'd earn a living doing it.'

'What did you do before?'

'Delivery work for my uncle.'

Chet put his glass on the table. Tully seemed to be waiting for him to expand on his answer, but Chet didn't want to give too much away about his uncle's business. Rosalie interjected changing the subject. 'The crowd loved the Revolvers, that's the name of Chet's band. Everyone reckons they're gonna to be big.'

Rosalie was gushing with pride, but her father didn't seem impressed. He took another drag on his cigarette and kept the same deadpan expression. 'Is it true that rock and roll bands indulge in wild parties, drug taking and drinking to excess?'

Chet was tempted to laugh. He thought that Mr. Tully was acting like a prosecuting attorney. 'I ain't into drugs, I get a big enough buzz from playing the music and hearing the fans applause.'

Tully continued the interrogation. 'If you get more successful will that mean spending more time on the road travelling to different venues?'

'Possibly, but we've only played locally, so far.'

'Won't that change if your popularity increases? That sort of nomadic lifestyle is hardly ideal for anyone wanting to settle down and raise a family.'

Chet rubbed his hand across the back of his neck. 'I ain't thinking that far ahead.'

'What are your intentions towards my daughter?'

Rosalie sat forward in the chair. 'Pop, that's not a fair question to ask Chet. We've only been seeing each other a short while.'

Chet touched Rosalie's arm. 'That's okay. I can answer that. To be frank, Mr. Tully, I've never met anyone like Rosalie and feel fortunate that she's my girlfriend. I reckon you and me want the same thing for Rosalie, to make her happy.'

Mr. Tully slowly and deliberately blew a ring of smoke into the air. 'Fine sentiments, Chet, but I'm not sure that we do want the same things. I've always hoped Rosalie would marry a doctor, or a lawyer.'

Rosalie stood up. 'I can't believe you said that, pop. You're acting so pompous.'

'I only want what's best for you, Rosalie.'

'You mean you want what's best for you?' she replied.

Tully ground the butt of his cigarette into the ash tray. 'Let's not argue, sweetheart. I'm only trying to find out more about Chet.'

Rosalie stormed out of the room leaving Chet to face the music. He seemed relaxed and if he was concerned about the grilling, that he was getting, he didn't show it. He sat back in his chair. 'I'm just a country boy trying to make it in the city, Mr. Tully.'

'Don't you miss your family?'

'My pappy and me don't get along too well. My mom died when I was young, and I moved in with my uncle. My brother's in the army. That's pretty much all the family I got. I was going nowhere fast in my home town.'

'What happened between you and your father?'

'My brother is the apple of his eye, but he's never liked me. He considers me his worst nightmare.'

'Why's that?'

'We just don't see eye to eye.'

Mr. Tully was leaning forward as if the conversation was turning more interesting. 'Are you unpopular with anyone else back home?'

'Some like me, others don't. I'm not the kind goes out of his way to be cordial to people I don't like. There's some mean son of bitches in this world that ain't worth a cent.'

'We can't always pick and choose the individuals we have to associate with.'

Chet fidgeted, and his eyes narrowed, he seemed to be losing his calm demeanor. Rosalie came back into the room. Chet thought that she too was looking anxious. He assumed that she was embarrassed about all the scrutiny he was getting. She took advantage of the pause in the conversation. 'Chet's boss really likes him. He's rented him a room in his house.'

Chet said, 'Bill Sanders and me hit it off, right from the get go.'

Tully said, 'It's useful to have influential people in your life. Your boss must see something in you.'

'He gave me a break when others didn't. I think everyone deserves to be given a chance.'

Chet watched Mr. Tully stroke his chin. Chet wondered if he sensed that the response was directed right at him. Tully stared back intently and said, 'Perhaps, Chet.'

Chapter 54

Aaron paid the bar fine, as was the custom if he wanted the pleasure of Choi's company for the night. Choi looked as beautiful as ever and she slipped her arm into his, as they walked out into the hot night air. They were on the way to her apartment and he felt good with his porcelain doll by his side. The man walking towards them looked familiar. It was the limey that started the bar fight a few months back. He was swaying slightly which suggested he'd been drinking. When he saw Aaron, he did a double take and the two men made eye contact. Aaron felt Choi's grip tighten and decided it was best to ignore the drunken bum. They walked right on by.

'Fucking Yankee bastard.'

Aaron stopped dead in his tracks, clenching his fists as he turned to look at the Brit grinning at him through gritted teeth. Aaron took a step towards the limey, but Choi tugged hard at his sleeve. 'He not worth it. Let's go.'

Aaron peered into Choi's imploring eyes and he knew she was right. Why waste time on the jerk. They had better things to do. He smiled sarcastically and turned away. Choi linked his arm again as they proceeded on their way. Aaron's eyes opened wide in astonishment when he felt the stab in his back. He let go of Choi, turned around and the Brit stuck the blade in his chest, this time. Choi screamed, and Aaron swung his right fist knocking the man backwards. He followed up with three more punches which caused the limey to crumple to the ground. The pain in Aaron's chest was excruciating and he started to feel faint. He dropped to his knees. Choi was screaming and shouting for help and a crowd began to gather around. Aaron held his chest. Blood was seeping out from his wounds and a siren was heard in the distance.

Choi didn't know how to stop the bleeding. She was crying like a baby as she waited for help to arrive. She couldn't believe what had just happened. Aaron was her possibility for a better life. She liked his quiet, confident manner and gentle disposition. Aaron made her feel warm inside and she was happy in the knowledge that she always fulfilled his desires. Whenever he arrived at the bar she felt her heart flutter. They always said that they would be back, but there was no guarantee. That was how it was. That was the reality of the job. All she could do was enjoy the good times and dream about the future. Her family were poor, and her choices were limited. She knew that she was attractive, and men would always pay for her services. The owner of the bar had already shown an interest in her. Fortunately, he had not made any advances, so far. She hoped he wouldn't as he was old and fat and if he came on to her she would have to find somewhere else to work. Every two months she took money back to her family in the village. Every time she slept with a customer she thought that there must be a better life. She thought that Aaron may be the one to take her away, and now he was dying in her arms.

Chapter 55

The place was full, and it was hot and sticky. Clarence described the venue as intimate and atmospheric. Sweat dripped off Ryan's forehead as he blasted out the song and took off his shirt showing his skinny body. The girls screamed all the same.

Before they had gone on stage Jimmy had passed the drugs around. Chet declined but Ryan took two swallowing one and putting the other into his pocket, before slipping it into Chet's beer when he wasn't looking. Chet was really enjoying being in the band and was now feeling more confident. Out front, the drink was flowing like a speakeasy. Bar tenders working flat out serving whisky, beer and cocktails to a crowd who were drinking it as fast as they could pour it. It was as if the bar was about to run dry, or they were trying to drink their fill before the cops raided the joint. But prohibition was long gone, and alcohol was now legal, except for kids under twenty-one. If the truth be known, most of the audience were teenagers with false ID, but as long as their pockets were full of dollars the owners of this small club in downtown Memphis didn't care. The Revolvers were nearing the end of the session. They were playing a longer set than at the last gig and they'd practiced hard all week. Ryan paused waiting for the applause, echoing around the room, to subside.

'This is gonna be our last song. It's also gonna be our first record. It's called, S*ee you later.'*

Clarence had told the guys that he would monitor the crowd's reaction to the song and he gave a thumbs-up sign, as they walked off to cheers, whistles and cries of *more*. After a while Ryan led them back on stage. 'You guys have been great. You ready for another?'

'You bet' and 'hell yes' came right back at him.

Ryan shouted. 'We love you Memphis and we're gonna finish with a Chuck Berry number.'

Chet strummed the tune and Ryan came in with the vocals. 'Maybelline, why can't you be true.'

Jimmy provided the beat on the drums and the crowd clapped along. At the end of the song Jimmy lifted his drum sticks high in the air indicating to the rest of the band to finish together. Applause erupted around the room. Ryan bowed and waited several seconds before he held up his hand to hush the multitude. 'You've been a fantastic audience. We hope to see you later, remember that's the name of our single that'll be hitting the record shops any day now.'

The crowd were still baying for more. Chet could barely hear Ryan speak above the noise. Ryan said, 'Okay, we'll do one more. You've been 'something else,' and so we're gonna finish with '*something else*.'

Chet thought how cheesy Ryan sounded but the crowd didn't seem to mind. The band belted out Eddie Cochran's *'something else,'* then skipped off stage with applause ringing in their ears. Chet was relieved that, early in the set, Ryan had introduced him to the audience along with the rest of the band. Clarence hugged the members of the band, one by one. 'You killed them, guys. That was awesome.'

They were covered in sweat and as high as skyscrapers. Ryan said, 'Reckon it's time to go celebrate with a few beers.'

At the bar Jimmy was buying and it wasn't long before a group of girls came over. Chet looked them up and down, but he didn't show any interest. He was disappointed that Rosalie couldn't make it and took a long swig of his beer, while he watched Ryan go to work.

'Hope you girls are gonna buy our new record?' said Ryan.

The redhead stood with her hands on her hips as if to challenge him. 'I'd need to hear it a few more times.'

She was tall and slim with lips as red as her hair. Ryan, as always, was quick with his retort. 'Maybe I can arrange a private session.'

The red head said, 'Just for us girls?'

'No, for you and me, honey.'

The redhead punched Ryan on the shoulder, playfully. 'Just because you're a rock and roll singer don't mean you get a piece of me that easy.'

Ryan frowned. 'Guess I'll look elsewhere if you're gonna play hard to get, honey.'

'Some girls think you're the new Elvis, but I ain't buying.'

Ryan glared at her and she stared right back at him, neither one blinked until Jimmy broke the spell by handing Ryan another beer.

'Get out the candy, Jimmy,' said Ryan.

Jimmy gave the guys what looked like cubes of sugar. Chet shook his head, but the others accepted. Jimmy turned to the girls. 'What about you, Red, you want a sweetener?'

'Don't mind if I do,' she replied.

No one else refused and Jimmy gave Chet an opportunity to change his mind. 'You sure you don't want one, Chet?'

He shook his head again, but the redhead put her arm around his neck and with her other hand she tried to put the cube in Chet's mouth.

'Come on, Chet, don't be such a party pooper.'

Chet kept his mouth closed.

'Open those sweet lips for Ruby?'

She moved her lips towards his and he opened his mouth to kiss her. Ruby slipped the LSD onto his tongue. He hesitated a second then swallowed it, washing it down with a swig of beer, and said, 'What the heck.'

Ruby said, 'You're such a good boy, you deserve a kiss.' She pulled Chet's head towards her and they kissed. Chet felt a little dizzy. He didn't realize that drugs would affect him so quickly. Ruby kissed him again, this time placing her tongue inside his mouth. Chet glanced over at the guys. Steve and Jimmy grinned and wagged a finger at him, letting him know he was being a naughty boy. Ryan glowered at all the attention Chet was receiving. Ruby put both arms around Chet as if she was claiming him for the night. He thought about Rosalie and felt a pang of guilt. Ruby broke her hold to take a sip of her drink. 'Where'd you learn to play guitar like that, Chet?'

'Self-taught, sugar.'

'You're new, ain't you? I've seen the band before and I'd have recognized you for sure.'

Chet stroked her hair, 'Probably won't forget you either. Don't often see hair that red.'

Ruby said, 'You like it?'

Chet smiled, cheekily. 'I prefer girls with black hair and brown eyes.'

Ruby pouted her lips like a baby that had just lost its pacifier. She moved closer staring deep into Chet's eyes. 'You gonna buy me a drink?'

'Sure, what do you want?'

'I'll have a martini.'

While Chet was at the bar Ryan came over and stood next to Ruby. 'Chet's got a steady girlfriend.'

Ruby shrugged. 'So.'

'He ain't interested in you.'

'He's playing hard to get, is all.'

Ryan shook his head. 'Don't say I didn't warn you. Good looking girl like you don't need to be wasting time on someone who don't wanna know.'

Ruby said, 'I like a challenge.'

She looked unperturbed as Ryan put his arm around another girl. It was getting late and some of the audience had gone home. The band members found an alcove, with comfortable chairs set around a low table, which had been vacated. Chet took a while getting served and when he came back with the drinks he couldn't see the guys. Jimmy spotted him and called him over. The guys each had a girl sitting by them. Ruby tapped the space next to her, indicating that she'd saved it for Chet. He gave her the martini and sat down.

Ruby said, 'Your lead singer thinks I'm wasting my time with you.'

'He's right. I already got a girl.'

She put her hand on his knee. 'I think he wanted you out of the way, so he can move in.'

Chet looked over at Ryan who seemed to be getting along fine with the girl next to him. 'Maybe.'

Ruby said, 'You don't have a girlfriend here, tonight. Not right now.'

'Guess not,' Chet replied.

She smiled like a cat that was about to get the cream and sipped her cocktail. She moved even closer to Chet and rested her head on his chest. He could smell the sweet perfume of her hair. She gave him a sultry look and he responded by putting his arm around her. He still felt a little light headed as he took a swig of his beer. She snuggled against him and he could feel his heart pounding. He pulled away. 'This ain't gonna work, honey.'

She fluttered her eyelashes at him. 'I think I may be able to persuade you otherwise.' She put her hand on his chest and lifted her leg over Chet's leg to get even closer.

'You ain't got nothing to tempt me, honey.'

Chet knew that was a bare faced lie. Desire was rushing through his veins like a tidal wave. He looked deep into her half-closed eyes. Then he tried to turn away as Rosalie flashed into his mind, but Ruby held his chin and turned his face towards her. He could feel her warm breath. She slid her hand slowly up his leg until she could feel his firm pecker beneath his pants. 'I beg to differ.'

There was no point denying that he wanted her, and they kissed long and hard. Her soft wet lips tasted good. Chet kissed her neck. Rosalie had disappeared from his thoughts as he put his mouth next to her ear and whispered.

'You win.'

Chapter 56

Thelma was washing the dishes when the doorbell rang. 'My hands are wet, can you get that Jethroe?'

Jethroe took off his reading glasses, put down his book and went to the door. He looked the man up and down. He was wearing an army officer's uniform.

'Are you Jethroe Carter?'

'Yep.'

'Can I come in?'

'Is it about Aaron?'

'Yes, sir.'

Jethroe moved inside and the man took off his hat and followed him into the family room. With a wave of his hand, Jethroe indicated a chair and the officer sat down. Thelma came in wiping her hands on her apron.

'It's best you both sit down,' said the soldier.

Thelma sat next to Jethroe on the couch and he took hold of her hand. She looked anxiously at Jethroe's impassive face, then turned her attention to the officer when he spoke.

'I'm afraid I've got some bad news.'

Jethroe squeezed Thelma's hand as his body stiffened. 'You best spit it out.'

'I'm sorry to tell you your son, Aaron has been killed.'

As Jethroe heard the words he punched the side of the couch and tears formed in his eyes. Thelma put her arm around him and he placed his head against her bosom.

Shortly after the officer departed Thelma went back into the kitchen to make some strong coffee. Jethroe sat, lifelessly, with his head slumped against his chest. When she came back in with the drinks the silence that filled the room was deafening. She clung on to him tightly as he started shaking, and for the first time ever she saw him burst into tears.

Chapter 57

Chet woke up with a sore head. The effect of too much beer was familiar but the surroundings were not. It dawned on him that the girl lying next to him wasn't Rosalie. He ran his hand through his hair as he tried to piece together the events of the previous night. As the implications of his infidelity became clear he felt like shit. Ruby was fast asleep, and he quietly eased out of the bed to rescue his clothes that were strewn all over the floor. As he was getting dressed he looked at Ruby's red hair sprawled all over the pillow. She still looked attractive, but he no longer felt aroused by her. He wished he could snap his fingers, make Ruby disappear, and wake up from this bad dream. She rolled over in her sleep onto his side of the bed and he remembered caressing her shapely body. He continued getting dressed thinking that no one needed to know. If the guys in the band kept quiet Rosalie wouldn't find out. He was putting on his shoes when Ruby opened her eyes. 'Are you leaving already, Chet?'

'Yeah.'

She sat up. 'Want me to make breakfast?'

'Thanks, but no.'

'How about some coffee?'

Chet finished trying his laces and moved closer to the bed to kiss her goodbye. 'I gotta go, Ruby.'

'Are you okay?'

Chet rubbed his face. 'This shouldn't have happened.'

Ruby sniggered like a school girl. 'I won't tell if you don't.'

Chet didn't find it funny. He was not in the mood for silliness. His head ached, his throat was dry, and he felt like a rat. Nevertheless, he was pleased that Ruby wasn't about to go running at the mouth. He said, 'I sure would appreciate that, Ruby.'

'A night of passion best forgotten.'

'Something like that.'

Ruby touched his hand. 'We had fun, though, didn't we?'

It was a great night, what he could remember of it, but paradoxically it was one he wanted to forget. A tiny smile struggled to break out on his worried face. By contrast Ruby's grin was as wide as the Grand Canyon. Chet remembered Ruby ignoring his assertions that he'd already got a girlfriend. She was the kind of girl that didn't take no for an answer. Last night she was determined to sleep with one of the Revolvers, and he had been easily persuaded. That was the truth but there was no point trying to put the blame on her. His overriding feeling was guilt. 'I reckon I'm gonna need a cab?'

'Why don't I drop you off?'

Chet shook his head. 'Not a good idea.' He didn't want anyone to see him with Ruby.

She said, 'Soon as I get dressed I'll call a cab. You look as though you could use some coffee.'

'Okay.'

Suddenly, coffee seemed like a good idea. Chet had no idea how he'd got to Ruby's place, or how to get home. Ruby slipped out of bed and put on a robe. He couldn't help staring at her shapely breasts and remembered his mouth covering those large, protruding nipples. She went into the bathroom brushing against him as she walked passed. He felt himself getting hard again. For a split second, he thought about getting back into bed with her and continuing where they'd left off last night, but this time he resisted the temptation.

The studio apartment was small, but it had everything a single girl needed. A bedroom that doubled as a lounge with a kitchen separated from the rest of the room by long worktop. They sat on stools, adjacent to the counter top, drinking coffee while they waited for the cab. Even without make up, and with her hair all over the place, Ruby was still extremely desirable. Chet stared into his cup to avoid ogling her.

'How are you feeling now, Chet?'

'Rough.'

‘The coffee helping any?’

‘A little.’

‘I enjoyed last night.’

‘Yeah. The gig was a blast.’

Ruby’s smiled widened. ‘I enjoyed the après gig too.’

Chet looked up at her succulent lips and sparkling eyes. ‘I did too, Ruby.’

She smiled and tousled her russet hair the way models did when posing for the camera. She oozed sex appeal. He was tempted to take her by the hand and lead her back into the bedroom.

‘I’ll give you my number in case you want a repeat performance,’ she said.

Chet didn’t answer. He screwed his eyes tight, trying to think of something other than Ruby’s naked body. He needed to get out of there fast. She looked at him, waiting for an answer, and he gave a slight nod of his head.

She said, ‘I’ll take that as a yes,’ and picked up a pen and note pad from the counter top. She wrote down her number, tore off the page and handed it to Chet. He quickly put it in his pocket without even looking at it. When the cab arrived, he pulled her to him and kissed her slowly. ‘So long, Ruby.’

‘Until we meet again, Chet.’

Chapter 58

Bobby was in the barn sweeping, but he stopped and leant on the brush when Bart walked in with a crate of empty mason jars, Duchess followed close at heel.

'I'm done unless you got anything else needs doing?' said Bobby.

Bart spat into the saw dust. 'Looks like all that sweeping has done wore you out. Sure, you don't wanna lie down?'

Bobby kept quiet rather than rise to the bait on this occasion.

Bart said, 'Go fetch some more jars from the kitchen drainer. I'm gonna fill these jars with moonshine from the barrel.'

Bobby returned with the mason jars. 'When are you gonna give up this illegal racket and move in with Jethroe?'

'And let down all my loyal customers?'

'They'd find some other poison to rot their guts.'

Bart pointed at him. 'Watch your mouth, boy. Folk in these parts have acquired a taste for my moonshine.'

'Yeah, I seen them good old boys with their rotted teeth, stinking breath and dirty hair.'

'And them's the good-looking ones.'

Bart nearly choked as he laughed at his own joke, spitting out whatever caused his congestion into the dirt. Bobby smiled as he thought how aptly the old man fitted the description he'd just outlined. 'Guess it's a coin toss whether moonshine, or chewing tobacco, kills them first.'

'Careful who you're maligning, son. Most hillbillies I know can shoot a jay bird at fifty paces.'

Bobby took a step back. 'Not if they're down wind. The bird would fly off before they could take aim.' He anticipated

Bart taking a swipe at him, but he had made sure he was out of reach.

'I've a mind to fill your fat ass with buck shot. Mountain men may be simple folk but anyone with a half a brain knows not to mess with them.'

Bobby could see that Bart was getting a little tetchy. The banter started off light hearted as usual, but Bart now seemed to be in fighting mood. He thought of all the times he'd seen Bart shoot down vermin. He rarely missed. Bobby wondered if the old man was up to shooting anything, nowadays. He was getting a hunched back from all the bending and lifting. His face showed the strain every time he straightened up. 'Just kidding, Bart.'

'You'd betta be, son, or I'll stick my gumboot up your sorry ass.'

Duchess squatted and took a pee in the corner of the barn. Bart shouted at her and she ran off. He scratched his unshaved chin.

Bobby said, 'You're a stubborn old timer. You could be sitting in a rocker on Jethroe's porch.'

Bart stepped closer to Bobby. 'Don't think you understand the importance of quenching the thirst of the inhabitants living in these parts.'

He slapped Bobby hard across the back of his head, cackling like an old woman. Bobby should have seen that coming. Nevertheless, he was pleased to see that the good old boy seemed fighting fit again. He snatched the dirty baseball cap off Bart's head and ran out the barn.

'Give me my hat, jackass.'

Bart chased him into a small field behind the barn where he'd ducked down to hide. Duchess followed, jumping up and down trying to see over the rows of corn that came up to Bobby's waist. When she located him she stood barking, her tail wagging wildly showing she was enjoying the game. Bart went towards where Duchess was barking and saw Bobby crouching down. He shook his fist. 'I'm gonna kick your ass when I get hold of you.'

Bobby stood up, poked out his tongue and threw the cap at Bart. It landed several yards away from the old man, and as he bent down to retrieve it Duchess grabbed it at the same time. They played the tugging game that all dogs seem to love.

'Quit, Duchess.'

Duchess let go and Bart put his cap back on his head, tweaking it until it fitted snugly. Duchess kept barking at Bart, wanting the old man to continue the game, but Bart didn't oblige. Bobby stood a while, admiring the corn. The beards were turning brown which meant they were nearly ready for harvesting. There was enough corn to supply the inhabitants of the county with hooch for at least another year. It was obvious that Bart planned to continue in the distillery game. It would be a while before he let Jack Daniels have the monopoly over the good people of Tennessee.

Bart went back to the barn and Duchess chased after him. He continued filling the jars from the barrel. Bobby walked to the house to rinse all the empty jars. Duchess was sniffing around the yard. Her ears pricked up, and she howled, when she heard a vehicle's wheels crunching in the dirt. Bobby wandered out and was surprised to see Jethroe pulling into the driveway. Duchess ran up yapping, as Jethroe climbed out of his truck. He ignored the hound and walked towards Bobby. 'Where's Bart?'

'In the barn.'

'Need to talk to him, you too.'

Bart had evidently heard voices and he poked his head out of the barn. When he saw Jethroe he stepped into the sunlight. 'You come to buy some moonshine, brother.'

'Got some bad news. Let's go into the house.'

Bart led the way. Bobby could see from the frown on Jethroe's face that something was wrong. Bart headed for the kitchen and said, 'Want some coffee, Jethroe?'

'Black, no sugar.'

'What about you, Bobby.'

'White with sugar. I got a sweet tooth.'

Bobby grinned but no one else was smiling. Bart said, 'Go sit in the den while I make it.'

In a few minutes Bart brought in the coffee on a metal tray, placed it on the coffee table, and sat back.

Bobby said, 'Got any cookies?'

'Yeah, but you ain't getting any,' Bart replied.

'Why not?'

Bart said, 'Just stay quiet. I wanna hear what Jethroe's got to say.'

Bobby was starting to pick up on the despondency emitting from Bart. Jethroe took a sip of his coffee and placed the cup back on the table, He looked ashen. 'Ain't any easy way to say this, Bart.'

'Just spit it out, brother.'

'Aaron's been killed.'

Bart sat up and raised his eyebrows. 'Holy shit. How?'

'Murdered by some drunken bum.'

Bart said, 'You sure it ain't mistaken identity.'

'There's no mistake.'

Bobby rubbed his hand across his forehead. 'Don't know what to say, Mr. Carter.'

Jethroe put a hand on Bobby's shoulder. 'I want you to call Chet, Bobby. It won't be the best way for him to find out his brother's dead, but it's right he knows as soon as possible.'

'Chet's gonna fall apart. He worships Aaron.' Bobby replied.

Jethroe said, 'We're all devastated.' He swallowed hard and Bart put his arm around his brother to console him. Tears formed in Bobby's eyes and his head drooped. Bart took a sip of his coffee.

'We need something stronger.' He went to a cabinet and took out a bottle of moonshine and some glasses, the ones he only ever used on special occasions. They weren't anything special, in fact he'd stolen them from Guthrie's, but they were better than the mason jars from which he usually supped.

Chapter 59

The band was rehearsing at the studio when Clarence walked in. They finished the song and Jimmy put down his drumsticks to hear the latest news. Clarence said, 'S*ee you later'* should be in the record shops any day now.'

Ryan clenched his fists and raised his arms aloft in celebration. 'When we gonna be hearing it on the radio, Clarence?'

Clarence said, 'I've been talking to some radio show producers, we should be getting some air play soon. I hope the American public are gonna like it enough to buy it.'

'I guess the fans that come to our shows will buy it,' said Jimmy

The Revolvers next gig was sold out and the guys were looking forward to performing again. Ryan gave Chet a sly look. 'Is your girlfriend gonna be coming this time, Chet?'

'She only missed before because she'd got a prior engagement.'

Jimmy had a smile like an alligator on his face as he glanced at the others. 'Which girl are you bringing?'

'Only got one girlfriend, Jimmy. You know I'm crazy about Rosalie.'

Ryan said, 'What about the redhead?'

'What about her?' Chet replied.

Ryan looked at the others and sniggered. 'You and her were getting hot and steamy at the last gig.'

'I was high as a kite, that LSD you guys pushed on me messed with my brain.'

'No one forced you, you just succumbed to the red head's charms,' Ryan insisted.

Chet said, ‘It was a big mistake.’ He glanced over to see if Clarence was listening to the banter, but his face wasn’t showing any emotion.

Ryan seemed to want to pursue the point. ‘I take it you spent the night with her?’

Chet looked around nervously. ‘I’d appreciate it if you guys don’t mention Ruby when Rosalie’s around.’

Ryan said, ‘You okay if I hit on the red head if she’s at the gig?’

‘Go ahead, Ryan, far as I’m concerned Ruby’s nothing more than a fan.’

Chet was hoping that Ruby wouldn’t be at the show. If she turned up and saw him with Rosalie he expected her to have enough class to keep away. He looked at Clarence again, to see if he was showing any reaction. He was mindful that Clarence was a friend of Rosalie’s family. Ryan must have noticed Chet glancing at Clarence. ‘What do reckon about our new guitarist cheating on his girlfriend, Clarence?’

Clarence had his hands in his pockets and a stern expression on his face. ‘I’m not impressed.’

Chet said, ‘My head was spinning from drink and drugs when this girl came on to me, Clarence.’

‘I thought you weren’t into drugs?’

‘Ruby promised him a kiss if he swallowed the candy.’ Ryan’s remark was greeted with sniggers by the other band members.

Chet snarled at his adversary. ‘Shut the fuck up, Ryan.’

He took a step towards him, but Clarence stood in his way. ‘I thought you had a mind of your own, Chet.’

‘I got caught up in the moment. Are you gonna tell Rosalie?’

Clarence took Chet into the corner of the room, out of earshot of the others. He said, ‘It’s not my style to tittle-tattle, Chet. I’ve already spoken to George Tully and told him that I’ve been impressed with your hard work and honesty. I didn’t think you could be coerced into doing something that you didn’t want to do. I don’t see you as someone who bends with the wind. I guess your resolve don't extend to turning down a pretty girl.'

Chet said, 'It won't happen again, Clarence?'

'If it's a one off, I'll forget it. On the other hand, if you make a habit of sleeping with groupies, I may have a word in Mr. Tully's ear.'

Chet took a deep breath. He felt relieved that Clarence wouldn't spill the beans. He was not so sure about Ryan. He hoped Ryan would focus on making a play for Ruby, but he was worried about him. He needed to take Ryan aside and give him a little friendly advice.

After the band practice, the guys usually went to the bar up the road. Clarence said, 'I'm not coming to the bar, tonight I've got paperwork to finish at home.'

Ryan was the first to leave as he didn't have any instruments to pack away. Chet put his guitar in his auto and ran up the street after him. He slowed to walking pace as he got closer, but Ryan heard his footsteps and turned around. Chet grabbed him and pushed him into an allcyway, slamming him against the wall. Ryan said, 'What the fuck?'

'If you wanna keep those baby face good looks, you betta keep quiet about Ruby.'

Ryan struggled to break free. 'Get your fucking hands off me.'

Chet had him pinned so Ryan brought his knee up into Chet's groin. Chet winced with the pain, but he didn't let go. He pushed Ryan back harder, cracking his head against the brickwork. Then he punched Ryan hard in the stomach and slapped him around the face, before grabbing hold of his collar with his left hand and drawing his right fist back. 'I've been waiting for an opportunity to slam my fist into your face ever since we met.'

Ryan stuttered. 'I ain't scared of you.'

Chet punched him in the stomach again then let him loose, holding his clenched fists high in a boxer's stance. 'Let's get it on, Ryan.'

Ryan shook his head. 'I ain't gonna fight.' He held his stomach and then stroked the side of his stinging face,

Chet didn't expect him to respond to the invitation. He knew that he'd scared Ryan, which was what he planned. 'Wise decision, be a shame to ruin your looks before the next gig.'

He heard footsteps and the other band members peered into the dark alleyway. He brushed off his jacket and stepped away from Ryan who followed him out of the alleyway. Jimmy narrowed his eyes as he looked at Ryan. Under the light of a street lamp he noticed red streaks on his cheeks. Jimmy said, 'What's going on?'

'Fucking jackass jumped me.'

Jimmy said, 'Are you fucking crazy, Chet? Last thing we need is you slapping Ryan around.'

Chet had been careful not to cause any disfigurement to the leader of the band. 'Ryan ain't got no worries as long as he keeps his big mouth shut, Jimmy.'

'We were only messing with you earlier, Chet. You gotta calm down,' Jimmy replied.

Chet gritted his teeth and pointed at Ryan. 'That son of a bitch has been riling me since the day I joined this band.'

Jimmy got into Chet's face and pushed him backwards. 'I told you to take t easy, Chet.'

Chet didn't want any trouble with Jimmy, but he wanted to make sure that Ryan had received the message loud and clear. 'I will, but you better make sure Ryan don't cross me, or you'll be rolling him on stage in a wheelchair.'

He strode back to his car leaving Jimmy scratching his head. Steve rolled his eyes skywards and poked a finger at Ryan. 'You got stripes on your face, Ryan?'

'That crazy bastard slapped me around.'

Steve said. 'I don't think he's bluffing, Ryan. You betta watch your mouth.'

Ryan shrugged his shoulders. 'He don't scare me none.'

Jimmy said, 'Your face tells a different story, Ryan.'

Chapter 60

The phone was ringing in the workshop. Chet had a wrench in his hand as he stepped from under the Buick, that was hoisted in the air. Bill was already walking towards the office to get the call.

'Sanders auto repair, Bill speaking.'

'Is Chet there? I'm his friend, Bobby.'

'Chet's busy at the moment, Bobby. I'll get him to call you back in his lunch break.'

'Tell him it's urgent, Mr. Sanders.'

Bill left the office, as he walked past Chet he shouted. 'Call your buddy, Bobby at lunch time. He said it was urgent.'

'Okay.'

Chet spent the rest of the morning worrying, as he knew Bobby would only call in an emergency. Was Bart in trouble again? As soon as the clock showed 12 noon he made his way to the office to call his best friend. 'What's going on, Bobby?'

'Picked up your station wagon from the repair shop.'

'Is it fixed?'

'Yeah.'

'Leave it at Bart's place. Is that why you called?' Chet was starting to get exasperated, thinking that he had been worrying for nothing.

'No, I got some bad news.'

'What?'

'There's no easy way to tell it.'

Chet drummed his fingers on a table. 'I ain't got all day, Bobby.'

'Aaron's been killed.'

Chet was stunned to silence. He felt like he'd just run head first into a tree.

Bobby continued, 'Jethroe visited when I was helping Bart load the Dodge. An officer from the army came around Jethroe's place with the news.'

'What happened?'

'Aaron was murdered by a drunk with a knife.'

Chet wanted to hit something. He held the phone down by his side and looked up to the heavens, feeling the tears forming in his eyes. In his mind's eye he saw himself sitting by the riverbank fishing with Aaron, who was smiling at him, rustling his hair. Then another flash back to when they found his mom dead in the barn. Jethroe sobbing like a baby. He could hear Bobby's voice in the ear piece and he put the phone back against his head.

'You okay, Chet?'

'I ain't able to take this in, I'll call you back.'

Chet put the phone down and stood frozen to the spot, staring down at his feet. Suddenly he shouted at the top of his voice. 'Fuck.'

Bill heard the profanity and hurried to the office to investigate. He opened the door and saw Chet with fists clenched hard by his side and tears in his eyes. 'Bad news?'

'My brother's been killed.'

'Holy cow. You betta sit.' Bill eased Chet into a chair, 'I'll get some coffee.'

Chet sat, zombie-like, slumped in the seat. A few minutes later Bill came in with two mugs of coffee and sat next to him on the cheap metal chairs.

'I'm gonna have to call Jethroe to confirm this, Bill.'

'Go ahead.'

Bill watched him dialing the number. The phone seemed to ring forever before Jethroe answered. 'Hello?'

'Pa, it's Chet. Bobby just told me Aaron's dead.'

'We're all devastated, Chet.'

'It must be some sort of mistake, pa.'

'Wish it was, son.'

The silence only lasted a few seconds, but it seemed longer, before it was broken by Jethroe. 'I'd like you to come back for the funeral.'

'Let me know when?'

'You better give me your number.'

Chet gave Jethroe the number of the auto shop. He could empathize with how Jethroe must be feeling and for once in his life he wanted to be with him. He slowly and deliberately put the phone back into its cradle. 'Jethroe's gonna organize a funeral service.'

Bill put his hand on Chet's shoulder. 'You need to be with family at a time like this. Go home whenever you're ready. Best you just sit here a while longer.'

Bill left him and went back into the shop. Chet closed his eyes and put his middle finger and thumb over both lids to further block out the light. He sat with his head lowered and all of a sudden nothing seemed to matter, not the job, nor the band. He just wanted his brother. He remembered back to when he started high school. He had been running in the school yard, not looking where he was going, when he ran into an older boy. He had been about to apologize, but the jerk pushed him away aggressively and walked off laughing. Chet called him an asshole and the boy came back and said, 'What did you call me?' Chet replied, 'You heard.' The older boy grabbed his shirt and was about to hit him, but he hesitated, studying Chet's face. 'Are you Aaron Carter's little brother?' Chet said, 'You better believe it.' He patted Chet on the head and told him to go away. Chet pushed his hand away, then flew at him swinging his fists like whirlwinds. The older, bigger, boy knocked him to the ground, then sat on top of him, hitting him in the face until another boy pulled him off. At home that evening Aaron noticed Chet's bruised and bloody face and asked what happened. Chet told him that he'd had a fight with an older boy at school. Aaron said, 'That temper of yours is gonna keep getting you into trouble, little brother.' Chet knew that Aaron was right but took pride in the fact that he didn't back down. From that day on he knew he would always stick up for himself. Two days after the fight Chet saw the boy walking in the school yard. As he got close he noticed that the boy had got two black eyes and knew right away where he'd gotten them. He had no longer needed the backing of his big brother, but it was there all the same.

Now, Chet contemplated on how much he was going to miss his brother. He thought about finishing off the muffler on the Buick to try and take his mind off the tragedy, but he wasn't in the right frame of mind to complete the job. His thoughts turned to Rosalie. He wanted to be with her.

Chapter 61

The sparkle had gone from Chet's eyes and the smile was missing from his face, as they sat on the bed in Rosalie's room. When he told her about Aaron she wrapped her arms around him.

'I'm so sorry, Chet.'

Chet said nothing and lowered his head.

Rosalie said, 'What you gonna do?'

'I plan on driving back at the weekend.'

Rosalie touched his hand. 'Do you want me to come with you?'

'It ain't gonna be very exciting.'

'I feel I ought to be there to give you some support, Chet.'

'I'm gonna be staying at my Uncle Bart's house.' Chet managed a smile. 'It ain't the Hilton.'

'Does he live on his own?'

'Yeah, he ain't had a woman since I've known him. The first time I met Uncle Bart was when he visited Jethroe's place. He had brought his hound dog, Duke. I didn't know at the time, but Bart had needed money to pay off a debt and Jethroe was his last resort. Bart introduced himself and went off to find Jethroe, who was out working in the fields. He left Duke with me. I found an old piece of rope, that was lying around, and we played tug. Eventually Uncle Bart returned to the yard, collected Duke, and told me I could visit him any time and play with the dog. From that day on, I often cycled over to my uncle's place. I'd take Duke hunting raccoon and the hound would howl when he located a coon up a tree. Other times we'd play hide come seek in the woods. That's why I sought sanctuary in my uncle's house when I left home. I didn't care that my daddy and Bart weren't on speaking terms.'

Rosalie said, 'Your uncle seems an interesting character.'

Chet forced a small smile. 'My uncle's a likeable old rogue and he likes meeting new people. One time when Jethroe was scolding me he remarked that Bart and me were like two peas from the same pod. He didn't mean it as a compliment, but I took it as one, all the same. I consider that my relationship with Uncle Bart is like the way it should have been between Jethroe and me.'

'What's your uncle do?'

Chet said, 'He works for himself.'

He had omitted to mention that his uncle made and sold illegal liquor. The more he thought about the trip the more he realized that his family might be a culture shock to Rosalie. They both lay back on the bed in silence. Eventually they kissed, and Chet started to unbutton her dress, but she held his hand to stop him.

'Not here, Chet.'

He realized that she was worried about her parents. Chet was behaving habitually, he wasn't really in the mood for sex. He said, 'I guess I just want to do something to numb the pain.'

Rosalie stood up. 'I know, but not here with my mom downstairs. Do you want to go back to your place?'

'Yeah.'

They went back to Chet's room and lay in each other's arms, kissing gently, but not having intercourse. After a while, Chet took out his guitar and started to play the blues.

Chapter 62

Chet got to band practice early. He was tuning his guitar when Jimmy and Ryan arrived. Ryan looked at Chet then quickly averted his eyes. Jimmy didn't seem to have any problem with Chet. 'You ain't ever been first one here, Chet.'

'Ain't been to work today.'

'Why not?'

'Had some real bad news so my boss told me to stay home. My brother's been killed.'

'Damn,' said Jimmy. He touched Chet lightly on the shoulder.

Ryan sat down and shook his head, sympathetically. 'That's a bummer Chet.'

When Steve and Clarence walked in, Jimmy put them in the picture. Clarence stood next to Chet, whose eyes were welling up. 'You gonna visit your folks?'

'Going back tomorrow, Clarence.'

Clarence said, 'Sure you wanna practice, tonight?'

'Playing guitar might help numb the pain.' Chet played a few chords. The other guys took the hint and got ready for the rehearsal. Clarence sat in a comfortable chair and prepared to observe. They practiced for just under an hour before Clarence put an end to the proceedings. 'Let's call it a night, guys.'

They looked at him with eyebrows raised. Ryan said, 'Why we finishing so early?'

'I've got some bad news too, Ryan, our next gig has been cancelled. Some idiot doubled booked the auditorium. We lose out because the other band made the first booking. We ain't been able to find another venue at such short notice. At least it will give you guys more time to prepare for the big college gig we got coming up. If you play the way you sounded tonight, you'll tear the roof off the joint. Let's go to the bar and I'll buy you all a beer.'

'That's like music to my ears,' said Jimmy.

'I'm only buying the first round, Jimmy, then you're on your own.'

Steve butted in. 'Jimmy can get the second round.'

'I'm only gonna have one beer, Steve. I gotta drive home and my drinking and driving days are over.'

Steve shook his head. 'You're such a cheapskate, Jimmy.'

Ryan punched Steve lightly on the shoulder and laughed. 'Jimmy's got it right, Steve. No drinking and driving for me either, I gave up driving at the start of the year.'

Steve wagged a finger back at Ryan. 'You got a DWI, more like.'

'Same shit, Stevie. Jimmy don't drink more than one beer and I don't drive, so neither of us is gonna get pulled over for drunk driving.'

'Yeah, you expect Jimmy and me to take you everyplace.'

'It's no big deal, Jimmy lives in the same apartment block.'

Jimmy was packing up his drums. He usually made several trips to the car and he was invariably the last one out. 'That's as maybe, Ryan, but when you get your license back you're gonna be the designated driver for a change.'

'No problem, Jimmy.' Ryan replied as he helped Jimmy with his drum kit.

Chet figured that Ryan didn't want to be outside on his own, as he was scared. But Chet wasn't in the mood for fighting. He hadn't joined in with the banter and was still slumped in a chair, when Jimmy tapped Chet on the shoulder. 'You wanna get drunk, Chet?'

'I think I'm gonna go home.'

'Clarence is buying. Don't you feel like some company?'

Chet held up his guitar. 'The blues will accompany me tonight.'

'You really can make that guitar sing, Chet.'

'It will be my comfort blanket tonight, Jimmy.'

Jimmy slapped him on the back. 'Let us know soon as you get back in town.'

Chapter 63

The first thing Chet saw when he pulled into Bart's place was his old station wagon gleaming in the sun. Bobby must have cleaned and polished it. He climbed out of the Ford, went around to the passenger side, and opened the door for Rosalie. Out the corner of his eye he saw a little critter dashing around chasing chickens. 'Well I'll be, looks like Uncle Bart's got himself another dog.'

The little hound was soon at the car barking and jumping up in excitement, nipping playfully at Rosalie's ankles. She said, 'What a cute little dog.'

Chet squatted down to make a fuss of the hound, rubbing her belly like he did with old Duke. Bart must have heard the commotion as he stuck his head around the barn door. When he saw he'd got company he made his way over. 'You always did know how to spoil a dog.'

'She's a beauty, uncle.' Chet threw his arms around Bart. He struggled to hold back the tears. 'Aaron would have loved her to bits.'

Bart said, 'It's hard to comprehend that your brother ain't with us no more. Ain't no rhyme nor reason to it.'

Chet shook his head. 'I keep asking myself, why Aaron?'

Bart grabbed hold of Chet's shoulders and looked at him, anger burning in his eyes. 'No one deserves to be cut down like a dog. There's some mean sons of bitches on this earth.'

Rosalie bent to stroke Duchess. 'She a fine-looking dog. What's her name Mr. Carter?'

Chet was pleased that Rosalie had changed the subject. He wanted to know more about the dog. Bart seemed happy to oblige and a smile appeared back on his face, 'You can call me Bart. I named the bitch, Duchess. You could call it a family tradition.'

Chet ran his hand all over the dog, feeling the sinewy muscles. She was a lean hound, very athletic, with skin still to grow into. He visualized her bounding through the woods, tail in the air, ears flapping in excitement. The look on Chet's face, as he looked into the dog's bright eyes, was the same expression that he could see on his uncle's face, pure admiration. Chet said, 'She's gonna be a mighty, fine hunting dog and I'm pleased to hear she got the royal seal of approval.'

'She's just like Duke when he was a puppy, got that same energy and appetite to match. She spends most of the day harassing the chickens.' Bart grinned at Rosalie showing his crooked, stained teeth. 'How about introducing your young lady?'

Chet said, 'This is Rosalie.'

'What's a pretty gal like you doing with this good for nothing?'

Bart slapped Chet on the back and he responded by putting the old man in a neck hold. The play fighting helped to put aside the grief that they were both feeling. Chet enjoyed grappling with his uncle again and he pushed him away pretending to be mad with him, while rolling his eyes at Rosalie, who seemed bemused. 'Thanks for the glowing reference, uncle.'

'You're welcome, son.'

Rosalie said, 'Chet's speaks highly of you, Bart.'

'You gotta be kidding. He only humors me because I let him do what he wants most of the time. You gonna be staying a while?'

'Just until the funeral.' Chet replied.

'You gonna work to earn your keep?'

That remark and his cheeky smile proved that Bart was back to his old self. Chet noticed that the old timer looked healthier than the last time he'd seen him. 'Suppose you want me to run moonshine?'

'You can help Bobby. He'll be over later.'

'Don't wanna leave Rosalie on her own too long.'

'You ain't gotta worry on that account, I'll keep her company.'

Bart put his arm around Rosalie and escorted the youngsters to a couple of nearby benches, partly in the shade of a tree. Chet thought this was as good a time as ever to let Rosalie know how his uncle earned a living.

'Uncle Bart makes and sells his own liquor and we transport it to customers all over the county. Since I've been gone my best friend, Bobby, has been helping him.'

'Best moonshine you ever did drink. Wait there while I fetch you a sample.'

Bart shuffled over to the barn and picked up a mason jar. He held it under a tap protruding out of a barrel that was raised on a table. When he'd filled two jars he returned and gave one to Rosalie who looked furtively over at Chet before taking a sip. She coughed and spluttered as the liquid burned her throat.

'Good, ain't it?' said Bart.

The old man held out the other jar for Chet, but he took a swig first. He licked his lips and wiped his mouth with the outside of his hand. 'Ahh.'

Chet took a good swallow of the mountain dew then gave the jar back to his uncle. 'I better not drink any more if I'm gonna drive the Dodge.'

Bart nodded, took another swallow and gestured for Rosalie to do the same. She acquiesced and put the jar to her mouth again. This time she was at least able to stifle a cough. 'I won't be able to drink all this, Mr. Carter.'

'Told you to call me, Bart. You like it don't ya?'

'Yeah, but it's awful strong.'

'You better believe it, honey. My moonshine will make your toes curl.' The old man laughed and slapped his thigh. 'Drink as much, or as little, as you want. I ain't gonna be offended.'

Rosalie said, 'I think I've had enough, thanks.' She gave the jar back to Bart who screwed on the top.

'It ain't gonna go to waste, gal.'

Rosalie watched him take another long gulp from the other jar. He smacked his lips and screwed his eyes tight before yelling. 'Ooohwee.'

Chet grinned at Rosalie and she smiled weakly back at him. 'Uncle Bart's been making moonshine since he was a teenager.'

'I started working for Jake Schneider until some hoodlums injured old Jake so bad he was forced to give up the distillery. The bastards were planning on helping themselves to free hooch but me and my brother, Luke, soon put a stop to that. After Jake retired he handed the business over to me.'

'You had any trouble since?' said Rosalie.

Bart wagged his finger. 'Folks round here know not to mess with the Carters.'

Chet said, 'Uncle Bart's got a reputation.'

Bart supped his drink. 'Ain't just me, everyone knows the Carters look after their own. No one messes with your daddy, either.'

Chet was curious about his uncle's remark about Jethroe. 'Thought you was the rough diamond in the family and Jethroe was the upright, honest brother.'

'We were all pretty wild when we were young. After Jethroe got wed his rowdy drinking days ended for good. When he took over the farm he became a hard-working family man. He put his heart and soul into working the land.'

'Ain't Jethroe always been teetotal.'

'He only started to abstain after he got drunk one night and walked around with your ma on his shoulders. He was fooling around but he tripped and fell, and she hit her head on the ground. Jethroe rushed her to hospital fearing the worse, but it turned out she'd only got concussion and some bruising. Even so, he made a promise never to touch alcohol again.'

'Ain't ever seen my daddy take a drink. Now I know the reason why.'

Bart squinted as he was facing the sun. 'When you planning on visiting your old man?'

'Tomorrow.'

'He's in a bad way. He took Aaron's death hard.'

Chet said, 'Me too.' He lowered his head and Rosalie reached for this hand.

Bart got to his feet. 'Don't know what a body can say at a time like this, I'm gonna load up the Dodge.'

'I'll do it uncle, it'll help take my mind off Aaron.'

Duchess, initially, followed Chet towards the barn before turning tail and catching up with Bart and Rosalie who were on their way to the house. They were almost at the door when Duchess turned and ran into the yard, barking, as a car pulled in. Her tail wagged at Bobby as he climbed out of the auto. Bart wandered over to greet him. Bobby had spotted the Ford in the drive 'Chet here?'

'In the barn loading up the Dodge. You might wanna split the round, Chet can do the north side of the county and you do the south.'

'I'll do the first run.'

Bart said, 'Sort it out with Chet' He beckoned Rosalie to join them. 'By the way, this pretty, young thing is Chet's girl, Rosalie.'

'Pleased to meet you, Rosalie. I'm Bobby.'

'Chet talks about you a good deal.'

Bobby went to hug her, then changed his mind. 'Yeah, I'm his best friend.'

They ended up shaking hands. Chet emerged from the barn and threw his arms around his best friend. When they broke from the hug, Bobby said, 'Hard to believe what happened to Aaron, Chet.'

'Ain't no justice in this world, Bobby.'

'You can say that again, you gonna run moonshine?'

'Yeah.'

'Bart reckons we oughta split the round.'

'That'll work for me, as I won't have to leave Rosalie on her own for as long.'

Bart cuffed Chet around the head. 'She won't be on her own, jackass, I'll be entertaining her.'

'That's what worries me, uncle.'

Rosalie eyes were open wide in apprehension. She glanced across at Chet who was smiling. 'Want me to come with you, Chet?'

Bart put his arms around Rosalie. 'See, now you're frightening the girl.' He grinned at her. 'You don't mind Chet being gone a while, do you, gal? Stay and keep me and Duchess company.'

Chet saw Rosalie's nose turn up. It was probably Bart's alcohol reeking breath. He wondered if she'd noticed that his uncle was missing a few teeth. The pegs that remained were far from white. Rosalie looked at Chet who just shrugged his shoulders. For once in his life Bobby took the bull by the horns. 'I'll do the first run, I wanna get finished early, and while I'm gone you can decide whether you're gonna take Rosalie along.'

Chet said, 'Go ahead Bobby, I ain't even showed Rosalie around the house, yet.'

Bobby climbed into the Dodge, Bart had left the ledger on the passenger seat, so Bobby could check off what he did. Chet put his arm around Rosalie and they followed Bart to the house. Bart opened the porch door and stopped unexpectedly, turning to face Rosalie. 'Hope you ain't picky, sweetheart, never been particular about cleaning.'

The outside of the house could do with a lick of paint. Inside wasn't as dusty as the yard, but it came a close second. Bart led them into a large room where a few threadbare rugs covered most of the floorboards. The furniture was old and had seen better days. 'Take a seat while I make coffee.'

Bart went into the kitchen as Rosalie surveyed the room. There were several chairs, but Chet plumped for the battered old couch. Rosalie sat next to him, sinking deep into the soft leather. He put his arm around her. 'Bart makes his coffee strong.'

'Anything's betta than the moonshine.'

Chet screwed his face at Rosalie, mimicking his uncle 'You liked it didn't ya?'

She grinned at his lousy impression. 'Only had a couple of sips.'

'Probably a wise move.'

Bart walked in with two mugs of coffee and set them down on an old wooden table.

'Is the bed made up in my old bedroom, uncle?'

'Go see for yourself, if you remember where it's at.'

Chet stood up and took hold of Rosalie's hand to rescue her from the depth of the sunken couch. After he pulled her up, she brushed dust from her dress.

Chet said, 'Gonna give Rosalie a tour of the house, while the coffee cools down.'

Bart had a sly grin on his face, 'Don't be lingering too long in the bedroom.'

Chet pulled in Rosalie close and kissed her, smiling mischievously at his uncle, before heading for the bedroom. Duchess bound up the stairs after them, causing Bart to holler, 'Duchess, get here.'

The hound ignored him until she heard the lid being taken off the cookie jar. She scampered down the stairs and sat in front of the old man looking up expectantly.

It was still light when Bobby got back. Duchess let out a high-pitched howl to let everyone know there was a visitor on the premises. Chet went out to help Bobby unload the empty jars. He said, 'How'd it go?'

'Okay,' Bobby replied.

'Everyone paid up?'

'We had a problem with Tom Williamson last week. He was behind with the payments, so I told Bart and I believe he paid him a visit?'

Chet put a crate on the ground. 'Did he take his gun with him?'

'Never saw him go. All I know is old Tom's paid up now.'

'Figures.' Chet stacked the empty crate in the corner of the barn. Bobby followed him with another crate. 'Got something to tell you, Chet. It may be nothing, but I think you oughta know.'

'What?'

'I reckon Carl Morgan's letting Sullivan know when you get back in town. He was asking questions about you, so I followed him to the pay phone. He hung up when he saw me. When I confronted him, he said he was calling family.'

'If you don't have proof then don't fret it. I do believe Joe Sullivan's in jail and Aaron gave his brother, Michael, a beating he won't forget any time soon.'

Memories of his dead brother came into his Chet's head. He rubbed his eyes trying to hold back the tears. He picked up a full crate and was about to put it onto the Dodge when he hesitated. 'You better tell Uncle Bart about Carl, just in case. I'm gonna run this hooch as quick as I can, so I ain't leaving Rosalie too long.'

Bobby helped Chet finish loading the Dodge. When they'd put on the last crate Chet settled into the driver's seat. Bobby waved so long and went into the housc for a conversation with Bart before he departed. He waited until Rosalie visited the rest room before confiding in the old man. 'Michael Sullivan may be snooping around this weekend.'

'How come?'

'I think Carl Morgan may be his informant. Just wanted to forewarn you.'

Bart's face turned ashen, the memory of their last encounter still fresh in his mind. 'Appreciate the warning, Bobby. I'll keep my shotgun close at hand and if that bastard comes around I'll let him have both barrels.'

Chapter 64

They slept in Chet's old bedroom. The bed was only just wide enough for two, but it was comfortable. It creaked some and Rosalie asked Chet if Bart might hear them. Chet told her he slept like an overfed dog. Chet hadn't sleep well since he'd heard the news about Aaron and now he'd got Sullivan on his mind.

In the morning Bart hollered up from the bottom of the stairs. 'Get your sorry ass down here if you want breakfast.'

They could smell the coffee as they entered the kitchen. Chet poured them both a cup and they sat, eagerly awaiting whatever Bart was about to serve up. Chet was starving. 'Need me to do anything, uncle?'

'It's all done.'

The sun shone through the large kitchen window. Duchess was outside mooching around the yard. It was a beautiful Tennessee morning and it was gonna be hot. The old man brought in eggs and toast. Rosalie said, 'Are you gonna say grace, Mr. Carter.'

Bart had his fork half way to his mouth and he stopped with his mouth open. He looked at Chet who nodded. Bart put down his fork and said, 'Thank you, Lord,' Then he started shoveling food into his mouth.

Chet figured that Rosalie was used to her dad saying grace before they ate breakfast. He thought 'culture shock', and tucked right in. There was a lot of eating going on and precious little talking. Chet and Bart seemed to be in a race to see who could finish first. Chet put his fork onto the empty plate and looked at his watch. 'As soon as you get done eating, Rosalie, we gotta visit my old man.'

Bart grinned. 'That'll be a rare treat for Rosalie, meeting my younger brother.' He looked at Rosalie before continuing. 'Jethroe looks like me, only he ain't as good looking.'

The old man screwed up his face making himself look even more grotesque. Rosalie turned towards Chet to see if he was laughing, but he just shook his head in bewilderment. 'You gonna be okay while we're gone, uncle?'

Bart glanced over at the rifle leaning against the wall, 'Why wouldn't I?'

Chet nodded and noticed that Rosalie had a puzzled look on her face.

On the drive to Jethroe's house Chet was silent. He felt apprehensive about meeting his old man. He hoped Jethroe would at least be civil. Even if he wasn't, Chet was determined to keep his cool.

Rosalie sad, 'You're awful quiet, Chet.'

'Ain't been on good terms with Jethroe.'

Chet wondered what Rosalie was thinking. She probably had a mental picture of someone looking like Bart, but with the angry scowl of a gangster. He remembered how horrified she had been when Chet told her about Jethroe taking off his belt to him. They turned into the drive, parked, and walked to the front door. Before they had a chance to push the bell Thelma opened the door and threw her arms around Chet. He was just as pleased to see her, as Jethroe was less obnoxious when Thelma was around. She opened the door wider, ushering them inside. 'Good that you could make it, Chet, and you bought your girl too.'

'Yeah, Rosalie this is Thelma.'

Thelma hugged Rosalie as if she was a long-lost friend. Then she led the way into the family room where Jethroe looked up from his newspaper at the visitors. 'Well, well, the prodigal son returns,'

Thelma said, 'And he's got himself a pretty girlfriend.'

'Hope he's treating you right, gal?'

'He sure does, Mr. Carter.'

Jethroe beckoned the visitors to sit down. 'Call me Jethroe. Thelma, fetch some coffee, we got some catching up to do.'

'Hope you guys can stay for dinner, I'm making meatloaf.'

'Long as it ain't any trouble, Thelma?' Chet answered.

Thelma smiled. 'I enjoy fixing dinner for guests, and It'll be a rare treat to see you and Jethroe sitting at the table together.' She turned to Jethroe who nodded showing his endorsement of Thelma's offer.

'It will be an opportunity for us all to get acquainted,' said Jethroe.

Chet went over to Jethroe and touched him lightly on the shoulder. 'It ain't gonna be the same without Aaron, pa.'

Jethroe took off his reading glasses. 'It's hard to come to terms with, son. Ain't a day gone by, without me thinking how much I miss him. Anyways, how you doing since you moved away?'

'My band's cut a record and it's gonna be on the radio.'

Jethroe raised his eyebrows. 'No shit?'

Thelma said, 'Please don't cuss when we're entertaining visitors, Jethroe. What must the young lady think?'

'Only showing how pleased I am for Chet. I hope you ain't offended, Rosalie.'

'I've heard a lot worse, Mr. Carter.'

Jethroe looked at Thelma who was holding the door and still hadn't left the room. 'I thought you were gonna fix coffee, Thelma.'

She replied, 'I don't wanna miss any tittle-tattle.' She rushed into the kitchen, switched on the kettle, and came back in and sat down while waiting for it to boil. She folded her hands neatly in her lap as she waited.

Chet figured she was poised to react to whichever whistle blew first, the kettle, or Jethroe's temper. 'How's the farm, pa?'

'We need rain bad, been watering the crops from the creek.'

'Still got the same hands working here?'

'I've been lucky in that regard. I've hired good people who ain't afraid of hard work.'

Chet narrowed his eyes, thinking that Jethroe was making a dig at him. 'Not like me, then?'

'Farming ain't for everybody, son. I believe fixing autos is hard work.'

Chet was surprised that on this occasion his old man chose not to rebuke him. He looked over at Rosalie as he continued the conversation. 'Jethroe wanted Aaron and me to be farmers, seems we both let him down in that regard.'

Jethroe said, 'Aaron was gonna manage the farm when he ended his term of duty. Always been a waste of time trying to get you to do something you didn't want to do.'

Thelma bolted upright giving Jethroe a stare that would warn off a grizzly. The kettle whistled, and Thelma went into the kitchen.

Chet said, 'Seems like nothing I ever did was ever good enough for you, pa.'

'I just wish you were less impetuous, is all.'

'I got a mind of my own.'

Jethroe sighed, 'You got that right, son.'

Chet gritted his teeth. 'I ain't one to follow the herd and I don't cow down, neither.'

Jethroe said, 'Nature's got a way of breaking that which won't bend.'

The pair locked eyes as they'd done many times before. 'Ain't seen much flexibility from you, pa. I'd say being stubborn is a family trait.' Chet waited for his daddy to snap back at him, but Jethroe's face was not set hard in the usual snarl.

'Maybe, anyways, ain't no point dwelling on the past. It's time for you and me to start appreciating the importance of family.'

Thelma returned from the kitchen with a tray full of cups. Jethroe looked over at her, as she placed the tray on the table. 'Thelma and her kids are gonna be moving in soon, ain't you, honey?'

All eyes were on Thelma who nodded as she handed a coffee to Rosalie. Chet thought that the atmosphere was more relaxed now that Jethroe was adopting a more conciliatory attitude. He smiled, as he enquired, 'How old are your kids now, Thelma?'

Thelma sat down. 'Ten, twelve and fifteen. old enough for them to stay home alone without needing a sitter.'

'You've met them before ain't you, Chet?' said Jethroe.

Chet's thought about Jethroe taking on Thelma's family. He knew that if Jethroe was mean to her kids she'd be out the door quicker than she came in. Maybe if his mother hadn't died things would have been different between him and his pa. 'Sure have, hope you're gonna look after Thelma's kids better than you treated me.'

Rosalie glared at Chet. Thelma looked at Jethroe, appearing to be waiting for a reaction, but all he did was sigh. She answered for him. 'No need to worry on my behalf, Chet, Jethroe's always done right by me and my family, ain't you, sweetheart?'

Jethroe nodded.

Chet said, 'I don't doubt that, Thelma, but he ain't showed me that same courtesy.'

'You can't let it go, can you?' Jethroe exclaimed.

Thelma moved her hands onto her thighs and sat forward. Chet assumed she was getting ready to spring into action if the argument got out of hand. She said, 'Jethroe's got an issue with you, which is why he gave you a hard time, Chet.'

Jethroe ran his hand across his brow. 'Let's not get into this, Thelma.'

'It's time you let the boy know why you've been so hardhearted.'

Chet frowned as he tried to figure out what Thelma was implying. Jethroe fidgeted in his chair and the tension in the room was thick as molasses. Like a dog with a bone, Thelma continued. 'Go on, Jethroe, tell him.'

Chet said, 'Tell me what?'

Everyone looked at Jethroe as he took his hand away from his face and fixed his eyes on Chet. 'Always held it against you for your ma's death.'

'I wasn't even there when it happened.'

'That was the problem. You'd gone fishing with Aaron and you were supposed to get back before dark, but the sun had gone down, and you still weren't home. You were only nine years old and your ma was worried sick when Aaron came back without you. He said you'd ran after a raccoon and he couldn't find you.'

'I got lost.'

'Chrissie sent me and Aaron out looking for you in the woods. While we were gone she must've needed some vegetables from the barn. As no one was around she went to get them herself. She needed a ladder to climb up into the loft where we stored the root crops. The trouble is, she picked the ladder with a broken wrung, that I'd never gotten around to fixing. Chrissie hardly ever went in that barn and she must not have seen the new ladder standing in the corner.'

'I knew about the broken ladder, you warned me and Aaron not to use it,' said Chet.

'Sure did, son, but I guess I never told Chrissie. When she climbed that old ladder she must have snapped the wrung and fell to the ground. Doctor said she broke her neck and died instantly. If I weren't searching for you she'd never have had cause to go in the barn.'

Chet shook his head. 'So, you reckon it was my fault?'

'I should have fixed the ladder, or put it somewhere out of harm's way. I was responsible, not you.'

'But you've always blamed me?'

'When we got back and found Chrissie dead on the floor all I could think of was the time we'd spent traipsing around that wood, shouting your name. We found you sitting under a tree with a big smile on your face. I was mad at you, but you didn't give a damn, just kept on about all the critters you'd seen. When we found your ma's body I felt like wiping that smile off your face with the back of my hand.'

Chet snarled, 'Why didn't you?'

'You were nine years old. I was racked with guilt and I kept telling myself you should've come home with your brother. Reckon I needed another shoulder to help carry the burden.'

'I had no idea you held it against me, pa.'

'You kept asking me if she was in heaven, but I lost my faith long ago. Aaron withdrew into himself and the next day, at school, he beat the crap out of a kid who said the wrong thing at the wrong time. How could I punish him for being angry because his ma was dead?'

Tears fell from Jethroe's eyes and Thelma put her arms around him. Chet was close to tears too as Rosalie held his hand in hers. He said, 'I miss ma more than words can say, but I never thought anyone was to blame. I always accepted it was a tragic accident.'

Jethroe tapped the table with his fingers. 'That was another thing that riled me, while I was consumed with guilt you just carried on, as if nothing had happened. You should have been hurting like me.'

Chet held out his hands, palms up. 'I was, pa, but I didn't know how to show it.'

'You should have cried like a baby and apologized for not getting home on time.'

'Guess, I didn't think that was the Carter's way.'

Jethroe rubbed his eye. 'Now we've lost Aaron and I ain't mad anymore, just sad and bewildered about why these things happen? If there is a god, his plans don't make sense to us mortals. You and Bart is all the family I got left.'

The two men hugged. Chet realized that he'd never heard Jethroe make any reference to god, before. He just assumed his father was a non-believer in contrast to most folk in Tennessee, who were affiliated to some religious denomination. Rosalie's family went to church every Sunday. Chet believed that the Carters put their faith in their resolve to stand up for themselves. Chet saw the importance of his family uniting together. His war with his father over.

Chapter 65

After clearing the table, the two women went into the kitchen to wash the dishes, while Jethroe and Chet relaxed on the couch in the family room. Rosalie seemed to be getting on fine with Thelma and Chet was beginning to feel that his daddy liked him.

Two men walked up the drive getting closer to the front porch with every long stride. They were big men, walking side by side, with a look of steely determination on their faces. The smaller of the two was six-foot-tall, weighing two hundred pounds, and he was carrying a shotgun. The bigger man was carrying nothing, but the threat of menace. Thelma took the trash out to the garbage can, but when she saw the unwanted visitors she dropped the bag and turned tail to retreat into the house.

'Hold it right there, lady,' said the man holding the gun. She froze, paralyzed with fear. The bigger of the two men grabbed hold of her. The other man was pointing his gun at Thelma's back. Jethroe and Chet heard voices outside and stiffened as they looked at each other. Chet jumped up, as if the house was on fire, and looked through the window while Jethroe went to the rack on the wall to grab his rifle. Chet turned and spoke quietly to his pa. 'Sullivan's.' He pushed open the door, and stood staring at his nemesis. Joe Sullivan, who was holding a knife against Thelma's throat. She looked petrified.

'Step outside, Carter. Easy now,' said Joe Sullivan.

Chet took a pace outside and Jethroe followed but he stopped abruptly when he saw Michael Sullivan's gun pointing at him and the knife against Thelma's throat. Joe Sullivan had the smug look of a school bully who'd just beaten a fellow student and stole his lunch money. Jethroe stood next to his son with his rifle in hand. Joe Sullivan said, 'Drop the gun, or the lady gets it.' The smile on his face showed that he was enjoying himself, whereas Jethroe's face was ashen. He dropped the rifle as instructed and Joe Sullivan let go of Thelma, who ran into Jethroe's arms. Sullivan turned his attention, and his knife, towards Chet. 'Reckon you hoped you'd seen the last of me, but that was never a possibility. The Sullivan's don't forgive, or forget.'

Chet heard Rosalie moving inside the lounge and he tried to usher her away with a backward wave of his hand. Sullivan must have noticed the movement. 'Get out here, whoever you are.'

Chet said, 'Your dispute's with me. No need to involve anyone else.'

'You and me got unfinished business for sure, but I ain't about to leave any stone unturned. Get out, now,' Sullivan repeated.

Rosalie came outside and put her hand to her mouth with a gasp as she surveyed the scene.

Joe Sullivan said, 'Who's the pretty lady?'

Chet stuck out his chest. 'Just leave her be, she ain't a part of this.'

'That's for me to decide. Anyone else inside? My brother Mick was hoping that brother of yours might be here as he's got a score to settle, too. You know how brothers like to keep their promises.'

Chet said, 'He's dead.'

The smirk on Joe Sullivan's face got bigger. 'Ain't that a shame. He's gonna miss all the fun. Now you listen up because my older brother's about to give you a history lesson. Go ahead, Michael.'

'Our mother used to live in this shit hole town. Her given name is Marie Donnelly, and something happened to her family long ago, right on this very spot.'

Jethroe nodded his head slowly. Chet glanced over at his pa and recognition, at hearing the mention of the Donnelly name, dawned on him too.

'I do believe they already know the tale of how the Carter's massacred the Donnelly's, Joe. You could say that, today, we'll be fulfilling our destiny. Our whole family were shot dead on this very property, so it's payback time.'

Michael Sullivan was still pointing his rifle at Jethroe. Joe put the knife back in its sheath and took a rag out of his side pocket. He lit it and, as the rag burst into flames, held it high in the air. Sullivan laughed like a man possessed and snarled, 'We're gonna burn this place to the ground like our forefathers aimed to do. After we've all watched it smolder we're gonna deal with you.'

Chet and Jethroe were rooted to the spot, helpless to intervene, but the sound of a speeding vehicle's tires screeching on the driveway made Joe Sullivan turn around and Chet slammed his fist into the side of Joe Sullivan's head, making him drop the burning rag. He responded by punching Chet hard in the belly, doubling him up in pain, then kneed him hard in the face, knocking him to the ground. Jethroe bent to pick up his rifle and Michael Sullivan shot him. Thelma screamed as Jethroe stood holding his arm, the rifle still lying on the ground. Bart climbed out of the Dodge. Michael Sullivan turned around and saw Bart's Winchester rifle pointing at him. Sullivan must have thought he had the upper hand. 'Drop the gun, old timer.'

Bart said, 'Was about to ask you to do the same.'

Joe Sullivan placed his foot on Chet's neck and took his knife out of the sheath. 'Better do what my brother says, or I'll gut him like a fish.'

Three shots rang out in quick succession. Michael Sullivan fell to the ground, Thelma screamed when she saw the hole in his head. Mick Sullivan's bullet had taken out the windshield of the pickup, and Joe Sullivan dropped the knife as a searing pain went through his shoulder. Bart spat in the dirt as he surveyed his handy work and he cocked the rifle for a third shot, should it be necessary. A smile formed on his face as he looked at Michael Sullivan. 'That's for old Duke.'

Joe dived on the ground in an attempt to pick up his brother's gun and Bart shot him in the leg.

'The next bullet's going in your head, Sullivan.' Bart was clearly enjoying himself.

Joe Sullivan accepted that the situation was hopeless. Even if he managed to pick up the gun he knew Bart would kill him before he could get off a shot. He watched a pool of blood seep around his brother's body and he roared like a raging bull. 'One-day you Carters are gonna get what's coming to you.' His leg was smarting with pain, and his arm rendered useless, but he slammed his good hand hard into Chet's face.

Bart hollered back at him. 'You hard of hearing, Sullivan. I ain't gonna warn you again, you so much as twitch and you'll be lying dead alongside your, piece of shit, brother. Chet, pick up the knife. Thelma, call the sheriff to come collect this piece of garbage.'

Chet grimaced in pain as he picked up the knife. He knew that Sullivan would have inflicted a lot more hurt, if not for Bart's timely arrival. His uncle was clearly in control off the 0situation and he thought back to the hunting trips where critters fell to the ground whenever Bart fired his rifle. His ability with a firearm had never been in doubt. Thelma took Rosalie inside and sat her on the couch. She was shaking as if she was freezing her butt off. Thelma said quietly, 'It's over, honey. I'm gonna call the cops.'

Jethroe shouted to Thelma, 'We need paramedics, too.'

Chapter 66

One year later

A family reunion was arranged to mourn the anniversary of Aaron's death. It was a year to the day since his life was snuffed out so needlessly. But Jethroe, Bart and Chet were determined to remember the happy times spent with Aaron. They had something else to celebrate as the Revolvers latest record had made the charts. The success of the band meant that Chet gave up working full time for Bill Sanders. He still rented the room from Bill and helped him out whenever possible, but his focus was playing in the band. They had a busy schedule of gigs and were spending more, and more, time rehearsing. On top of that Chet was collaborating with Ryan, writing songs. They had become friends.

Rosalie had moved out of state to do a college degree as her parents always wanted. Chet knew that they were also happy that she'd put some distance between herself and him. When Rosalie told them about the fight with the Sullivan's they were horrified, and Chet figured that this confirmed their belief that he wasn't right for their daughter. She had even kept some of the gruesome details to herself. Chet hadn't given up on her, as she was the only girl that he'd ever really loved. He preferred to think that their relationship was on hold while she was at college. In the meantime, he wasn't going short of affection. There were plenty of girls available at every gig. Occasionally he saw Ruby and they both enjoyed each other, without any strings. Ruby wasn't the settling down type, anyhow.

Thelma was busy preparing the meal while Chet sat on the porch describing the latest Revolver's concert to her children, who were listening intently. Jethroe sat on the couch in the sitting room next to his brother, who seemed to be irritating him. 'Why you keep looking at your watch?'

‘I’m so hungry, I could eat a frozen dog, Jethroe.’

‘You’re just gonna have to wait, Bart.’

Finally, Thelma hollered that dinner was ready and they all sat at the long table in the kitchen. She brought out the pot roast and everyone tucked in. Thelma said, ‘You gonna say grace, Jethroe?’

He nodded at Thelma. ‘For what we are about to receive may the lord make us truly thankful.’

Chet smiled at the new house rules Thelma had established. As soon as grace was finished the dishes were passed around and everyone had their fill. As a testament to Thelma’s cooking all the plates were scraped clean. After dinner Jethroe and Bart went into the yard, taking their weapons with them, stopping at the prearranged location. Chet followed close behind carrying some empty cans. Jethroe said, ‘Set them up, Chet.’

Chet placed the cans along the fence before trudging back to stand alongside Jethroe and Bart, who were sixty paces away from the targets. Jethroe was first to shoot, and a can went flying off the fence.

Bart said, ‘Good shot, brother, believe I’m next.’ He took aim and he too sent the can airborne.

Chet stepped up to the plate. It had been a while since he fired a gun and the challenge brought back familiar memories of Jethroe teaching him how to shoot, in the same way that all the Carter fathers instructed their sons. This was a tradition that went back for generations. Chet was never passionate about shooting, but as a child he enjoyed hunting and fishing as he loved being outdoors. Jethroe handed him the rifle and he took aim and fired. Nothing moved off the fence and Bart slapped him on the back and laughed. ‘You forgotten how to shoot, boy?’

Chet shook his head and fired again. This time he dislodged a can and a grin appeared on his face. It was like riding a bike, some things you don’t forget. Chet thought that one day he would be raising his own family. He pictured three or four children and he didn’t care if they were boys, or girls. If he was blessed with sons he wondered whether he’d instruct them to shoot like Jethroe showed him, or his granddaddy had taught Jethroe, Bart and Luke. He thought not. The first thing he'd teach his kids was how to play guitar, like Aaron taught him. As dusk settled they went back inside. Bart fetched some more moonshine from the pickup and Chet played his guitar.

Two men strode purposely up the drive. They were big men, wearing dark blue padded jackets with white writing across the chest. Thelma was clearing up in the kitchen, when she saw them through the window and hollered at Jethroe. 'We got visitors.'

Bart and Chet turned to look at Jethroe. He raised his eyebrows and shrugged. 'I ain't expecting no one.'

Nevertheless, he fetched his rifle, just in case. Bart did the same and said, 'Get the door, Chet, I'll be right behind you.'

When Chet opened the door, he tried to keep the surprise from his face as he read the writing on the men's jacket, DEA.

'We're looking for Bartholomew Carter. We've been to his house but he ain't home. As you're kin we thought he might be here.'

The revenue men had finally come looking. Chet fixed the men in the eyes. 'He ain't here.'

'Know where he's at?'

'Sorry, sir. We ain't seen him for a while, we ain't on speaking terms,' Chet lied.

'When you do, let him know the Drug Enforcement Administration wants to speak to him.'

Chet said, 'Sure will.' He closed the door and went back into the lounge. Jethroe and Bart were sitting with eyebrows raised waiting for Chet to reveal what happened.

'Looks like the government want to shut you down, Uncle Bart.'

Bart stroked the gleaming Winchester which he lovingly held in his hands. 'We'll see about that.'

The End

About the author

Charles was born in Coventry, England. He has been a metallurgist, teacher and soccer coach. He attended a creative writing class in 2007 and started writing short stories. After completing a novel writing course at Warwick University, he gained the tools to write his first novel, 'Brothers Lost and Found.'

26308761R00153

Printed in Great Britain
by Amazon